A-LIST

Also by D. P. Lyle

The Jake Longly Series

Deep Six

The Dub Walker Series

Stress Fracture
Hot Lights, Cold Steel
Run to Ground

The Samantha Cody Series

Original Sin
Devil's Playground
Double Blind

The Royal Pains Media Tie-In Series

Royal Pains: First, Do No Harm
Royal Pains: Sick Rich

Nonfiction

Murder and Mayhem
Forensics For Dummies
Forensics and Fiction
Howdunit: Forensics; A Guide For Writers
More Forensics and Fiction
ABA Fundamentals: Forensic Science

Anthologies

Thrillers: 100 Must-Reads(contributor); *Jules Verne, Mysterious Island*
Thriller 3: Love Is Murder (contributor); *Even Steven*

A-LIST

A JAKE LONGLY THRILLER

D. P. LYLE

OCEANVIEW ◯ PUBLISHING
LONGBOAT KEY, FLORIDA

This book is a work of fiction. Names, characters, businesses,
organizations, places, and incidents either are the products of the author's
imagination or are used fictitiously. Any resemblance to actual events,
businesses, locales, or persons living or dead, is entirely coincidental.

ISBN 978-1-60809-270-3

Published in the United States of America by Oceanview Publishing
Longboat Key, Florida

www.oceanviewpub.com

10 9 8 7 6 5 4 3 2 1

PRINTED IN THE UNITED STATES OF AMERICA

To my late father, Victor Wilson Lyle, who taught me everything. But most importantly—work first, play second, always. And he truly loved New Orleans. A day doesn't go by that you are not greatly missed.

ACKNOWLEDGMENTS

To my wonderful agent and friend Kimberley Cameron of Kimberley Cameron & Associates. KC, you're the best.

To Bob and Pat Gussin and all the wonderfully dedicated people at Oceanview Publishing. Thanks for your friendship and always spot-on insights, making my writing the best it can be.

To my writers group for helping make this story work. Thanks, Terri, Barbara, Craig, Donna, Sandy, and Laurie.

A-LIST

CHAPTER ONE

I LIKE A lot of things. My 1965 Mustang. Burgundy with black Pony interior. Captain Rocky's Surf and Turf, my bar/restaurant that squats on the sand in Gulf Shores. Living on the Gulf Coast, where I've been most of my life. That's pretty cool, too. And then there are memories of a few epic games during my career as a major-league pitcher for the Texas Rangers. That was me. Jake Longly. Baseball stud. Ninety-plus mile-an-hour fastballs with just enough tail to make batters whiff, corkscrewing themselves into the ground. But that was another life, long gone, blown away on a cold Cleveland night by a ripped rotator cuff. Few pitchers recover from that. I surely didn't.

But right there at the top of my "like" list would be watching a gorgeous, nearly naked woman roll around on the floor. Well, not exactly rolling around. More like twisting, flexing, and stretching in a Pilates or yoga or some such fashion. I never could keep all those straight. But whatever you call it, it surely looks better than six-count burpees.

The woman in question was Nicole Jamison. My latest girlfriend. I guess that's what she was. Though we'd only known each other a few weeks, it seemed longer. Like we'd always been together. Sort of scary. Definitely not my norm, which was more or less hit and run. Yeah, I know, piggish, but at least I'm honest about it.

Anyone could see why I hung around with her. I mean, stunning didn't quite cover it. That blond hair, that perfect smile, and those eyes. Oh yeah. Bluer than blue. Deep, lively, and intelligent. And, of course, that body. Oh my.

Why she tolerated me was a whole different story. I could be a little difficult. According to her, anyway. My ex-wife, Tammy, would agree wholeheartedly, while adding a string of well-chosen expletives. Not undeserved, of course, but our experiment in marital harmony collapsed years ago. You'd think she would've mellowed by now, but Tammy doesn't do mellow.

I should probably be down there on the carpet with Nicole going through the same routine, but no way I could contort my body into some of the positions she adopted. Not now. Not even back when I was a young stud baseball player.

Clad in a form-fit peach sports bra and black shorts that must have been electroplated on her firm hips, she made it all seem so easy. Easy on the eye anyway. My, my.

Instead of risking a permanent back injury and a visit to an orthopedic surgeon, I lounged on her sofa, sipping coffee and pretending to read the newspaper, but in fact watching her every move.

"Stop oogling me," Nicole said.

"Oogling?"

"Okay, drooling." She rolled up onto her shoulder blades and bicycled her legs at a pace that would make those Tour de France dudes jealous. A patina of perspiration frosted her perfect face.

"I would never do that."

She smiled. "That's not what you said last night."

She had a point. Last night had spilled well into the new day. Two a.m. or so, if I remembered correctly. Of course, my memory of last night was suspect at best. We had started with rum at Captain Rocky's, moved on to tequila at her place, in the hot tub, and then smoked a blunt in bed. Followed by all that sex, which, with Nicole, was an athletic event. More or less turned my brain into oatmeal. She could do that. Add all that up and it explains why I was having trouble getting my motor started this early.

I folded the paper, laid it on the coffee table, and massaged one shoulder.

"Still stiff?" she asked.

"A little."

We were only a week removed from a thirty-foot, middle-of-the-night jump from the stern of the *Sea Witch*, the 100-foot mega yacht owned by the late Victor Borkov. Right into the cold, dark, storm-churned waters of the Gulf. We didn't make the leap by choice, mind you. But it was either that or be tossed in while chained to a massive iron ring that would have planted us in the silt that collected several hundred feet below any fresh air. Apparently Borkov's preferred method for flushing those who opposed, or even simply displeased, him. Like the Wilbanks brothers. Our ride to the Gulf floor would have been courtesy of Borkov's hit men, Joe Zuma and Frank Boyd. They, too, could be filed in the "late" category, the trio now the property of the Escambia County Coroner's Office over on 9th Avenue in Pensacola.

Hitting angry water from thirty feet is not a pleasant event. I wrenched a shoulder and tweaked my back; Nicole torqued her hip and sprained her neck. We hadn't known it at the time, adrenaline forcing our brains to focus on other things like survival, the pain not appearing until the next day. But all in all, we survived, so there was that.

"That's why you should be down here stretching with me," she said. "Work out those kinks."

"With you in that outfit, that might lead to something else altogether."

She rocked into a sitting position and mopped her face with a towel. "Time for a shower." She stood. "Join me and we'll see if something else altogether happens."

Even at seven thirty in the morning, that sounded like a plan. My brain might be oatmeal, but the rest of me was good to go.

Never happened though. Her cell chimed. She picked it up from the kitchen counter and answered.

"Uncle Charles?" She frowned. "I can barely hear you. Hold on a sec." She crossed the living room and pushed through the French doors, stepping out on the deck.

Uncle Charles would be her uncle Charles Balfour. Big-time movie producer, director, and everything else A-list. A full-house backfield of Oscars and an army of other awards.

"That's better," she said as she kicked the door closed.

I walked to the kitchen, refilled my coffee cup, leaned against the counter, and watched her pace, phone to one ear, a finger in the other.

This house belonged to Uncle Charles. A massive stilted construction on the sand in The Point, a high-dollar enclave in Perdido Beach on Alabama's Gulf Coast. I knew he was in some remote location in Europe, shooting a big-budget film. I figured that explained why she couldn't hear him well.

For the next ten minutes, I watched her pace, her expression and body language bouncing between concern and shock. Had something happened to him?

When she stepped back inside, she simply said, "Let's go."

"Where?"

"To see Ray."

Ray would be Ray Longly. My father. Longly Investigations. The PI firm Ray ran from his home down in Gulf Shores. Not far from Captain Rocky's and my own house.

"Why?"

"I have a job for us," Nicole said.

"A job? For us?"

"Well, technically for Ray. But, yeah, us."

"We don't work for Ray," I said.

"Sure we do. I still have my ID card Pancake made for me. That makes me official."

Good grief.

"Okay, Mata Hari, what is this job?" I asked.

"Kirk Ford."

"The actor?"

"That would be the mega-buck, A-list, franchise actor to you."

"What did old Kirk do?"

"Got himself arrested for murder. It seems some local girl was found strangled in his bed this morning."

"I really hate it when that happens."

"Don't be a smart-ass—and get a move on."

CHAPTER TWO

THE SHOWER WASN'T nearly as much fun as it could have been. I was hoping for "something else altogether" but instead Nicole was all business. Slapped my hands away more than once. At least she let me wash her back.

So, we dressed, climbed in her new Mercedes SL, and were on the way. For Nicole, on the way meant warp speed out of the neighborhood and onto the highway, much to the consternation of other drivers. Blowing horns and extended fingers fell in our wake.

Her old SL, the one Victor Borkov's thugs Zuma and Boyd trashed with the massive bumper of their even more massive SUV, had been red; this one, the replacement coughed up by her insurance company, was white with a sedate light gray interior. I hoped the less aggressive coloring might slow her down. That was a dream doomed to failure. Nicole only had one speed.

Regardless, we survived the trip.

Ray ran his business from his home, a stilted, two-story affair on the sand in Gulf Shores. As we pulled in, I saw Ray's black dually pickup nestled among the support pylons. Nicole parked. We climbed the outside stairs to the first floor. As usual, Ray sat at his teak, umbrella-shaded deck table, laptop, phone, and a Mountain Dew in easy reach.

"What brings you guys by so early?" he asked.

"I have a case for us," Nicole said.

"Us?" Ray asked.

"You know—you, me, Jake."

"Oh, that us." Ray looked at me and then back to Nicole. "So, you guys still work for Longly Investigations?"

Nicole: "Yes."

Me: "No."

Nicole ignored me. "Yes, we do. I even have my ID card." She pulled it from the back pocket of her jeans and held it up.

"Hard to argue with that," Ray said.

No, it wasn't, I thought. And was going to say exactly that, but Ray moved on.

He leaned back in his chair and looked toward me. "You on board with that?"

"Yes, he is," Nicole said.

I guessed I didn't have a speaking role in this family scene.

"He'll go wherever I go," Nicole added.

I would? Of course, I would.

Ray laughed. "I suspect that's true."

I tried to come up with a witty response but found none.

"So, what is it?" Ray asked. "Did you lose your purse?"

She glared at him and then me.

Me? I didn't say anything. And since Ray and I rarely got along, it couldn't be guilt by association. Could it?

Apparently so. Nicole shook her head. "Apple—tree. You two are both asses."

Ray laughed. "Sorry. Couldn't resist." He took a slug of Dew. "So, tell me."

Nicole sat in the chair opposite Ray. "Kirk Ford was arrested for murder this morning."

"The actor?"

She nodded. "He's in New Orleans shooting his latest *Space Quest* movie. My uncle, Charles Balfour, is one of the executive producers for the franchise. He called and asked me to look into it." She shrugged her shoulder. "Actually asked me if I'd ask you to look into it."

Ray stared at her a beat. "How does he know me?"

"I told him," she said. "About that whole Borkov thing and how you saved us from the Gulf."

"I thought that was me," I said.

She smiled and patted my arm. "You, too."

"Why isn't he, your uncle, doing it himself?" Ray asked.

"He's still in Europe. Just outside Paris. Shooting another movie."

Ray spread his hands on the table. "What do you know so far?"

"It looks like Kirk hooked up with a local girl. This morning she turned up dead in his bed. Uncle Charles said the police believe she had been strangled."

"Does he make a habit of that?"

Nicole stared at him. "What? Strangling women?"

"No," Ray said. "Picking up local girls when he's on location?"

"He's an actor. It's what they do."

"So I see in the tabloids at the grocery store." Ray drained and crushed the Dew can, dropping it in the nearby wastebasket. "But Kirk? Is this something he does often?"

Nicole nodded. "He's a player, as they say. He leaves a lot of broken hearts in his wake."

"I take it you know him?"

"For many years."

"And?"

"He's actually a nice guy. He screws around, no doubt there, but he's not malicious about it. At least that's how I see it."

Ray asked, "Any other details?"

She shook her head. "That's all I know."

"I take it, it's your uncle who wants to hire us?"

Nicole nodded.

"Aren't the police on the case?"

"Uncle Charles doesn't trust them. At least not to do a quick and thorough investigation. Quick being the operative word." She brushed her hair back over one shoulder. "Location shooting can burn through millions very quickly. If Kirk is locked up, the production will have to be shut down until he's out."

"Your Uncle Charles? He's aware of our fees?"

"He is. He said he'd triple it. More if necessary."

"I like the sound of that." Ray raised an eyebrow. "But isn't he overreacting a bit?"

Nicole rested her elbows on the table. "Do you know who Kirk Ford is?"

"Yeah, he's an actor who makes some goofy space movies."

She shook her head. "Goofy? The *Space Quest* franchise has raked in nearly two billion dollars so far."

Ray whistled. "That's adult money."

"This is the sixth episode. Supposed to be the biggest and best yet. But if Kirk's taken out of the picture—no pun intended—the entire thing collapses."

Ray massaged his neck. "Okay, why don't you two head over to New Orleans. See what the story is. I'll round up Pancake, and we'll start digging around."

She stood. "We're on it."

On it? She even sounded like a PI.

Ray looked at me. "Want to fly or drive?"

Fly popped in my head, but before I could say it, Nicole piped up.

"Drive," Nicole said. "We can get there faster."

Oh, Lord. I saw speed and fear in my future. Maybe a cardiac arrest. Which brought up another point. Why did I continually subject myself to her driving? I looked at her. Tight jeans, halter top, wonderfully toned abs. Well, there was all that.

"I'll call and get you a room somewhere," Ray said.

"Already done. Uncle Charles called Marty Ebersole. He's the director. We have a suite at the Monteleone. And Uncle Charles is leaving and headed there as soon as he can grab a flight."

Ray picked up the phone. "You guys get rolling. I'll track down Pancake."

"You got it," she said.

"And be careful," Ray added. "I saw on the Weather Channel site that there's a storm in New Orleans and it's headed this way."

Great. Wet roads, Nicole in hot-rod mode.

CHAPTER THREE

IT TOOK US the better part of two hours to get out of Gulf Shores.

First stop was Captain Rocky's. I checked in with Carla Martinez, my manager, to let her know I'd be away a few days and that she was in charge.

Her response: "I'm always in charge. You just own the joint."

And that was true. She did run the day-to-day business, but if need be, I could do it myself. But that would cut into my playtime. And playtime was important. Of course, Ray didn't see it that way. To him, playtime was wasted time. He even considered that my owning a bar was foolish. Felt I should throw in with him and work as a PI. Yeah, like that was going to happen.

But, while Carla was giving me the thumbnail of last week's receipts, expenses, and pending liquor and food inventory orders, and while I nodded as if I were truly listening, it dawned on me that once again Ray had pulled me into his orbit. Here I was, headed to New Orleans. To work for Ray. How the hell did that happen?

Then I glanced toward Nicole. Through the windows. She was on the deck, leaning on the rail, gazing out over the Gulf. That crystallized it. I mean, just look at her.

I had the kitchen whip up a pair of breakfast burritos and a thermos of coffee for us, and we headed to my place and then Nicole's to pack a few things. Took me twenty minutes; Nicole ten. Never seen a woman pack so quickly and efficiently.

We spun out of The Point, and twenty minutes later were soaring west on I-10. Warp Factor 4. Nicole had the 429 horses under the hood in full stride. I held on and shut up.

For a while, anyway.

"What's the story on Kirk Ford?" I asked, as we rolled through rural farmland. It had begun to sprinkle, and the horizon ahead looked dark and menacing. Great.

"Just what I said. He's a big deal. Pulls in a ton of cash for the studio."

"Thus, the franchise moniker."

"You got it. His *Space Quest* series began with *Hidden World*. It was about some cloaked planet that waged war against a neighbor."

"I hate it when that happens."

"It grossed over three hundred million."

"I guess there's big money in conquering cloaked planets."

"Kirk and crew swooped in and saved the day in that one. All the other episodes, too." She blew past a convoy of five semis.

"Somehow, I missed seeing them," I said.

"You're not his demographic anyway. He's big with the high school and college crowd. Very loyal fan base."

"This could put a dent in that. Whether he's guilty or not."

"That, of course, is Uncle Charles' concern. He has big money riding on this."

"What is this one?" I asked. "Little green men attacking Commander's Palace?"

She laughed. "No. It's called *Swamp Wars*. That's why they chose New Orleans. Lots of swamps to choose from."

"So, exactly how well do you know him? Kirk Ford?"

"We went out a couple of times."

"And?"

"And what?" She glanced at me.

"Were you two an item?"

She laughed. "No way. Of course, the tabloids tried to make it so. Even *People* magazine had a red-carpet pic of us together."

"The Oscars?"

"No, some minor award thing. I forget which one." She raised an eyebrow. "You jealous?"

"He is a hunky superstar."

"So are you." She laughed.

"I still hate him."

"You don't even know him."

"So? I can still hate him. It's a free country."

She rolled her eyes. I wished she wouldn't do that at eighty-five miles an hour on a slick highway.

"Truth is we had no chemistry," she said. "He's a nice guy but too pretty."

"Pretty? Not sure that's a term for a guy."

"It is for him. He's more pretty than handsome." She swerved around another eighteen-wheeler. "And no girl wants to be around a guy who's prettier than she is."

"Not possible in your case."

"You trying to garner points for the suite later?"

"Never hurts to plan ahead."

"You're such a good Boy Scout."

"That's what I was going for."

She shook her head. "In case you forgot, I'm easy."

"I'm going to hold you to that."

"Of course you are." In rapid succession, she dropped a Corvette, a Lexus, and a jacked-up SUV in her wake.

"You said Ford is a nice guy?"

"Yes. He is."

"Nice enough not to kill a lover?"

"Not the Kirk I know." She sighed. "I can't imagine he did this."

"Love and sex make folks do some awful stuff."

She nodded. "True."

I somehow missed Mississippi. The entire state. Seemed like it only took a couple of heartbeats, or in my case a couple of million, to cross the state and power into Louisiana. As we blew past the Slidell exit and charged headlong into the storm, Nicole kept her horses running. Soon we were out over Lake Pontchartrain, where the wind whipped the water into foam and some of the waves looked as if they might wash over the road. Sheets of rain battered the windshield at a low angle, the wipers barely able to keep up.

Didn't bother Nicole. She drove with one hand, the other twisting a strand of hair near her left ear. I would've preferred she used both hands, at the ten-and-two positions of course, but was smart enough to stay silent on that point.

The storm was powerful but short-lived. By the time we exited into the French Quarter, the rain had settled into a drizzle. I could even see patches of blue sky to the west.

A few twists and turns, and angry drivers, and Nicole slid to a stop in front of the Monteleone. White with gold trim and little curly things all over the front. Very French. Very wedding-cakey. Is that a word? Regardless, it's a good description.

A valet and two crisply attired bellmen appeared. The valet climbed in the Mercedes and whipped it around the corner toward the parking garage while our luggage rode a rolling cart through the front door. We followed.

Inside, the wedding cake was pretty cool, too. The Monteleone's lobby looked more like a palace on the Cote d'Azur. Vaulted ceilings, chandeliers, and a parquet floor. Behind the reception desk stood an attractive young lady whose name tag indicated she was Katrina. Nothing like the hurricane, nothing wind-blown or out of place, she was also crisply dressed, and offered a welcoming smile.

Took her all of a minute to tell us our suite was ready and another five minutes before a bellman opened the door to our room. It, too, belonged in a French palace. Uncle Charles did good. Very good.

While we unpacked, Nicole called Marty Ebersole. He said he'd meet us in the bar in thirty minutes. Not long enough for a nap, a shower, or "something else all together," so we decided a trip down-stairs to the bar was in order. A drink or two could only help. Right?

CHAPTER FOUR

THE MONTELEONE'S CAROUSEL Bar, a New Orleans icon, drew tourists like spilled sugar on a countertop attracts ants. Today was no exception, every seat occupied, drinkers loitering and laughing three deep around its perimeter, bartenders working in a chaotic but efficient rhythm to fill the stream of drink orders. New Orleans and alcohol were more or less synonymous. Especially the French Quarter where folks drank themselves into stupors, anger, or silliness on a nightly basis. Kept the NOPD busy, I suspected.

A canopy of carnival lights, mirrors, and painted Mardi Gras figures topped the circular bar and stools, each with hand-carved wooden backs inlaid with mosaics of big-game animals, perched around the perimeter. Lions and tigers and elephants. Like a real carousel, the entire arrangement rotated, making a complete circle every fifteen minutes. I wasn't sure alcohol and orbiting a bar were a good combination. I checked the stools for seat belts but didn't see any. No airbags either.

We bypassed the carousel and moved into a more normal area of the bar where we settled into comfortable leather chairs around a pair of thick glass coffee tables that didn't rotate but did wobble slightly on the old floor.

In a heartbeat, a pleasant waitress named Tracey arrived. Nicole ordered the house Cab; I a Maker's Mark, on the rocks. In no time, the bubbly Tracey returned with our drinks. No bar in the Quarter allowed fists to stay empty very long.

A family of tourists grabbed a nearby table. A couple and three kids, early teens I guessed. Each carried a stuffed plastic shopping bag. The kids were jabbering about one of the street performers they had seen. Apparently one of those statue dudes. This one painted silver from head to toe and standing motionless on an inverted metal can, from what I could gather. The patriarch of the group looked like he hadn't missed a meal while in New Orleans. Probably not in his entire life, for that matter. His gaze kept devouring Nicole. Pervert. But then again, I'm guilty of the same thing.

I called Ray, told him we had arrived and were waiting for Marty Ebersole. Ray and Pancake were on his deck, no shock there. He said he'd turned up a couple of things.

"The victim is Kristi Guidry," Ray said, "nineteen."

"You're kidding. Nineteen?"

Nicole started to say something, but I held up a finger. She frowned.

"Afraid so," Ray said. "She was nearing the completion of her freshman year at Tulane. Don't know much else about her yet, but Pancake's digging around. I'm sure he'll come up with something. The detective in charge is a guy named Troy Doucet. I have a call into him. Waiting to hear back. I did talk with one of the uniforms who was at the scene. Sounded like a rookie, or at least someone without a ton of experience. Did know enough to keep his mouth shut and not draw the ire of his bosses, though. All I got was that he felt Ford was in a world of shit."

"That's putting it mildly."

"Pancake and I'll keep at it and let you know what we dig up."

"Hopefully Ebersole can fill in some of the blanks."

"Later," Ray said, and ended the call.

"What did the boss say?" Nicole asked.

"The boss?"

"Okay, Ray."

"Not much. The girl was nineteen. A college freshman."

Nicole sighed and shook her head. "Kirk's dick is going to be the end of him."

"If it isn't already."

I saw a man round the carousel, scan the room, locate Nicole, and head our way. Ebersole, I assumed.

It was. Nicole made the introductions and he sat. Short, thin, and wiry, he had rust-colored hair in tight curls that looked like a shower cap of sorts, and intense blue eyes. And speaking of intense—he seemed in perpetual motion. One knee bouncing, gaze flitting here and there, never really locking on anything, as if his eyes remained stationary for more than a second his retinas might burn out. He wore jeans, an open-collared blue shirt, and a black leather jacket. Seemed a bit warm for the weather, but it did look cool. And being a Hollywood type, I suspected cool trumped all else. He appeared very director-y. Is that a word?

"So, anything new?" Nicole asked.

He shook his head. "The twins and I went by the PD to see Kirk."

Nicole must have sensed the question that came to my mind because she jumped in. "The twins are Tara and Tegan James. Kirk's sidekicks in *Space Quest.*"

I should have known who he meant. I mean, their blond hair and lean bodies appeared on every *Space Quest* poster I'd ever seen. Not to mention every checkout counter tabloid in the country. I think I remembered an article about one of them being impregnated by a space alien. And that was one of the more believable tales about the two.

I nodded. "Ah, yes."

"Anyway," Ebersole continued, "they wouldn't let us talk to him. Said he was still being booked." He rolled his eyes. "Really? He's been there eight hours. Either they're the slowest people on Earth or they're just screwing with me."

"When can we see him?" Nicole asked.

"Tomorrow morning. He's going to be arraigned and have a bail hearing at ten."

"That's fast," I said.

"Ben Kornblatt. The studio's legal council. He made a few calls, got some local legal eagle on the case." His leg stopped vibrating, and the finger tapping his knee fell silent for a few seconds. He glanced toward the ceiling as if recalling something. "Can't remember his name." All parts went back into motion. "Kornblatt's flying in tonight."

Tracey the waitress appeared. Ebersole ordered a Manhattan and Nicole and I refills.

"What about the girl?" Nicole asked. "What do you know about her?"

"Nineteen." He shook his head. "Kirk's usual dalliance."

"And?"

"What do you mean *and*? She's dead."

Nicole tossed him a slight frown. "What I meant is what's her story?"

"Name's Kristi Guidry. Worked mornings over at Café du Monde. That's where Kirk met her."

"When?" I asked.

"Maybe a week ago. She's been around essentially daily since then."

I assumed around meant in Kirk's room.

Our drinks arrived.

"Anything else?" Tracey asked.

Ebersole raised his glass. "I'll need another one of these in a minute."

She smiled and walked away.

Ebersole took a sip of his drink. "Girl's two older brothers are making a stink. Talking to every TV news reporter they can find. Saying Kirk is a predator. That sort of thing."

Well, in a way he was, I thought. I didn't express that opinion. Truth was I knew how this worked. Hollywood and Major League Baseball have that in common. Young women following the team, appearing in considerable numbers in whatever bars and restaurants the players frequented while traveling from stadium to stadium. I know I'd had my share. But that was another story, another life almost. Part of me missed that, most of me didn't.

"Can't say I blame them," Nicole said. "Big brothers are usually protective of little sisters."

Ebersole shrugged. "True." He took another slug of martini. "Rumor is their uncle, Kristi's too, of course, is some local badass." He shook his head. "With my luck he's probably a gangster or drug dealer or methed-up motorcycle dude."

His luck? Wasn't it Kirk who was locked up for murder?

Ebersole drained his glass just as the next one appeared. He smiled and nodded a thanks to Tracey the waitress. She gathered the empty and headed back toward the bar.

"We didn't shoot today," Ebersole said. "A storm blew through."

"We know," I said. "Nicole flew through it."

"Flew? I thought you drove."

"Semantics," I said.

She slugged me. Hard. On the arm.

"I see." Ebersole smiled. "I forgot. I rode through LA with her. Once."

I gave her a smug look. "See? I'm not the only one."

She rolled her eyes. "Wimps."

"The main thing is that he has to make bail tomorrow." Ebersole massaged one temple as he spoke. "We can't afford to hang around while the wheels of justice grind along." He sighed. "Kornblatt will need to work his magic and get Kirk back on the set, pronto."

"I'd bet the bail tab will be high," I said. "If he gets it at all."

"Doesn't matter as long as there's bail. The amount is irrelevant. We can cover it."

I suspected a two-billion-dollar franchise would allow that. I also wondered how much pull some slick LA attorney would have down here in the Big Easy. I flashed on an image of a shiny three-piece suit facing a stern judge, jeans, tee shirt, and a .45 beneath his black robe. Could be a hell of a show.

"It happened here?" I asked. "In this hotel? Right?"

Again, Ebersole's movements abruptly ceased and he nodded. "Kirk's room is just down the hall from yours." His knee kicked back into gear. "Want to see it?"

That didn't compute. It'd been less than a dozen hours since the crime was reported. I couldn't imagine the police and the forensic dudes had released the scene yet. I said so to Ebersole.

"No problem," he said. "I have a key."

"You do?" Nicole asked.

"Of course. I'm paying for the room." He smiled. "Actually, the hotel gave me one today."

I couldn't believe it. "They gave you a key to a crime scene?"

He shrugged. "The cops took Kirk's, and I didn't want to be locked out, so to speak. The room's in my name, and I guess the girl at registration didn't get the memo on Kristi Guidry's murder. Regardless, she gave me a copy."

"Still, I'm not sure contaminating a crime scene is a good move," I said.

"Then don't touch anything." He drained his drink and waved Tracey the waitress over.

Ten minutes later, we faced the door to Kirk's suite. None of that yellow crime scene tape slashed across the entry, rather a simple sign that said, "Out of Service." You think? Guess the Monteleone had some pull. Didn't want to upset the clientele and a crime scene banner would do exactly that.

Ebersole opened the door and we entered.

I hesitated just inside. The term breaking and entering seemed appropriate. If we got caught, we would end up in a cage with some of New Orleans' finest miscreants. Didn't seem to bother Nicole and Ebersole, though.

Kirk's suite was an exact copy of ours. Two rooms: a spacious living area and, through a pair of open, glass-paned French doors, the sleeping quarters. Even had the same green curtains, and cream-colored sofa and floral chairs around a wrought-iron, glass-topped coffee table.

Of course, our suite didn't have fingerprint powder splotching the entry door and frame. Nor was our bed stripped to a mattress that sat slightly askew on the frame. A trash can roosted on the cabinet next to the TV, and beneath it, the in-room fridge stood open and empty. More fingerprint powder smudged the bathroom doorjamb.

"The cops took the sheets, and Kirk's and the girl's clothing. They were piled on the sofa." He pointed back toward the living room area. "They found two empty wine bottles and a couple of condoms in the trash can, and a pair of wine glasses by the bed. Also, three joints, one half smoked. Took all that, too."

"The girl was strangled, right?" I asked.

Ebersole nodded. "When Kirk called and told me what had happened, I came running. The girl was in bed, her bra wound around her neck."

Nicole swallowed hard. "What did Kirk say?"

"That he remembered nothing. They had been in here drinking and smoking and having sex and fell asleep. When he woke up, she was sprawled next to him. Dead. Cold."

"They didn't have an argument or anything like that?" I asked.

"He said they were having a good time. Maybe too much of a good time."

Nicole walked around the bed. "And he doesn't remember anything?"

Ebersole shook his head. "Nothing. Said he must have been hammered. Said this morning he had the worst hangover ever."

I suspected finding a dead nineteen-year-old in your bed could easily do that. Hell, my head was beginning to throb. What was it Ray had said the rookie cop told him? That Kirk was in a world of shit. From where I stood, it was all that and then some.

CHAPTER FIVE

As HE LOCKED up Kirk's room, Ebersole said he had set up dinner for us at seven thirty. Meant we had an hour or so to kill. Nicole and I moseyed down the hall to our room. She busied herself doing Nicole stuff, and I stretched out on the bed with a book, Sports Center on TV, the volume cranked down to a barely audible whisper.

"What are you reading?" Nicole asked.

"Some self-defense book Ray gave me. He said I needed to be tougher. His word."

She sat on the edge of the bed and mussed my hair. "Poor baby."

"I'm tough."

She laughed. "Jake, you're a lover, not a fighter."

I tried to pout, but it didn't work.

"But I will say," she went on, "you sure handled Borkov's baddies. On the boat that night."

That was true. I still had a few fastballs in me and I threw a couple of beauties that night. I could still see the surprise on Joe Zuma's face as first one and then the other ball approached at eighty miles an hour. Forehead, then throat. Two perfect pitches.

"So, all I have to remember is to keep a couple of baseballs around."

She raised an eyebrow. "I think you have enough balls already."

"Funny. But I'll take that as a compliment."

She smiled. "As it was intended." She glanced at the book. "Are you learning anything?"

"Just where people are vulnerable. How to incapacitate them if need be."

"Balls," Nicole said. "That always works."

"Unless it's a woman."

"What, you're afraid of a woman?"

"I'm afraid of you." I was. She was into kickboxing. I'd seen her work out on a bag a couple of times. From what I saw, those long, wonderful legs could be positively lethal.

"You'd better be." She laughed. "So, if it's a woman, what do you do?"

"The eyes. Says here that a simple flick of your finger at the eye will stop anyone."

"So Ray's big bad self-defense book recommends thumping someone with a finger?"

"Not thumping. Flicking. And in the eye."

"Still sounds wimpy to me."

"Unless it's your eye."

"You better read a few more chapters." She smiled. "Later." She peeled off her top, jeans, and black thong and stood naked, eyeing me. "Ready for a shower?"

I looked her up and down. "Since you put it that way." I rolled out of bed.

I loved showers. Particularly when they turned into something else altogether.

Afterwards, we slipped on the robes the hotel provided and stretched out on the bed. Nicole flipped the channel to Fox News, and I picked up my self-defense book. I managed to read all of one page before my cell chimed. It was Ray.

"Okay," he said. "That detective, Troy Doucet, called back. Seemed like a nice enough guy. Not too shy about chatting with me."

"Really?"

"Well, I had my guy at the local FBI field office give him a call. Let him know we were legit."

"What do they have?"

"Let's see. Ford found the girl dead. In his bed. The door was locked. Just the two of them. Told Doucet he remembered little about the entire evening."

"Ebersole said Kirk told him he was hammered. Wine and marijuana. Did Doucet say they turned up any other drugs?"

Nicole muted the TV and rolled to her side, facing me, questions in her eyes.

"Ford admitted to wine and marijuana but nothing heavy," Ray said. "The toxicology stuff will take a couple of days."

I shifted my phone to the other ear. "Kirk must've had a shitload of wine."

"Guess the lab guys will tell us that. Anyway, there's an arraignment and bail hearing in the morning."

"Yeah, we know. Ten a.m."

"Be there," Ray said.

"We will."

"Doucet said he'd meet with you afterwards."

"Great. And Kirk's attorney—actually the studio's attorney—some guy named . . ." I drew a blank.

"Ben Kornblatt," Ray said.

"Yeah, Kornblatt. He's flying in on the red-eye and he'll be there, too. He's got some local hotshot on the case as cocounsel."

"Walton Greene," Ray said. "He's with one of the big New Orleans firms."

Damn, Ray was good. More likely Pancake. Sounded like something he would dig up.

"Sounds like Kirk's well represented," I said.

"The best big money can buy."

"Do you think they'll give him bail? On a murder beef? And he's not local?"

"Not to mention the judge is known to be a bit of a hard-ass," Ray added.

"Who is it?"

"Let's see." I heard Ray push some papers around. "William Booth. Been on the bench for nearly twenty years. Law and order type."

"Doesn't bode well," I said.

"Guess we'll see. You guys hit the court tomorrow. Pancake's digging around in the girl's world. I'll let you know what we find."

"One other thing," I said. "The girl's two brothers are making waves. Talking with the press about how evil Ford is."

"Expected."

"And their uncle is supposed to be some tough guy. At least, that's what Ebersole heard."

"I'll get on it."

"Okay."

"Be cool." He disconnected the call.

CHAPTER SIX

NICOLE AND I arrived at Mr. B's Bistro a few minutes late. It was Nicole's fault. She changed outfits three times. I innocently sat on the edge of the bed in black boxer briefs and watched the show. I mean, really, how could I not? She wriggled in and out of various colored jeans, finally settling on white, and an untucked dark-green silk shirt. She did a 360 before the mirror, and then looked at me, saying, "You going like that?"

"I might."

"Maybe some pants?"

"Not what you said earlier."

That got a shake of the head. But she had a point. Jeans, black golf shirt, sneakers, good to go.

Getting to Mr. B's was easy. It was directly across the street. We pushed through the glass entry doors and were met by a hostess, young—I mean she looked about twelve—and attractive in black pants and a crisp white shirt, smiling from behind the reception stand.

"Welcome to Mr. B's," she said, her smile warm and genuine. "How may I help you?"

"I think the reservation is under Martin Ebersole," Nicole said.

"Yes. The others are here. Please, follow me."

She led us to a secluded green leather booth near the back where Ebersole and the James twins, Tara and Tegan, were sipping wine. Nicole hugged the girls and then introduced me.

"Sorry we're late," Nicole said, taking her seat. "Jake had trouble getting dressed."

Really? I started to complain that I was distracted but decided on silence. I simply smiled and sat.

"You look nice," Tegan said. Or was it Tara?

I did look nice. Even cool. My humble opinion.

"And hot," her sister added. "Just as Nicole said."

"She did?" I asked.

That got a shrug and a smile from Nicole.

Our waiter materialized and handed Nicole and me menus and took our drink orders.

"Anything new from Ray?" Ebersole asked.

I shook my head. "Nothing you don't already know, but he and Pancake are working on a couple of things."

"Pancake?" Tara asked. Or was it Tegan?

I explained the unexplainable. Tommy Jeffers, aka Pancake. Big, redheaded, and a whole lot smarter than most people gave him credit for on first blush. Looked like a big dumb jock, but his computer skills were legendary. Could dig into areas that for most were inaccessible. Not to mention you wanted him on your side in a brawl. Big chest, big arms, big fists. He could definitely bring the pain if need be.

"He sounds cute," Tara/Tegan said.

Cute is not a word I had ever heard used to describe Pancake. Charming? Sure. Even affable worked. Sometimes scary was a better fit.

"First dibs," one twin said.

"No way," her sister fired back. "It's my turn."

"Turn?" I asked.

They laughed in unison.

The twin on the left elaborated. "We have a deal."

"Not really," the other said.

"Do, too."

"You always say that."

The left twin took a sip of wine. "'Cause it's true."

The twins were stunning. Even more so in the flesh than on the posters and in the tabloids. Straight blond hair, similar to Nicole, blue eyes, similar to Nicole, and lean, mean bodies, like Nicole. And they were also disturbingly identical. Even their all-black attire and simple gold necklaces matched. I had known a few identical twins, and in each case, there were subtle differences. Not just in clothing and mannerisms, but in the face. Slight differences that allowed some degree of distinction. But Tara and Tegan looked, moved, talked, laughed, everything I could see as if one was the reflection of the other.

"I'm sorry," I said. "But which of you is which?"

Another unified laugh.

"I'm Tara," the left twin said. "And Tegan is my younger sister."

"Younger by about a minute," Tegan said.

"More like three minutes."

"Whatever."

Okay, so Tara left, Tegan right. Now, if they didn't move, I'd be fine.

Our waiter returned with Nicole's wine and my Maker's. He asked if we were ready to order, but Ebersole said we hadn't even looked at the menu yet. He nodded, saying he'd check back shortly, and walked away.

"Don't worry," Tara said. "No one can tell us apart."

"And make no mistake," Tegan said. "We use that all the time."

Tara: "Drove our teachers crazy."

Tegan: "Boys, too."

Tara: "Oh, yeah."

"So you two date the same guys?" I asked.

Tegan: "Sometimes and they—"

Tara: "—never know the difference."

Tegan: "Almost never."

Tara: "Never."

Tegan: "Well there was that Jimmy what's-his-name dude."

Tara: "He didn't know."

Tegan: "Sort of."

"Sort of?" I asked.

Tegan: "Tara went out with this wannabe actor type. Jimmy . . . uh . . . somebody."

Tara: "Never can remember his last name."

Tegan: "Me, either."

"Bet he'd be thrilled to know he made such an impression," I said.

Tegan: "He didn't complain. But Tara got tired of him."

Tara: "After two dates."

Tegan: "But I thought he was cute—"

Tara: "—so when he next asked me out—"

Tegan: "—I went."

I nodded. "And he never knew?"

Tara: "Nope."

Tegan: "But he did note that the sex was better."

Tara: "You always say that."

Tegan: "Just telling it like it was."

Tara: "That's because you're a bigger slut."

Tegan: "Yeah, right."

I was glad we got that settled before our waiter returned. We ordered. He collected our menus and left.

"I understand you guys went by the jail to see Kirk," Nicole said.

Tegan: "Didn't get very far."

Tara: "They were dicks."

Tegan: "Not the cute one."

Tara: "In a blond-hair, blue-eyed—"

Tegan: "—hot body—"

Tara: "—sort of way."

Tegan: "Not to mention the uniform."

Tara: "Very cool."

My brain felt like it was suffering from a contrecoup injury as my head swiveled back and forth. These girls had the twins-finishing-each-others-sentences thing down to an art form.

"Bottom line," Ebersole said, "the twins tried their magic on this young cop, and it nearly worked. I think we might have gotten by him. His sergeant was a different story."

Tara: "No sense of humor."

Tegan: "None."

"Let me ask you girls something," I said. "You know Kirk well, I take it?"

Tegan: "Since we were fourteen."

Tara: "When the *Space Quest* series started."

"What do you think?" I asked. "Could he have done this?"

"No way," they said in unison.

Tara: "Kirk would never—"

Tegan: "—do anything like that."

"I take it you knew the girl? Kristi Guidry?"

Their heads bobbed in perfect sync. The Rockettes would've been jealous.

"And?"

Tara looked at her sister, hesitated, and then said, "We liked her."

"Pretty, smart, and funny," Tegan added.

"Any tension between the two of them?" I asked.

Tegan shook her head, while parking a wayward stand of perfect blond hair behind her ear. "She liked Kirk. That's for sure."

"I think she was in love," Tara said. "Never a good thing as far as Kirk's concerned."

"In what way?" I asked.

"Broken heart," Tegan said. "Kirk never gets involved. Mainly seeks out temporary distractions. The women he hooks up with always seem to think it's more than a fling, but Kirk doesn't really do love."

"More like lust," Tara added.

"I understand he has a habit of that? Hooking up while on a location shoot?"

"It's what he does," Tegan said. "But then, all actors do."

"But don't get the wrong idea," Tara said. "There's nothing malicious about it. Kirk is charming, if anything."

Tegan nodded her agreement. "And handsome. And hot. And totally cool."

I smiled. "Sounds like you girls have a crush on him."

Tara: "Big-time."

Tegan: "In a brotherly sort of way. He's like the big brother we never had."

Tara: "Really looks out for us."

Tegan: "Sometimes overly protective." She drained her wine glass. "More than a few times he's run off guys we tried to hang with. If he thought they were bad actors."

Tara: "True story. And he's usually right."

Tegan: "Especially the dudes you try to pick up."

Tara: "Yeah. Like you never do?"

Tegan tossed a mock frown at her sister. "But I will say that usually the girls only last a day or two, so, Kristi being around for a whole week meant he totally liked her."

"So, she was different than his usual?" I asked.

Tegan stared at me. "I think that's true." She glanced at Tara. "She's the first one I can remember who might've been able to steal him away?"

"Steal him away?"

"From us," Tara said.

"We're very protective of him, too," Tegan said. She smiled. "Him being our big brother."

Tara nodded. "Totally."

"Sounds like you guys are very close," I said.

Tegan swirled the wine in her glass and took a sip. "We love him madly."

Our food arrived and it was magnificent. Of course, I've never had a bad meal in New Orleans. Especially at Mr. B's. While we ate, we discussed the upcoming arraignment. Ebersole said we should get there early. He expected it to be a zoo with the media and Kirk Ford fans out in force, but added that Kornblatt had arranged spots for us just behind the defense table.

Front-row seats to the big event.

CHAPTER SEVEN

CAFÉ DU MONDE. No place like it. I never visited the Big Easy without at least one trip for their beignets and chicory coffee. The aroma of each hung thick beneath the green awning that covered the patio, as did the din of conversation. It was just after eight and the place was packed, as usual, but Nicole and I managed to snag a table along the railing. Out on the sidewalk a street performer, a guy dressed like a clown, face paint and all, squeaked together balloon animals that he handed to one excited kid after another. Parents dropped bills into the small aluminum bucket near his feet. Free enterprise, baby.

Our waitress, Patty according to her name tag, walked up, pad and pen in hand, and we ordered. Only took a couple of minutes before she returned and placed a plate of sugary beignets and two steaming cups of coffee on our table. Turnover at Café du Monde was rapid. Smooth, polite, friendly, but rapid. Keep the money train rolling. Patty asked if we needed anything else, and after we assured her we were fine, she waltzed away.

Here's the thing. There is no way to eat beignets without decorating your clothes with powdered sugar. Not possible. Nicole did a better job than I did, and still, her dark-green pullover looked like Christmas.

"Want me to brush the sugar off your chest?" I asked.

"Unless you want to lick it off."

All in all, not a bad idea. But maybe not here. Instead, I rolled my eyes.

"Just thought I'd throw that out there," she said.

Woman was evil.

We had a little over an hour before we hooked up with Kornblatt and Ebersole to limo over to the courthouse for Kirk's arraignment. And for Kornblatt to plead for bail. Of course, the fare was reason enough to visit Café du Monde, but my hope was that we could chat with someone with some insight into Kristi Guidry. She had worked here, so she must have friends on the staff. When our waitress spun back by, I asked her if she knew Kristi.

She hesitated, then said, "I heard about what happened. I mean, everyone has. Just awful. She was so nice." She looked out toward the street. "I still can't believe it."

"So you knew her?" Nicole asked.

"Yeah. Not well, but I knew her."

"Would anyone here know her better?" I asked.

"Why're you asking?"

"We're investigating her murder," I said.

Again, she hesitated. "You don't look like cops."

"We aren't," Nicole said. "Private investigators."

Private investigators. It rolled off her tongue so naturally. Like she'd said it a million times. She was really getting into this PI stuff. Ray had created a monster.

"Oh," Patty said, as if that had answered her question. "You might talk to Gloria. She and Kristi were tight."

"Is she here today?"

She looked around. "Yeah. Somewhere. I'll find her and send her by."

"Thanks."

By the time we finished the beignets and dusted the stray powder from our clothing, Gloria appeared. She was small, thin, with ebony skin, full cheeks, and dark eyes that were alive and expressive.

"Patty said you wanted to talk."

I introduced Nicole and me. "Is this a good time and place to chat?"

"Not really, but it'll do."

A couple at an adjacent table waved to get her attention. She raised a finger, saying, "Just a sec."

Patty came by and touched Gloria's shoulder. "I'll take care of them."

"Thanks." Gloria directed her attention back to us. "You guys are private investigators. Right?"

"We are," Nicole said.

"And you want to talk about Kristi?" Gloria asked.

"Just a few questions," Nicole said. "If you don't mind."

"Who're you working for?"

"My uncle. He's the executive producer for the movie being shot here."

"So, you're here to help that asshole that killed Kristi?"

"Not really," I said. "Simply trying to figure out what happened."

"Shit. I can tell you that. He killed her."

"Maybe," I said. "And if so, we want to know that. And why."

She looked at me, her eyes narrowing. "Kristi was good people. She didn't deserve any of this."

I nodded. "That's what we hear."

"Believe it. She was solid. Totally solid." Moisture gathered in her eyes. "What do you want to know?"

"Did you ever meet Kirk Ford?"

"Sure. He would come in here, flash money around, all smiles and good looks. People fawning all over him. Like a goddamn movie star. 'Course, I guess he is."

"Up until yesterday, what did you think of him?" I asked.

"Yeah, well, that was then. This is now."

I waited her out.

She sighed and wiped her eyes with the back of one hand. "Truth is, I was taken by him, too. I mean, he is a good-looking dude. And seemed nice."

"What about Kristi?" Nicole asked. "How did she feel about him?"

"Girl fell hard. I think she thought it was true love."

"Maybe it was."

Gloria let out a little explosive laugh. "He has a funny way of showing it, don't you think?"

"What about him?" I asked. "How do you think he felt about her?"

"I don't know for sure. But he seemed to be into her. I mean, they'd sit over there"—she waved a hand—"at that corner table. Get all moony-eyed and kissy-faced. Sort of embarrassing if you ask me."

"No arguments? Problems?"

"Not that I saw. And Kristi said he treated her like a queen. 'Course, I told her he probably does that to all the girls." A faint smile parted her lips, and she looked down as if thinking of something. "She wouldn't buy any of that. Said he wasn't like that."

"Drugs?" I asked. "Did Kristi use any?"

Gloria shook her head. "No. Never."

I gave Nicole a quick glance. "What about her family? I understand her brothers are making noises."

"Wouldn't you? Your kid sister gets murdered? Wouldn't that stir up your hornets?"

I smiled. "Sure would."

"Well, Robert and Kevin aren't guys you want to mess with. They ain't real bright but they're big and bad dudes."

Mister squeaky balloon the clown and the entourage of giggling and shrieking kids he had attracted were making it hard to concentrate.

Cute for about a minute, their racket was rapidly becoming annoying. Didn't seem to bother Nicole though.

"And her parents?" Nicole asked.

"Dead. Her mother died when Kristi was young. Maybe five or six. Some kind of cancer, I think. She didn't talk about it much. Just missed the hell out of her. Then in high school her father was killed when some drunk T-boned his car. On his way to work. Early in the morning." She shook her head. "Folks around here drink any time. Morning, noon, night, it don't much matter." She wiped her hands on the towel she had stuffed in her apron tie. "Her uncle took care of her and her brothers after that."

"Who's her uncle?" I asked.

She looked at me as if I were stupid. "For a couple of investigators, you don't know a whole bunch, do you?"

"That's why we ask questions." I smiled again.

That seemed to soften her a notch. "Sorry. This is just all too much."

"I understand. I lost my mom at an early age, too."

Again, her eyes glistened. "Well, her uncle is Tony Guidry. And you don't want to be anywhere near his bad side."

"You're the second person who's told us that," Nicole said.

"Believe it. It's true."

"What do you mean by bad?" I asked.

"He's the real deal. No make-believe there, from what I hear. Story is he's connected."

"Connected?"

"You know. The mob."

"Mob?" Nicole said. "I thought that was a thing of the past."

Another short laugh. "Where the hell you think you are? This is New Orleans. Gambling, alcohol, drugs, tittie bars. All that shit mob guys got their fingers into."

"And Uncle Tony is in all that?" I asked.

"I don't know what he's into and even if I did I wouldn't bump my gums about it. I ain't stupid." She paused a beat. "Look, I got to get back to work."

"Thanks for talking with us," Nicole said. "It really helped."

"Don't know about that, but I was you, I'd steer clear of her brothers and Tony and his guys. They just might find your ass rolling down the Mississippi."

What a pleasant thought.

She started to walk away, but I stopped her by asking, "Was Kristi seeing anyone else? During or before Kirk showed up?"

She turned back to me. "Yeah. Owen Vaughn. Good guy. I thought he and Kristi might be in it for the long haul. They've been an item for years."

"But?"

"He did what guys do. Cheated on her. So she dumped him."

"When was that?"

She looked up as if recalling. "A few months ago."

"How'd he take it?" Nicole asked.

"Not well. Came by and begged her to forgive him. Saying it was a stupid mistake. She agreed with that alright. But she wouldn't take him back." She sighed. "Still, he came around and tried to snag her."

"Was he upset?" I asked. "Angry? Anything like that?

She shook her head. "Not really angry. Owen's not an angry guy. I'd say more crushed than anything."

"So, no threats or anything like that?" Nicole asked.

"Not Owen's style."

"What is his style?"

"You know—quiet, soft-spoken. Very polite. That's my take anyway. Of course, I was wrong about Kirk Ford, too."

"Do you know how we could reach him?" I asked. "Owen?"

"His dad owns a car repair shop. Over off Esplanade. Vaughn's Motor Works or something like that. Owen works there."

Nicole reached out and touched Gloria's arm. "And I'm truly sorry about your loss."

She scrunched her eyes, holding back tears, followed by a short sniff. "Yeah, life's a big old bitch sometimes." She spun and weaved her way through the tables toward the kitchen.

CHAPTER EIGHT

DIRECTOR MARTY EBERSOLE expected a zoo at the courthouse. He got one. Big-time.

The Orleans Parish Criminal District Court covered an entire block of Tulane Avenue just north of the Pontchartrain Expressway in a neighborhood populated by rows of shotgun houses. An array of Corinthian columns gave it a certain majesty as did the series of age-tarnished double doors that led inside. The press, well represented with cameras, shoulder-held video equipment, and slickly dressed, live-remote-ready reporters, jostled for position with what I guessed was well over a thousand other folks.

The throng packed the broad entry staircase and the grassy areas that flanked it. Several uniformed officers maintained a line along the curb in a futile attempt to keep the crowd from drifting into the street. Only marginally successful from what I could see. The traffic along Tulane snarled as cars jerked to a stop to avoid pedestrians who darted across the street and many brushed dangerously close to other oblivious gawkers. Our limo crept along with the flow.

"What a mess," Nicole said.

"Sure is."

"How are we going to get through that?"

"Head down, straight ahead, and avoid eye contact."

She laughed. "Not sure that'll work." She looked out the window. "Reminds me of the mob outside Dr. Frankenstein's castle. All they need are torches and pitchforks."

There was truth in that. The good citizens did appear to be divided into two camps, some lifting signs that supported Kirk, his smiling face front and center on many of them; others waved placards that called him everything from a child molester to a serial predator and murderer. Nothing like a high-profile killing to divide a city. Especially if even a hint of sex is involved. I hoped the shouted verbal assaults they directed at each other didn't become physical. Particularly since we had to wade through them.

When the limo stopped, we clamored out and followed Ebersole and the twins through the wake created by a pair of NOPD uniforms through the crowd and up the stairs. Cheers and jeers followed us. Some screamed to Tegan and Tara and extended pieces of paper and flapping pads, begging for autographs; others directed stabbing glares and angry shouts our way as if we were guilty by our connection to Kirk. I grasped Nicole's arm tightly until we pushed through the entry doors.

Inside was quieter. Security tight. A dozen NOPD officers and four guys who looked like SWAT dudes—tactical gear, automatic weapons, alert eyes, no smiles—funneled us to a table manned by two uniformed officers. They checked our IDs and matched our names to those on a list. I wondered if our names hadn't made the list whether we'd be escorted out, handcuffed, or shot. Looked like it could go either way. To say everyone was tense didn't quite do it justice. Each of the officers attempted to appear relaxed, casual, but their sharp, intrusive stares said otherwise. Well, there was one who seemed distracted. His gaze kept sweeping over the twins, and Nicole. I wanted to tell him to stop oogling—where had I heard that word before?—but since he was armed, I beat that idea into submission.

Fortunately, we made it past the security check—metal detectors, pat-downs, purse searches—and were led down a long hallway to the courtroom. Before we made it inside, Nicole's cell chimed. She answered, walking away from us as she brought the phone to her ear. She chatted for a few minutes, slipped the phone back in her pocket, and returned to where we stood.

"Uncle Charles," she said. "Wanted an update. Also said he wasn't going to make it anytime soon."

"Oh?" I asked.

"Some big dustup at the remote site. Seems the owner of the property is threatening to toss them out. Uncle Charles thinks it's simply a shakedown for more money."

"Ah, money."

"Anyway, the entire production is on hold until he settles it."

"Ah, the French."

She smiled. "You got that right."

"Bet he isn't too happy about now. I mean, two productions in limbo."

"While the bills keep rolling in."

When we entered the courtroom, already packed, a soft, electric hum of voices filling the air, all eyes seemed to turn toward us. Well, Nicole and the twins anyway.

Ben Kornblatt greeted us, shaking hands with Ebersole and me and hugging the girls over the railing that divided the spectators from the business end of the courtroom. He was tall, with thick black hair, and wore a perfectly tailored dark blue suit—an Armani or something equally high-end—a white shirt, and red tie. Power and confidence. Kornblatt was a player. No doubt.

He introduced us to his local cocounsel, Walton Greene. Thin and wiry, brown hair that could use a comb, his tan suit a size too large and a little less crisp.

The prosecutor, an attractive woman, leaned, straight-armed, on the railing behind her table, and chatted with three men. Two younger guys, very large, very stone-faced, probably the brothers; and a shorter, thicker, older guy with dark hair, graying at the temples, and a three-piece, faintly pinstriped navy blue suit. Tony Guidry, the uncle. Had to be.

Though he looked at and talked directly to the prosecutor, I got the impression that much of his attention was on us. No glances our way, but I had the feeling he was sizing us up peripherally. I also suspected he was all Gloria the Café du Monde waitress had said he was. Dangerous. Face relaxed, hands folded calmly in his lap, he looked as if he was in control of all before him. The entire courtroom. I wondered if that extended to the judge, who had yet to make an appearance.

The two brothers were a different story. They looked at us with hooded eyes and tight jaws. No doubt we were the enemy. As if they didn't need a trial to declare Kirk Ford guilty—just take him out back and hang him—and anyone who even hinted at supporting him was fair game.

Their collective gaze left us and turned toward a door to the left of the bench as it swung open. Kirk walked through, accompanied by the bailiff. He wore a tan suit and blue shirt, no tie. At least he wasn't in jail garb, and no handcuffs. He caught Nicole's eye and offered a thin smile.

She leaned into me, whispering, "He looks scared."

He did. His face was tight, jaw set, eyes wide and almost glassy. "Nice suit though."

"Kornblatt's insistence, I'm sure," she said. "Probably leaned on the judge."

"Probably. Jail jumpsuits always make you look guilty."

Nicole was right about one thing. Despite the circumstances, and his obvious fear, Kirk was indeed pretty. No other word seemed to fit.

I mean, I'd seen his face in movies and on the covers of magazines, but none of those did him justice. He had that "thing." That "It Factor." That charismatic halo that made him the superstar he was. If it came to it, I wondered if the jury would hold that against him or melt before his charm. From the facts we had assembled so far, Kirk better hope for the latter.

Kirk moved behind the table, shook hands with Kornblatt and Greene, then took his seat, adjusting his collar so that it lay just right. He never looked toward the prosecution table.

"All rise," the bailiff barked. The black-robed judge, the Honorable William Booth, walked in, climbed behind his podium, sat, and said, "Please be seated."

The show had begun.

After all the preliminary mumbo jumbo, the judge asked the prosecutor to present her arguments. She introduced herself as Assistant DA Melissa Mooring and jumped directly into vilifying Kirk. Only he and the girl had been in the room, the door locked, no one else with access.

Well, that wasn't exactly true. Ebersole had a key card. Though, according to him, he didn't get it until later in the day, after the fingerprint dust had settled, so to speak. And, of course, the hotel staff had access. Did anyone else? Couldn't those things be cloned? I made a mental note to ask Ray. He'd probably know. Pancake would for sure.

Mooring continued, pointing out that the victim had been brutally strangled to death. That she was young and naive and just entering womanhood with her entire life before her. That she had been starstruck and manipulated into bed by a "seasoned predator" who had a history of such behavior. That Kirk's lack of "memory of these sordid events" was "convenient." She hammered the point that incapacitation and selective amnesia seemed to be his only defense. She closed by saying that Kirk had unlimited funds, was not local, was charged with murder, and definitely posed a flight risk. She asked that the judge hold him without bail.

No doubt Assistant DA Melissa Mooring knew her stuff.

Hell, Kirk sounded guilty to me. Was that merely perception or reality?

Now it was Kornblatt's turn.

He countered each point, quickly and efficiently. No flash, no theatrics, calm and professional. Kirk was innocent. He had been drugged or too drunk to have killed anyone. That he and the victim were both adults and had entered into a consensual affair. That the ME had yet to determine the cause of death and that stating it was due to strangulation was "speculation." That Kirk was no flight risk since his face was known worldwide. He compared him to Elvis Presley and Muhammad Ali. Kirk couldn't go anywhere without attracting a crowd. The collection outside the courthouse indicated that. That Kirk was here as a professional, working every day on the movie that had, and would, bring money to the community. That he was innocent and had no intention of running from something that he wanted resolved as quickly as possible. He asked for Kirk's release on his own recognizance, and if not that, at least some acceptable bail amount.

Judge Booth removed his glasses, rubbed one eye with a knuckle, and then replaced them. He shuffled through some pages before him, before looking up, his gaze over the half glasses that now rode low on his nose, his face grim.

"I've read through both the prosecution and the defense motions and listened to their clear and concise verbal arguments." He hesitated and looked around the room. "This is a difficult case. And one that has obviously caught the public's attention. I appreciate the prosecution's position. This is a murder trial. The defendant does have essentially unlimited resources. And, in general, this would represent a significant flight risk. I am also well aware of who the defendant is. How well known he is. And I agree this lessens any chance he could flee. I also understand that his continued incarceration could damage not only the production company but also the many folks they have employed while here in our lovely city." He again rearranged the pages before him, removed his glasses, and leaned his elbows on the bench. "My ruling is that bail will be offered in the amount of three million dollars. Mr. Ford will surrender his passport and will not be allowed to leave the city." He leaned back. "Any objections?"

I noticed that Kirk's shoulders immediately relaxed and his head dropped. I wondered if he might cry. Pretty boys never did well in jail. Especially if they were celebrities. There was always some yahoo trying to make a name of himself by whacking around such folks. Or worse."

Kornblatt responded immediately. "We accept your decree, Your Honor."

Mooring hesitated, then glanced over her shoulder. Uncle Tony gave an almost imperceptible nod. She turned her gaze back to the judge. "We agree, Your Honor."

Well, well, Uncle Tony was definitely large and in charge. Made me wonder how deep into the DA's office, maybe the court system, his fingers extended.

I flashed again on what Gloria had said about him. That you didn't want to get on his "bad side" and that he was "connected." Which raised the question—why would he want the supposed killer of his niece out of jail? On the street? Vulnerable?

I suspected that Tony could reach him even in jail. Out and about opened up even more possibilities. This could get very ugly.

But would he whack an international celebrity? Someone with a direct connection, through Kristi, to him? Seemed to me that could lead the cops right into his world. But right now, looking at his calm, relaxed demeanor, I sensed Tony had probably done worse. And obviously gotten away with it.

CHAPTER NINE

AFTER THE COURT adjourned, we followed the other spectators into the hallway. Kornblatt walked down the hall, away from us and the loitering crowd, to "make a couple of calls." I sensed a presence behind Nicole and me, and turned to face the two brothers. In the courtroom they had looked big, but now, standing in front of us, they looked even bigger. Thicker anyway. Each around six feet, a good four inches shorter than me, but they went about two and half bills each. Five hundred pounds to my 190—well, maybe a bit more after last night's meal at Mister B's. Where was Pancake when I needed him?

"So, you're with the murderer," one of them said. I didn't think it was a question but figured he expected a response anyway.

"Depends on what you mean by 'with,'" I said.

"One of his Hollywood types."

Nicole had moved to my side and I could tell she was revving up to engage him. Chin up, shoulders square, and those wonderful eyes shining with electricity. As if she might fire a bolt from them and vaporize the brothers. I gently touched her arm, signaling this wasn't the best time to go all Nicole on these two.

"Never met him," I said.

That caused a brief hitch. Not what he expected. His head cocked to one side. When he recovered, he asked, "Why're you here?"

Before I could answer, a tough-looking dude walked up and tapped the speaking brother on the shoulder. He wore jeans, an open-collar white shirt, and a blue sports coat. And sunglasses.

"Tony wants to see you," the man said. "Now."

The man never looked at us, never acknowledged that we even existed. Face flat, no frown, no smile, nothing. Reminded me of Ray's "be cool" attitude.

The brothers gave us an angry glare and then followed the man to where Tony stood with a similarly attired man. Probably Tony's muscle. Tony stared at me, his face expressionless. His gaze held mine for a beat and then he turned to the brothers, jaw set, eyes narrowed. He didn't look happy.

Nicole and I walked to where Kornblatt stood, leaning against the wall, phone to his ear. He was telling someone to round up Kirk's passport, saying it was in the top left-hand drawer of Kirk's desk at home, and to take it to the LAPD for holding. He asked that they "get the bail money together like an hour ago" and get the papers prepped for the court so "we can get Kirk out and back to work."

Priorties.

As Kornblatt wrapped up the call, I noticed that Tony now had his nephews pinned against the wall in what seemed to be a heated exchange. Not really an exchange. Tony doing the talking, wagging a finger that more than once tapped one and then the other of his nephews on the chest. His face was stone, his anger almost palpable.

Interesting. A good old family squabble.

Tony finally shook his head, spun on his heels, and headed toward the entrance. His two thugs, who looked and walked as if they didn't take shit from anyone, peeled off the opposite wall and fell in on either side of Tony. The nephews, shoulders rounded forward, heads low, followed in contrite shuffles. They swerved past the security setup and disappeared through the doorway.

Kornblatt ended his call. "Okay, the wheels are turning. My work here is done. For now, anyway. I'm going to go out and do a song and dance for the press, and then head back to LA."

"You're leaving?" Nicole asked.

He smiled. "Not much more to do right now. At least nothing that requires my physical presence. We'll be working on Kirk's defense, but I suspect any trial won't be for many weeks, more likely months. The police still have a lot of work to do before the DA could possibly get the case on the docket. We have time. Not to mention that Kirk's not the only fire I have going right now."

"We'll go out there with you," Tara said.

Distinguishing them was easy because Tara wore a green blouse and Tegan a blue one. If I remembered it right, anyway. I could've had it backwards. I needed to write this stuff down.

Kornblatt studied the twins and said, "I like that. Seeing Kirk's beautiful young sidekicks supporting him might engender at least some cred with the public."

"That's what we thought," I said.

He nodded. "Let's go."

"Nicole and I are supposed to have a chat with Detective Doucet," I said. "I think he's expecting to meet us here."

Kornblatt nodded, glanced at his watch.

"You guys go ahead," I said. "We'll grab a cab back to the hotel."

Another nod from Kornblatt, then Nicole and I watched as he and the twins exited the building.

"Mr. Longly?"

The voice came from behind me. I turned to see a man, looked midthirties, in jeans, black tee, and a blue blazer, cop written all over him. He was short, fit, with thinning blond hair and pale blue eyes. A gold shield hung from his belt.

"I'm Detective Troy Doucet."

I shook his hand and introduced Nicole, ending with, "Call me Jake."

"You're Ray Longly's son? The baseball player?"

I nodded. "Ex-player."

Doucet offered a brief smile. "I told Ray we would chat, so let's chat."

No nonsense. I liked that.

He led us down a hallway and around a corner to a bench seat along the wall across from a closed courtroom. We sat.

"I remember when you pitched for the Rangers. You were great."

"Thanks. Didn't last long, though."

"But you could bring the heat."

"He still can," Nicole said with a wicked smile.

Doucet glanced at her and laughed, then back to me. "Ray's some PI type from over in Gulf Shores?"

"That's right."

"Don't know him, but he must have some pull." He shrugged. "I mean, it's not every day I get a call from the regional director of the FBI."

"He has friends in the agency."

"And he's not bashful about reaching out to them."

I smiled. "Bashful and Ray don't know each other. Growing up, he'd call the FBI if I missed curfew."

That drew a smile from Doucet. He seemed to relax a notch. "What can I tell you?"

"How do you think all this went down?" I asked.

He took a breath, held it a second, then exhaled slowly. "It's not really our policy to discuss ongoing investigations. Not the details, anyway."

"I see."

"Why don't you tell me what you know, and I'll see if I can confirm any of it."

"That'll work," I said. "A couple in a closed room, alone. The girl, Kristi Guidry, strangled. Kirk Ford not remembering any of it. How's that?"

"So far so good."

"That's all we know."

Doucet stared at me but didn't say anything.

"I take it you know more than that?" I asked.

"Not much."

I nodded. "Look, we're here to help."

"Help? In what way?"

"Get to the truth."

He twisted his neck as if working out a kink. "I've never found a PI to be very helpful. In fact, just the opposite." He smiled. "The FBI, too, for that matter."

"I understand." I let it hang there and waited him out.

Finally, Doucet spoke. "Mr. Ford's lack of memory is convenient if nothing else. On first blush, it doesn't look good for him."

"On first blush?"

He shrugged. "I've been doing this job long enough to know that the simple answer is usually the right one. But I also know things aren't always as they seem."

"You have doubts?"

"Not really. I think he's as guilty as homemade sin. But an open mind is always wise."

I liked that, too. At least the lead detective was sniffing out other possibilities. Even if I didn't see another option right now.

"Any other real suspects?"

"Old boyfriend. One of my guys talked to him. Says he doubts he's involved. Pretty tore up though."

"But he's at least a possible suspect. Right?" Nicole asked.

"Sure." Doucet scratched an ear. "We're still early in all this so everyone with any connection to Kristi, or Mr. Ford, is a suspect."

"I believe there was no evidence of other trauma?" I asked. "Other than the strangulation? Not a fight or struggle? Anything like that?"

"No. But Ford said they were both hammered—his word."

"Wine and marijuana, I understand?"

"Looks that way. We found a couple of empty bottles and three joints. Only one smoked. Half of it, anyway."

"Doesn't sound like a recipe for a blackout," I said.

"True. The lab guys are doing their thing. Looking for anything else that might be in play." He twisted his neck again. "That'll take a while. A few days at least."

"No evidence anyone else was there?"

"No forced entry or anything like that. And in a more or less public area like a hotel room, fingerprints will be a bitch to track down. The techs found a couple of dozen different prints. Most are probably from the staff."

"It's never easy, is it?" I asked.

"Almost never."

"Anything else?"

"Yeah. Kirk had scratches on his arms and back."

"Really?" Nicole asked.

"Sure did. Some looked a few days old but a couple looked fresher. He said he got them on the set. Out there in the swamp where they've been shooting." He shrugged. "Could be that. But the ME will get fingernail scrapings from Kristi to see if his DNA turns up."

I thought about that. *So what?* was my conclusion and I voiced that thought. "But they had sex. Even if she scratched him, it could be part of the deal."

Doucet cocked his head to one side. "Gee, I never thought of that."

"Sorry. Just thinking out loud."

He smiled. "I'm messing with you."

"What about her uncle? Tony Guidry?"

"As a suspect?" Doucet asked.

"No. I mean, from what I saw in there, it looked like he had his fingers in the court proceedings."

"Tony Guidry has his fingers in everything. He and Assistant DA Mooring are tight."

"Tight?"

"Let's just leave it at that."

"There's a story there," Nicole said.

Doucet shrugged. "Ain't there always a story?"

"People've told us he's a bad guy," I said. "Maybe connected. That kind of thing."

"Tony Guidry is no doubt powerful and many think dirty to the core."

"Do you think he's dirty?"

Doucet hesitated, looked up and down the hallway, and then said, "I think Tony has no brakes and no boundaries. But don't quote me on that."

"Could he manipulate this case?" I asked.

"Wouldn't be the first time. He did arrange for Melissa Mooring to handle the prosecution."

"Arranged?" Nicole said. "He did that?"

Doucet shrugged. "I'm not sure there isn't anything he can't worm his way into. We've never been able to hang anything on him but we've looked into everything. Bribery, extortion, witness tampering. Even a couple of murders."

"Really?" Nicole asked.

Another shrug. "As I said, nothing we could ever prove." He leaned forward, resting his forearms on his knees. "But if I were you, I wouldn't go sniffing around in his world. Wouldn't be healthy."

"You're not the first person to tell us that," I said.

Doucet shrugged. "Then, there you go."

"What about her brothers?" I asked.

"Not running on all cylinders, if you know what I mean. Not too bright. And not very close to Tony."

"Looked that way," I said.

"He gets them work. Mostly in one or the other of his clubs. From what I understand, they aren't very good at much. Sure, Tony took them in after the death of their parents, but it's Kristi he really protected. Those two he simply seems to tolerate."

"Family drama," Nicole said. "Nothing quite like it."

"Anything else we need to know?" I asked.

Doucet stood. "That's all we have right now, but like I said, we're just beginning to dig around." He glanced at his watch. "I've got to run, but I'm sure we'll chat again before long."

I stood and shook his hand. "Thanks for filling us in."

"I hope I don't regret you two rooting around in my case."

"You won't. Anything we find out, we'll pass along."

He hesitated, nodded. "Just watch your six. You ask me, Tony has his own ideas about how this story should go."

"Do you think he might try to harm Kirk?" Nicole asked.

"With Tony Guidry, anything is possible."

CHAPTER TEN

ROBERT GUIDRY, JR. knew it was coming. Sure, Uncle Tony had chewed their asses outside the courtroom, but he wasn't finished with them. No doubt about that. That was Tony's way. Like a shark. Hit, damage, back off, and wait before striking again. Let the victim bleed a little, lose the will to fight, and the ability to escape. Mostly in a figurative sense, but with Tony it could just as easily be literal.

Robert knew from the way his brother gripped the edge of the limo's seat that Kevin felt it, too. How could he not? They'd been the focus of Uncle Tony's ire on many occasions. Knew the signs. Jaw set, chin slightly elevated, shoulders tensed, like a Serengeti lion crouching to launch at an unsuspecting gazelle.

One of Tony's robots, Reuben Prejean, drove; Robert and Kevin sat on the limo's rear, forward-facing bench seat; the other robot, Johnny Hebert, on the side seat across from the well-stocked bar; and Tony himself, back to the driver, facing them. In charge. Always in charge. King of the freaking New Orleans jungle.

Tony held his cell to his ear and jabbered about digging into someone's life. His eyes, however, were aimed at Robert and Kevin, and they had that dark, dangerous look Uncle Tony could lay on anyone at a moment's notice.

Sure, he had taken them in after the death of their parents, had paid for their schooling, gotten jobs for him and Kevin, and was, of course, footing the bill for Kristi's college. He could afford it. No doubt about that. Robert might have been grateful for all this if Tony wasn't such a dick. To Kevin and him anyway. Not Kristi. Never Kristi.

Tony never had kids. Maybe he didn't want them, but the scuttlebutt was that Tony shot blanks. Or maybe it was Aunt Anita. Robert preferred to believe Tony was the issue. Wouldn't that be a hoot? Big bad Uncle Tony with an empty gun? Somehow that'd make all his bullshit tolerable. Mostly, anyway.

At first, Uncle Tony's conversation made no sense to Robert, but then he said, "Yeah. Tall good-looking guy and a very attractive blond chick. They were in court today. Came in with Ford's attorney. Maybe they're just friends or Hollywood hanger-ons. But, maybe not. Either way I want to know who all the players here are. I don't want anyone screwing up the plan." He listened again. "Let me know what you find."

He disconnected the call and stared at Robert. "Any questions about what I said?" Tony asked.

Robert shook his head.

"You sure? I don't want you two fucking this up."

"She was our sister," Kevin said.

Tony's eyes narrowed. "And my niece."

Robert almost jumped on that, but let it ride. There was no doubt that Uncle Tony merely tolerated Kevin and him, maybe out of some sense of obligation to his brother, their father, but he loved Kristi. And he made no bones about it. She could do no wrong, Robert and Kevin no right. In truth, Kristi did no wrong, never a misstep. Until now, anyway. But he and Kevin always seemed to piss Uncle Tony off.

"I'll say it again," Tony said. "I don't want you two to open your mouths. Not to the media, not to anyone. Don't approach anyone associated with Kirk Ford or anyone even tangentially connected to Kristi's murder. Am I clear?"

Robert looked at him, knowing not to respond, but somehow, he couldn't hold back. "We have every right to find out what happened to her. To lean on her killer and his friends."

"And then what? You piss them off. Maybe attract the attention of the police. For what purpose?"

Robert had no response for that.

"I'll handle this." Tony leaned forward, his eyes seeming to settle deeper beneath his brow. "Like I do everything else. The courts will take care of Mister Ford. He'll never see the light of day again. And if by some miracle, he slips out of this, I'll fix that, too."

And there it was. Tony's go-to fix for everything. Manipulate the legal system, and if that failed, go all street on whoever had dared to twist his tit. That's where Johnny and Reuben came in, street justice being their speciality.

He almost felt sorry for Kirk Ford. Not much, but a little, Robert thinking maybe Kirk would be better in max lockup than on the street. Even if it meant the life of a pretty boy in a cage with serial predators. Who knows, maybe the judge would toss him into the hellhole of Angola. Even that might be better than dealing with Tony's wolves.

CHAPTER ELEVEN

NICOLE AND I said our good-byes to Detective Troy Doucet, again thanking him for not only his time but for talking so candidly with us. He shrugged, saying it was a two-way street and that if we uncovered anything useful to keep him in the loop. Will do.

"I like him," Nicole said.

"Me, too," I added. "Seems like a straight shooter."

We stood in the hallway, watching as he headed toward the rear entrance and the gated and guarded parking area beyond. He had his cell to his ear and walked with purpose.

The relationship between cops and PIs was always complicated. And delicate. Ray had offered his opinion on the subject often enough. His take? Badges made some people an agent for truth, justice, and the American way, but others simply became arrogant, aggressive assholes. Gave them a certain swagger, deserved or not. Sure, both cops and PIs worked toward the same goal—to find the true facts of what had happened—but each had their own rules, methods, and restrictions. PIs seemed to resent the access to info and evidence that law enforcement enjoyed; while cops often resented, envied, disdained, pick your word, a PI's ability to bend and ignore the rules. It could lead to epic clashes. But I hadn't read Doucet that way. He seemed to keep his eye on the prize—the truth—and didn't concern himself with who dug up the evidence. I hoped my assessment was correct.

"What now?" Nicole asked.

"Let's get out of here. I need to call Ray and then we can track down a cab and go grab your car. Maybe swing by and have a chat with the boyfriend. Owen what's-his-name."

"Vaughn. Owen Vaughn."

"Yeah, him."

"What about the uncle? Tony Guidry?"

"That's one of the things I want to talk to Ray about."

We exited the courthouse. No evidence of Kornblatt or the twins. Probably on the way to the airport so Kornblatt could head west and deal with his other fires. Now, Assistant DA Melissa Mooring faced the media, giving them her side of the story. I wondered how much of her script had been penned by Tony Guidry. She gave us a quick, expressionless glance as we weaved through the crowd, descended the steps, and turned up Tulane.

Nicole hooked her arm in mine. "This is really going to be a media circus, isn't it?"

"All that and a barrel of squirrel monkeys."

"Not that bad, I hope." She banged her hip against mine.

We crossed South Broad, away from the crowd, and stopped before a row of shotgun houses—narrow, deep, interior rooms stacked one behind the other, the doors between often lined up as straight as a gun barrel. Made life interesting. I mean going from the kitchen to a bathroom might require passing through a bedroom or two. Privacy a pipe dream.

I called Ray.

"Tell me," Ray said when he answered. Obviously, I had popped up on his caller ID.

"He got bail. Three million."

That raised a soft whistle from Ray. "I expected it would be high. I assume Ford can cover it?"

"The studio. They want him back on the set ASAP."

"Yeah. God forbid the production schedule gets wonky."

"Time is money."

"True," Ray said. "And here I imagine it's big money."

"Kornblatt's getting the cash together and arranging to get Kirk's passport over to the LAPD. That's another condition of the parole. _bail_ The judge said that as soon as the LAPD has possession of it and the funds are secured, Kirk will be out."

"Standard procedure. What's the turnaround here?"

"Kornblatt said a few hours."

"Sounds good."

"Another thing," I said. "Kristi's uncle was there. Guy named Tony Guidry. Seemed to have some sway with the DA. Maybe the judge. A friend of Kristi's said he might be mobbed up. Probably an exaggeration, but that's what she said."

"She ain't wrong," Ray said.

"What?"

"Pancake and I are way ahead of you. We started digging into Kristi's life and Tony popped up. And it does appear he's connected to some faction of the old Dixie Mafia."

"I thought all those clowns were dead."

"Mostly. Or in prison. But there're remnants laying around. Anyway, Tony's a bad dude. Doesn't seem to take prisoners. Implicated in everything from bribery and extortion to drugs, girls, influence pedaling. Obviously, none of it was ever proven."

"You're just full of good news."

He laughed. "That's what I'm here for."

"What about her brothers? They were there. Tried to give Nicole and me some shit, but Tony's sidekicks intervened."

"Yeah. Robert and Kevin. A couple of goofballs. Definitely not part of Tony's operation. In fact, I'm not sure Tony cares much for them."

How the hell did Ray and Pancake find all this stuff? I should be used to it—they always find stuff—but this quickly was pretty damn good, even for them. So, I asked.

"Pancake cracked into their Facebook pages, Twitter accounts, that sort of thing. They were at least smart enough not to say anything overt, but the sense we got is that they aren't big fans of Tony."

"Looked that way to me," I said. "Tony was giving them a ration of shit before they left the courthouse."

"Tony must be up to something—as far as Ford is concerned—and doesn't want those two clowns screwing it up—or attracting any unwanted attention."

"What does that mean?" I asked.

"They've yapped to the media. Saying all kinds of crap about Ford. Making threats. That's not Tony Guidry. He likes to stay off the radar and work his magic behind the scenes."

"You mean like controlling a DA, maybe bribing a judge?"

"Exactly. And if any of that comes to light, he would want to be insulated. Probable deniability. If his nephews are out there making waves and threats, Tony might not look so innocent."

"Makes sense."

"And Tony's guys—Johnny Hebert and Reuben Prejean—are different animals altogether. If Tony has had anyone whacked—as most believe he has—these would be the guys that did it."

"They seemed . . . what's the word? . . . professional."

"Bank on it," Ray said. "That's why Pancake and I are headed that way."

"Really?"

"Can't let you have all the fun. We're halfway across Mississippi already. See you in a couple of hours."

"Cool." I disconnected the call and slipped the phone in my pocket. Then to Nicole I said, "The cavalry is coming."

CHAPTER TWELVE

NICOLE FLAGGED DOWN a cab—she's much better at that than me—for obvious reasons—and then minutes later we were at the Monteleone. Ten minutes after that we were in her car zigzagging through the far reaches of the Quarter. The parts visitors rarely venture into, most sticking to Bourbon and Royal and a few other streets where bars, restaurants, shops, and music venues were plentiful. Which is too bad. There are some cool homes, small hotels, and cozy B&Bs in these less-trafficked areas.

Our meandering ultimately led us to Vaughn's Motor Works. It looked just as I expected. Messy, run-down, weatherworn. A place that worked for a living. It was a long, low, wooden, and corrugated metal structure with six bays, four filled with cars, two jacked up on lifts, workers doing their thing beneath each. The parking area was gravel, the office sitting at the left corner. Nicole crunched to a stop near the entrance and we walked inside.

A middle-aged man, phone clamped to his ear, stood behind a counter littered with papers and file folders. A computer to his left, mug of coffee near his right hand. His stained blue shirt had "Carl Vaughn" embroidered on one pocket. The boss man.

He looked up and nodded, while continuing his conversation. "Yeah. We got those in stock. Shouldn't take more than a couple of hours to get the work done." He listened for a minute and then said, "Sounds good. See you around three." He hung up and looked at me. "What can I do you for?"

"You're the owner, I take it?"

"Sure am."

"We'd like to talk with Owen if he's around."

"About what?"

"Kristi Guidry."

His eyes narrowed. "I see."

"It'll only take a couple of minutes."

He flattened his palms on the countertop, fingers spread, revealing grease-stained cuticles, a dirty and frayed Band-Aid wrapped around one knuckle. A workingman's hands. His thick shoulders bulged as he leaned forward. "Owen's already talked to the police. And you still haven't told me who you are and why you're here."

I introduced Nicole and me, then said, "We're private investigators. Trying to find out what happened."

"That's an easy one. That Hollywood pretty boy killed Kristi. A wonderful young lady. That's the truth of it."

"And if that's the case, that's what we'll find out."

"Nothing to find out. It's a fact. So, I'd say we are about done here."

"Mr. Vaughn," Nicole said. "We don't have an agenda here."

He straightened and folded his arms across his chest. "You don't? He the one paying you? Ford?"

She shook her head. "Not really."

He released a quick laugh that was more like a derisive snort. "Like I said, we're done here."

"We're not trying to cause Owen any grief," I said. "Just trying to get a handle on Kristi. Find out more about her and why this happened to her."

"Didn't I say she was a fine young lady? Not much else to know."

"That's what we hear. But I suspect Owen might know her better than just about anyone. He might have some insights that could help us."

He hesitated, shook his head. "Owen's had a rough time with this. He and Kristi had been together for years. Basically, since they were kids. So, I think you can see this ain't a good time to talk to him."

"It's okay," a young man said as he came through a curtained doorway behind Carl. "I'll talk to them."

Carl turned. "You don't have to."

"I know. But maybe it'll help."

Carl gave a quick shrug. "Your call."

A man, wiping greasy hands on a blue towel, shouldered through the door that led from the work bays to the office. "Boss, got a question on that old Plymouth."

"Be right there." Carl looked at his son.

"It'll be okay," Owen said. "I got this."

Another nod, and Carl followed the worker through the door.

"What do you want to know?" Owen asked.

I looked around. "Maybe someplace private?"

He hesitated, then said, "This way."

We followed him through the curtained doorway, down a short hallway, two bathrooms on the left, an open storage area stacked with boxes of auto parts on the right, and into the rear parking lot. It, too, was gravel and held a dozen cars in no discernible order. Some the employees' rides; others waiting to enter the work bays, I imagined.

Owen lifted a pack of Marlboros from his shirt pocket, shook one up, and clenched it between his teeth. He clacked open a Zippo, lit it, and took a long drag. He settled against the fender of a red Mustang.

"We're sorry about Kristi," Nicole said.

"Everyone is. She was special."

"That's what we hear," I said.

"Believe it." He took another drag, smoke escaping between his lips as he spoke. "I still can't believe it really happened."

His face, his entire being, seemed sad, slumped, as if he could barely stand under the weight of it all.

He sighed. "I told the police everything I know, which is close to nothing."

"How long had you and Kristi been a couple?" Nicole asked.

"Known each other since we started school. But we've been dating regular for about five years."

"But she ended it recently?" I asked.

"Couple of months ago." His eyes glistened. "I did something stupid." He looked at me. "Some chick I met in a bar. Onetime thing. Didn't mean nothing."

"And Kristi found out."

He looked down, kicked at the gravel, and then looked back up. "I told her."

I raised an eyebrow.

"Stupid. At least it sure seems that way now. Shoulda kept my mouth shut. Then maybe none of this would've happened." Another kick at the gravel. Another drag from the cigarette. "Truth is, I was eaten up with guilt. Figured if we were in it for the long run, honesty would be best."

"I take it she wasn't happy," Nicole said.

"You could say that. But furious might be more like it. Hurt, probably humiliated. Can't say I blame her."

"So, she broke it off," Nicole said.

"Yep."

"How did you feel about that?"

"Shocked. I thought she'd appreciate the honesty."

Nicole reached out and laid a hand on his arm. "Women don't usually take such things as lightly as guys do. At least, most don't."

"Kristi sure didn't." He looked up toward the cloudless sky. "I was so stupid." He looked at Nicole. "I knew it was wrong at the time. I knew that girl—funny—I don't even remember her name—I knew that girl didn't mean nothing. And could screw up everything. But I did it anyway." He took a deep breath and let it out slowly, puffing out his cheeks. "So stupid."

"Were you angry when Kristi broke up with you?" I asked.

"Not really. Mostly sad. Definitely shocked." He finished the cigarette with a final pull, dropped it to the ground, and crushed it with his boot. "I never thought she'd take it so hard."

"I assume you told the police about the breakup?" I asked.

"Sure did. I also told them that I know as the ex, so to speak, I'd be a suspect. But, that ain't true. That could never be true."

I believed him. I'm no psychiatrist or interrogator or anything even close, but I know people. Owning a bar allows for that. Alcohol makes some folks happy, funny, gregarious and others dark, moody, angry, and dangerous. Reading body language and moods can head off most problems before they blossom. Any bar owner or bartender could tell you that.

Looking at Owen, I saw a man crushed and destroyed. Not angry, or defensive, or evasive. Nothing that would even suggest guilt. I also knew his life had forever changed. From this point on, he would divide his earthly existence into the time before Kristi's death and the time after. I suspected the ones before would be brighter, happier memories. Some people never recover from such tragedies but rather get dragged into a deep sinkhole, like quicksand, that smothers them. No matter where life led after those moments, the darkness would always be there. I hoped Owen wasn't one of those. I hoped time would soften the edges of his pain. But I didn't think so.

"You knew she was seeing Kirk Ford, didn't you?" Nicole asked.

He nodded.

"How'd you feel about that?"

"Confused. As I said, I never dreamed she'd dump me for a single slip. Guess I misjudged that one." He shook his head. "As for Kirk Ford, Kristi was grounded. Never had stars in her eyes. I wasn't sure what to make of her taking up with him."

"Did you talk to her about it?"

"Once. She said it was nothing. I wasn't so sure. There was an excitement in her. Not right out there for all to see, but I did." He looked at Nicole. "I knew her better than anyone." He pulled out another cigarette and lit it. "It was like she was trying to hide her true feelings. Like she didn't want to hurt me."

"That's probably true," Nicole said.

"But deep down inside, I knew this was more than just a fling. To her, anyway."

"Did she say anything specific that led you to believe that?"

"Not really. I mean, she said he was nice and polite. And seemed like a good guy. But, it wasn't what she said but how she said it. She had that glow. The one she'd get when she was happy." His eyes glistened. "Truth is, I lived to put that look on her face." A deep sigh. "Can't believe I'll never see that again."

Life is weird. And a bitch sometimes. Unpredictable. Definitely unfair. I suspected that Owen's guilt, so evident on his face, was that this was all his fault. At least he felt it was. And I couldn't argue that point. No one-night fling, no breakup. No breakup, no Kristi and Kirk. And she would be alive and she and Owen would be planning a future. That load of bricks would be his forever.

"You weren't aware of any friction between them?" I asked.

He shook his head. "Like I said, I only talked with her about it the one time."

"Did you ever meet Kirk?"

"Nope. Didn't really want to." Another drag on the cigarette. "But I'd sure like to now."

"Why?"

He looked at me. "To ask him exactly that. Why'd he do it?"

I nodded. "Something we'd like to know, too. If he did it, that is."

He squared his shoulders. "Who else? From what I hear, they were alone in a hotel room. I don't think anyone else could've."

"We haven't talked to him yet, but I understand he said they were both out of it," Nicole said. "He doesn't remember anything."

"Convenient."

"What about drugs?" I asked. "Was Kristi into anything like that?"

He stared at me, a note of confusion in his eyes. "Why do you ask?"

"There were empty wine bottles and some marijuana found in the room."

"Look, Kristi barely drank. And drugs were definitely off-limits. In fact, she was active in our high school's anti-drug program. If any drugs were found in that room, they'd've had to come from him."

Made me wonder a couple of things. Were the joints found in Kirk's room only for him? Did Kristi also partake? Had Kirk led her into that world? Obviously, I didn't know Kristi, but the picture of her that was forming in my head was that of a nice, naive, inexperienced young woman who could have easily been swayed by the charms of an A-list Hollywood type. I made a mental note to ask Kirk those questions.

"I take it you know her uncle? Tony?" I asked.

"Sure."

"What do you think of him?"

"I like him. Always did. I know he's got a bad reputation." He looked at me. "I'm sure you've heard the rumors."

"We have."

"He was always good to me. And he worshipped Kristi. Like she was the daughter he never had."

"And her brothers?"

He smiled. The first emotion other than sadness I had seen from him.

"Robert and Kevin are okay. Not too bright, not overly motivated to do anything useful. But their devotion to Kristi was solid."

"I understand Tony took the three of them in after their parents died."

"He did. And Lord knows he tried to get Robert and Kevin to work. To focus on something. Anything. Moved them around from job to job. In one of his businesses or the other. But they always managed to screw up. Piss off the wrong people. That kind of thing." He flicked an ash to the ground. "Those two aren't easy to light a fire under. I think Tony tolerates them more than anything else."

"From what I hear, Tony doesn't suffer fools well."

That got another half smile from Owen. "Not even close. If they weren't family, he'd've kicked them to the curb a long time ago." He dropped the cigarette butt and crushed it. "Let's just say Tony isn't someone you fuck . . ." He stopped and looked at Nicole, embarrassment on his face.

"I've heard it before," she said.

He nodded. "Tony Guidry isn't someone you mess with."

CHAPTER THIRTEEN

NICOLE AND I left Owen leaning against the Mustang, working on his third cigarette. As she pulled away, I turned and glanced back to see a broken man, head down, shoulders slumped, the weight of life's inequities draping over his entire being. I decided I liked him. Good kid. Hard worker, it seemed. Head screwed on straight, dealing with a pain that no one should ever have to bear. I also knew his guilt over what had happened—more imagined than real—would haunt his nights for years, probably forever.

You couldn't help walking away from Owen's world without thinking that your own life was pretty good.

Nicole obviously sensed my internal despair. Maybe not despair, but a load of sadness, anyway.

"What is it?" she asked as she sat not-so-patiently waiting for a light to change. Fingers drumming on the steering wheel.

"I don't envy Owen."

"He seems to be taking it hard."

"And he always will."

"Unless he's acting," she said.

"What?"

"I mean, he wouldn't be the first killer to lie."

"Can't argue with that."

"All that sad and aw-shucks stuff could be a cover for something darker."

"You aren't very sympathetic."

"I'm just saying that he loved her, she dumped him and took up with a famous actor. I've read about murders with less motive."

"Nicole Jamison, homicide detective. Or is it criminal profiler?"

She tossed me a glare, then smiled. "No, just a PI."

"That's right. I forgot."

"Want me to show you my PI card?" she said. "Since I have one and you don't, I'm more official than you."

"Meaning?"

"I guess that makes me your boss."

"It's not the card that makes you boss." I looked her up and down. "It's all that other stuff."

"You are so easy." She laughed. "I like that."

The light cycled and we were off again.

"What do you want to do now?" I asked.

"When are Ray and Pancake getting in?"

I glanced at my watch. "An hour or so."

"Maybe we can wander around the Quarter for a while?"

"Or crawl in bed?"

"Animal."

"You complaining?"

She laughed. "No. But I need to walk."

That settled that.

She pulled into the Monteleone parking structure, and we jumped out. A valet materialized, slid in, and the SL spun away up the ramp. We walked the block over to Bourbon Street and turned toward Jackson Square.

Many US cities have iconic streets. Peachtree in Atlanta. The Sunset Strip in LA. Broadway and Madison Avenue in New York. None of them are even remotely like Bourbon.

Bourbon Street actually has three personalities, depending on the time of day. The one most folks equate with it is nighttime when it becomes one big street party. Stretching from Canal Street to Jackson Square, the neon blazes, the alcohol flows, and some of the best music in the world spills out of bar after bar. Not to mention the strip clubs. Ones that cater to any and all persuasions. Short of murder, few things are off-limits. Of course, the Quarter sees more than its share of homicides, too.

During the day, Bourbon is an altogether different experience. For sure, you don't want to see it around sunrise. It smells of garbage and stale alcohol, the detritus of the previous night. Like a decaying corpse. Refuse crews and street cleaners do yeoman's work to prep it for a new onslaught.

But by noon, the trash is hauled away, the pavement dries from the hosing it has received, and the stench magically evaporates. People appear, street performers take up their stations, and music begins to crank up.

Circle of life in the Big Easy.

We did a lap of Jackson Square, checking out the artwork that hung on the fence that embraced it, stopping to listen to the various street musicians. A five-piece Dixieland band, a stringy-haired guy in a forward-tilted cowboy hat beating out acoustic blues from a worn Gibson, and my favorite, a lanky black kid, couldn't have been more than sixteen, with dreds to his mid-back, who huffed out some great jazz on a clarinet. I dropped a five in the cigar box at his feet. He nodded, never missing a note. He could play the stick for sure.

While we completed our circuit of Jackson Square, I revisited the Owen situation.

"You don't really think Owen was involved in this, do you?" I asked.

"No. Just tossing out possibilities."

"Did he even know where Kirk was staying? And if so, how would he have gotten into the room?"

She shook her head. "I don't know."

"He certainly doesn't look or act like a Ninja killer."

"No, he doesn't."

"So, we're agreed—Owen didn't do it?"

"Mostly." She took my hand. "Let's shop."

Yes. Let's.

We visited several antique stores and clothing boutiques along Royal, Nicole purchasing an antique broach in one. It was cool. Overpriced, but cool. Of course, being smart, and maybe a little bit afraid to raise her ire, I told her it was perfect and a steal at that price.

A block later, we saw the gypsy. Not a real gypsy, but she was surely dressed like one. A loud floral dress, ropes of colored beads around her neck, and long fingernails, painted black. Her deep-set dark eyes added to the image.

She was a fortune-teller, her working name Madam Theresa. I know this because the sign over her door read: *Madam Theresa, Fortune-Teller, Tarot Reader*. I'm observant that way.

I was inclined to ignore her invitation to come inside, but Nicole stopped.

"Enter," she said. "And learn what the future holds for you."

Nicole grabbed my arm and tugged me inside.

The room was small with heavy drapes, dim lighting, and a round cloth-draped table where she plied her trade. There was a mustiness in the air and everything looked old and mysterious. The woman was also mysterious but not old. Couldn't have been over thirty. Made me wonder if she was a scam. I mean, didn't it take decades to learn to tell fortunes? Maybe she started at a young age. Like five.

We sat across from her. The tabletop was strewn with cards, dice, and what looked like a cluster of chicken bones. At least I hoped that's what they were. Surely she couldn't have human bones. But they looked sort of like finger bones. Creepy. I wanted to leave, but Nicole had that light in her eyes.

Before delving into the mysteries of life, she took care of business. "It'll be forty dollars." She extended an open palm.

I thought about taking her hand and telling her that she had a long lifeline and would live to a very old age and have great wealth and happiness, but I wasn't sure she'd see the humor in that.

And I had an uneasy feeling she just might be able to slap a voodoo curse on me. I mean, it was possible. This was New Orleans, after all. Instead I laid a pair of twenties on her. She folded them and slipped them into the top of her dress somewhere.

She reached across the table and grasped Nicole's hands, her eyes closing, her breathing deep and slow, her brow furrowed in concentration.

"I feel great love in you," she said. "For many. For the gentleman here with you."

I looked at Nicole and smiled. She tossed me a mock frown.

The woman continued. "And great success. Your future will be long and bright."

See, I could've done that.

The woman opened her eyes, released her hold on Nicole's hands, and gathered up the cards, giving them a quick shuffle. She began turning them over one at a time. With dramatic flair. She was good.

"The cards say you are healthy and happy. You are at peace with your world." She flopped down two more cards and her face tightened. "But there are dark clouds."

"Oh?" Nicole said.

"Not for you. For a friend. A friend that is in trouble. Do you know of such a thing?"

Nicole sighed. "Unfortunately, yes."

Two more cards. "But this person's troubles are even worse than they seem."

"Really?"

The woman scooped up the bones. I had hoped they were merely decorations, but she shook them in her hands and tossed them on the table. They clacked and scattered over the cards. She selected and slid her thumb back and forth along one and then another, running through a half dozen of them.

"This friend is male. He is accused of a heinous act."

I felt Nicole's body tense and she took in a quick breath.

She picked up one of the bones, folding it tightly in her hand. She placed the fist against her forehead, eyes closed. "But he is not the one. They did it. Not him."

"They who?" Nicole asked.

The woman opened her eyes and placed the bone on the table. "That I cannot say." She selected another bone and repeated the mystic reading process. "But your friend is in danger. Not from the act he did not do but from others."

"From the ones that committed the mur—act?" Nicole asked.

"Perhaps. But I think not. There are forces arrayed against your friend. Powerful forces."

"What can he do to protect himself?"

"Maybe nothing. Maybe his fate is set. But, maybe not." The woman leaned forward, her gaze stabbing at Nicole, a black fingernail tapping on the table. "It is possible that you are his salvation."

Nicole looked at me and then back to the woman. "What? How?"

She sighed. "I'm afraid that those are questions only you can answer."

Come on. Forty bucks and she couldn't even guess? I felt cheated and started to say something, but Nicole spoke first.

"Thank you. This does help."

It does?

The woman smiled, briefly, then her face turned darker. "What I give you is not only hope, but a warning. Tread carefully."

CHAPTER FOURTEEN

IF I HAD been a believer, the gypsy woman would have spooked me. I mean, bones for Christ sakes. I still wondered if they were human. Surely not—but then again, this was the Big Easy. A place where voodoo and ghosts and a bunch of other crazy shit were commonplace. Ever walked through a New Orleans cemetery? There are a bunch of them, and each even spookier than the gypsy lady and all her skeletal remains. If ghosts were real, those walled-off burial grounds would be a major hangout for them. Late-night postmortem dance clubs. And as opposed to being six feet under, I suspected all those aboveground crypts would be easier to escape from. Eerie even in daylight, if you visited after sunset you pretty much deserved whatever happened. I had done that exactly once—once—never again.

But, the gypsy lady had spooked Nicole. No doubt about that. When we left her standing in the doorway of her den of prognostication—like a spider waiting to trap and extract cash from the next unsuspecting soul—we walked two blocks in silence. Nicole gripped my hand with a little extra fervor, her gaze directed straight ahead as if deep in thought. I wasn't sure if she had blinked once the entire time.

Finally, she spoke. "What do you think?"

"About what?"

She glared at me.

I shrugged. "I think she just made forty bucks."

Nicole shook her head and let go of my hand. "Don't be an ass."

"It's what I do best."

"No argument there. But what about what she said?"

"Which part? About you being in love with me?"

"I don't think that's what she said."

"That's what I heard."

"Because that's what you wanted to hear."

"My point exactly." I was smart enough not to push that thought any further.

Another half block in silence, then, Nicole asked, "What about what she said about Kirk?"

"I didn't recall his name coming up."

"Come on, Jake. The friend in trouble? Who else could it be?"

"That's the beauty of fortune-tellers. They can tell you anything, carefully vague, of course, and you can interpret it as you wish."

"How did she know I had a friend in trouble?"

"Everyone does."

"Really? Do you?"

My mind went blank. Then I went to my universal fallback position. "Pancake."

"Pancake? He's not in trouble. He is trouble."

Hard to argue that point.

"She said Kirk didn't do it," she continued. "She said *they*."

"I'm sure the jury will buy that. Maybe Kornblatt can put her on the stand. Madam Theresa, can you tell us what you conjured from your bones?"

"Ass."

"Listen to yourself. A so-called fortune-teller says a bunch of generic stuff and you chose to apply it to Kirk."

She stopped and turned to me, a scowl on her face. Uh-oh. Then she laughed and shook her head. "You're right." She parked a wayward strand of hair behind her ear. "Look, I don't believe all that woo-woo stuff. But she did get me to thinking." She looked up and down the street. "Let's say she's right. If not Kirk, then who?"

"I have no idea."

Nicole took my hand again and we continued our walk up Royal Street. As we neared the Monteleone, two big guys turned the corner toward us. Kristi's brothers. Robert and Kevin.

"Well, well, look who we have here," one of them said.

We stopped. They approached, blocking the sidewalk, stopping ten feet from us. They didn't look friendly.

"Nice seeing you two again," I said.

"Probably not."

"I don't think we've officially met."

The one who had spoken before puffed out his chest. His large chest. "I'm Robert. This is Kevin. We're Kristi's brothers. But you already know that."

"Actually, we didn't. I'm Jake and this is Nicole. Nice to meet you."

"Probably not," Kevin said.

An echo of his brother. Likely meant Robert was the older of the two, and the more alpha. Kevin the follower, taking his cues from his big brother. Also made me wonder if Kevin was capable of independent thought. I had my doubts. He had a Neanderthal look about him, ears a bit low set, eyes dull. I suspected he didn't do well with math, but figured two against one was simple enough even for him. Tension gathered in my scalp.

"Why's that?" I asked.

"Because we're on opposite sides here," Robert said.

He shoved one hand in the pocket of his jeans. I wondered if he might pull out a gun. He didn't.

"You're with Ford," Kevin said. "That makes you all sideways as far as we're concerned."

"We aren't with anyone," I said.

That seemed to confuse them. Only for a beat, though.

"You were there," Robert said. "In court. Sitting right behind him. And then hanging with that fancy attorney he brought in from California."

"We were."

"That means you're in his camp."

"We don't work for Kirk Ford, if that's what you mean," I said. "Fact is, I've never met him."

More confusion.

"Then why were you there?" Robert asked.

"My uncle," Nicole said. "He hired us to look into Kristi's murder."

"Your uncle? Who's that?"

"Charles Balfour. He's the executive producer of the *Sea Quest* series."

Robert smirked. "And he expects you to save his boy from himself?"

"Not really. He expects us to get to the truth."

"Shit, I can tell you what's true. He killed our sister."

"And if he did," I said, "that's what we'll find out."

Robert took a couple of steps forward. He was maybe six feet tops, so I looked down on him, but he was thick and well muscled. I flashed on Ray's self-defense book and tried to figure which eye to go for. Somehow the flick technique pictured in the book didn't seem so simple right now. I should've read the next chapter.

"You scratch around in whatever haystack you want, but the fact is he'll pay the bail—it's what rich folks like him do—and he'll be on the street. That's our world."

"I suspect that kind of thinking won't be a good thing for you," I said.

"Worse for him," Robert said.

"That would be a mistake."

Robert didn't flinch, but he did smile. "A mistake is taking his side in this. Not very healthy."

"I take it your uncle knows you're here? Harassing citizens?"

Even more confusion settled over Robert's face.

I continued. "I mean, from what I saw over at the courthouse, he wasn't exactly thrilled with you two."

I guessed Robert ran out of clever banter as he took a step forward and reached for Nicole's arm. I slapped his hand away and moved between them.

"Maybe you guys should move along," I said.

Time seemed to come to a screeching halt. He froze; I froze.

The right eye. That's the one I decided on. Left-hand flick and then whack him with my right. We stared at each other. This could get real ugly, real quick. I braced my feet and balled my fists at my side, half expecting one of his own very large fists to come my way.

My brain contorted. Strike first, or try to tap-dance out of this? The first option would definitely end discussion. I rummaged around in my mind for something clever to say. Anything that might defuse this situation. I found nothing.

Then there was Kevin. Even if I managed to surprise Robert and get a fingernail in his eye, I didn't think Kevin would simply stand there and watch.

I noticed Nicole had eased forward. I also saw that her gaze was focused on Kevin's crotch. I might have been jealous but I also knew her kickboxing skills had ramped up. The way her feet were set, it looked like she was preparing to kick his balls up into his throat. Beauty, smarts, and a kick-ass attitude. What was not to love?

The little posturing dance everyone was doing seemed to hit a wall. As if no one wanted to make the first move. The air thickened, my chest hurt, and I realized I hadn't taken a breath for maybe an hour. At least it felt that way.

That's when the cavalry arrived. Pancake's truck lurched to a stop. Middle of the street. He ground the gear lever into park and he and Ray rolled out the doors.

"What's going on?" Ray asked.

Pancake said nothing. He settled at my side and squared his shoulders. His were even bigger than Robert's. Robert took a step back.

"Just having a chat," Robert said.

"Don't look that way to me," Pancake said.

"Maybe you misread the situation." His gaze jerked right and left as if looking for a graceful exit. Pancake had that effect on pretty much everyone.

"I would suggest that any misreading is on your part," Pancake said. "Bet you're pretty good at that."

"Look . . ." Robert began.

Pancake punched him square in the sternum. A short, quick jab that knocked Robert back against a storefront, took his breath way.

"You were saying?" Pancake asked.

He gasped in a breath. "Hey, man, you didn't have to do that."

Pancake shuffled toward him. "Seemed like a good idea to me."

Ray spoke up. "I take it you're Robert?" And then to his brother. "Kevin? Or do I have it backwards?"

"Yeah," Robert said, rubbing his chest. "And I just might sue this guy for assault." He nodded toward Pancake. "Maybe something worse."

"That wasn't an assault," Ray said. "But if you want to see one, I can turn him loose."

Robert hesitated as if weighing his options, meager as they were, and finally said, "We said what we needed to say."

Ray smiled. "Then maybe you should mosey along."

Robert jerked his head, indicating his brother should follow. We watched them go, Kevin glancing back over his shoulder as if he feared Pancake might not be finished.

"Too bad," Pancake said. "I was just getting warmed up."

Nicole hugged him. "You're the best."

"That I am."

"Hey," I said. "I had it under control."

Nicole laughed. "Jake, at the risk of saying something I've said many times, you're a lover, not a fighter. And I'd hate to see your pretty face messed up."

That got a laugh from Pancake.

My feelings were hurt. Really, they were.

Nicole ruffled my hair and then hugged me. "Actually, you did good. My white knight."

I felt better. Sort of.

"When will Kirk be out?" Ray asked.

"Not sure," I said. "Ebersole was hoping by the end of the day, but you know how those things go. Seems to take hours to move a few pieces of paper around."

Ray nodded. "I want to start with him. See what he says about what happened."

"I'll check with Ebersole and see if he has an update."

"We'll get checked in and then meet you guys in the bar."

"They have food there, don't they?" Pancake asked.

Nicole took his arm and led him to his truck, pulling the door open. "They have food everywhere in this town."

"Good. Ray wouldn't let me stop. All I wanted was a couple of Moon Pies. Maybe an RC."

"Poor baby." She slapped his butt. "Park this beastly truck and get checked in."

Pancake tugged open the back door and pulled out a baseball bat. "Look what I brought you," he said. He handed me the bat. "I was going to bring you a gun, but Ray said you might shoot yourself with it."

I get no respect.

I grabbed the bat. It was a Louisville Slugger. Ash, not one of those cheap-ass metal ones.

"This'll work," I said. "Thanks."

"What about me?" Nicole asked. "Don't I get a weapon?"

Pancake smiled. "You got those legs, darling. I've seen you kick the bag. You'll be fine."

She laughed. "You're such a charmer."

"That'd be me," he said.

CHAPTER FIFTEEN

THE SIT-DOWN WITH Kirk Ford took place in Ebersole's suite. The business sit-down, anyway. The social one happened in the Wine Room at Commander's Palace—the flagship of the extended Brennan family's gastronomic empire. Maybe my favorite restaurant anywhere. What's not to love about Commander's? I mean, it's been there over a hundred years and has served as the proving ground for such celebrity chefs as Emeril Lagasse and the late Paul Prudhomme. And the cuisine, as far as I could tell, hadn't suffered from their departures.

Kirk had been sprung from jail around five p.m. and had entered the Monteleone through a rear service entrance to avoid making a scene in the lobby and out on Royal where a handful of protesters and supporters held vigil. And made a general nuisance. Bet the Monteleone staff loved that. After a much-needed shower and a couple of drinks, Kirk was good to go so we climbed into Ebersole's limo and headed off.

For some reason, Ebersole felt this little social distraction would be good for Kirk—and everyone else. Sort of a get-out-of-jail party. Allow everyone to relax, decompress. Ray wasn't pleased. He wanted to "get to it" as he said. But that was Ray. Always work first and play second. This time I was actually on his side. I couldn't wait to hear what Kirk had to say, what he remembered, what he thought might have happened. Unless he already knew, of course.

At Commander's, we navigated another backdoor entry, courtesy of the maitre d'. Ebersole had made the clandestine arrangements with the crisp professional man who met us at the rear door. The two had also decided to make the reservation under a fake name. They chose Smith. I knew this because as we stepped inside Ebersole said, "Smith. Party of eight." The two men then exchanged a brief smile.

I wondered about their collective imaginations. I mean, I would have chosen the Manson family. Why not? Probably not a good idea though if staying off the radar was the goal. Still would have been fun.

We were quickly ensconced in the private Wine Room where we settled around a long wooden table surrounded by bins of wine that no doubt held bottles more pricey than my car. The meal was, of course, flawless as was the flotilla of waiters that made sure all was just so. The conversation had been light, but a current of tension hung in the air like a bundle of electrical cables.

Kirk was pleasant and smiled a lot—getting out of lockup would slap a smile on anyone's face—but he seemed subdued, as if part of him was elsewhere. That was my take anyway. But since I had never met him, I could've been wrong on that. Given the circumstances, I would've been surprised if he weren't apprehensive. I guessed that in the back of his mind, he was constantly assessing his future and all the ugly things that he might face down the road. The meal concluded with Commander's famous bread pudding and a bottle of Remy XO cognac. I was so stuffed I could barely fold into the limo. The twins didn't fare much better and moaned and complained all the way back to the Monteleone.

Now, we gathered in Ebersole's suite to discuss Kirk's "situation"—Ebersole's word. Not sure that was the right description. Not even close.

Ray took the wingback chair at the head of the long, low coffee table, Kirk in an identical one opposite him. Nicole and I sank into the sofa. Ebersole dragged over two chairs and offered them to the twins, but Tara—?Tegan?—said they were too full to sit up, so they stretched out on the floor. Ebersole grabbed two pillows from the bed for them, but they tossed one aside and shared a single one to prop on. Ebersole and Pancake took the chairs.

Ray first asked Kirk if he had any reservations about talking all this over in front of everyone, to which he said he didn't, that everyone there were friends, even his "new" friends.

Ray jumped right in. "Tell me," he said. "You and Kristi."

Kirk related how he had met her a little over a week earlier in a Bourbon Street bar and said they had an immediate chemistry. They had spent every night together since then, mostly in his room, but a couple of nights out on the town. They had been to dinner at NOLA the night of her death. With Tara and Tegan. They all returned to the hotel round nine thirty. Tara and Tegan dropped by the room and they had some wine. The twins left around ten. He looked at them. "Isn't that about right?"

The twins nodded and spoke in unison. "That's right."

Kirk continued, saying he and Kristi had sex "for a couple of hours" but after that things were fuzzy at best. He woke up the next morning and found her dead. In bed, next to him. He freaked, not knowing what to do, so he called Ebersole.

"Any issues between you two?" Ray asked. "An argument maybe?"

"No." Kirk shook his head to emphasize the point. "Look, I didn't kill her. Let's get that straight right up front."

Ray caught his gaze. "So, you remember not killing her?"

That stopped Kirk for a beat. He looked from one of us to the other before returning to Ray. "I don't remember anything after we crashed."

"How do you think a jury will react to that?"

Kirk's jaw tightened. "Whose side are you on here?"

"No one's."

"Then why am I talking to you? If you don't believe me, how can you help?"

"Because you don't need someone to kiss your ass right now. You need someone a shade more objective." Ray waved one hand. "I don't know you. Don't know the situation yet. Don't know what I believe. That's what the guy who signs your checks asked me . . ." he nodded toward Nicole and me . . . "us—to find out."

"Then how do I know I can trust you?"

"You don't. But I promise you the DA will ask these questions in court." Ray's gaze never wavered. "And a shitload of even more uncomfortable ones."

Kirk sighed and collapsed back into his chair, his shoulders sagging. He looked scared. Or was it beaten? It was as if the true flavor of all this had just wrapped him like a boa constrictor. Like maybe he hadn't considered that all that legal stuff he had seen on TV and in movies was now going to unwind his life. That he had the starring role in a true-life legal drama. Scary stuff.

"You're probably right," Kirk said, his voice low, tired.

"I'm definitely right," Ray said. "What's the first thing you do remember?"

Kirk massaged one temple. "A headache. A nasty taste in my mouth. Confusion. Like I didn't know where I was. Took a few seconds to figure it out."

"Then?"

"Kristi was laying next to me. The sheet was up to her neck. I rolled over and gave her a nudge. Nothing. She just lay there. I thought she was simply asleep, but when I nudged her again, she still didn't respond. I peeled back the sheet. That's when I saw her bra wrapped around her neck." He took in a ragged breath. "I touched her shoulder. It was cold." He closed his eyes and grimaced as if fighting back tears, then pinched the bridge of his nose, gathering himself. When he opened his eyes, they glistened with moisture. "That's when I knew she was dead."

"That when you went for help?" Pancake asked. "Called Mr. Ebersole?"

"Yeah. I mean, I shook her. Called her name. Praying she'd wake up. I placed my ear on her chest hoping to hear a heartbeat. But I knew. Her skin was cold—and rubbery."

I looked at Ebersole. "After you got there, how long before you called the police?"

"Ten, fifteen minutes. First, I had to calm Kirk down. He was a mess. Scared to death."

"Understandable."

"To be honest, the idea of getting rid of her, dumping her body somewhere, making it all go away, as if it had never happened, crossed my mind."

"Perhaps the worst thing you could have done," Ray said.

Ebersole nodded. "But it crossed my mind. Of course, getting a body out of the hotel and then—I didn't know what then. Anyway, I quickly let that idea go and called the police."

"Glad you did. A stupid move like that would have made this a whole different story."

"This one's bad enough," Kirk said.

Ray nodded. "Sure is. But things can always go from bad to worse."

"I don't see how."

A heavy silence fell over us. As if no one could think how this could really be any darker. Two people locked in a room and one ends up dead. It was like a B movie script.

"The police found two empty wine bottles," I said.

"And we had one earlier—with dinner."

"Who drank the most? You or Kristi?"

"Me. She wasn't much of a drinker. But I think she had maybe three or four glasses."

"And a little smoke?" I asked.

Kirk looked at me.

"The cops found three joints. One half-smoked on the bedside table."

"Yeah. We did."

"Both of you?" Nicole asked.

Kirk nodded.

"We talked to a friend of hers," I said. "And her ex-boyfriend. Both said she didn't use drugs."

"Fuck me," Kirk said. He leaned forward and rested his face in his hands.

We waited him out.

He looked up. "She didn't. Until she met me." He sighed.

"That night was her first time?" I asked.

"No. Not that night."

"Want to explain?" Ray said.

"The first time was our second date. She was reluctant, but I talked her into it."

"Jesus," Ebersole said. "The DA will paint you as a predator."

Ray raised a hand. "Just a second. So she tried it for the first time. And?"

"She liked it. We did it every time we got together after that."

"The joints were yours then?" I asked.

"Actually, no. Well, two were. She brought one. The one we actually fired up."

"She did?" I asked. "A girl who doesn't do drugs suddenly has a dealer?"

"All I know is she had one. That's the only one we smoked. And only a little of it."

"She say where she got it?" Ray asked.

"From a friend was all she said. Supposed to be good stuff." He shook his head. "That's an understatement. Sure fucked me up."

"What do you mean?" Nicole asked.

"I remember us taking a couple of hits. Then we started having sex again. I must've been really hammered because everything was . . . odd."

"In what way?" I asked.

"Like I was floating. Or flying. Or something. Like the world had shifted off axis." He looked at me. "Crazy, isn't it? I don't use it often but I have had some pretty good stuff. I mean, Hollywood? High-end everything rolls around out there. But this was different."

"The new stuff," Pancake said. "The product out there now ain't your daddy's Mary Jane."

"I can vouch for that," Kirk said.

"And toss in a bunch of fermented grapes and things can get wonky in a hurry," Ray said.

"Maybe. It's not like I haven't mixed those two before."

"You sure Kristi didn't say where she got it?" I asked.

"Not that I remember. But then, I don't remember much."

When Kirk had entered the room, he had shed his sports coat and now wore a black tee shirt. I had noticed several scratches on his arms and flashed on what Doucet had said.

"Those scratches." I pointed to his exposed arms. "How'd you get those?"

"From all the crap we have to wade through in the swamp and the underbrush out there."

The twins snapped to a sitting position. In unison. Like a Rockette's routine.

"We can attest to that," one of them said. Not sure which.

Her sister stretched her pullover off one shoulder. A nice shoulder. Covered with fine scratch lines. "We have them everywhere. I'm amazed we haven't been infected by some deadly swamp bug."

"True," the first twin added. She lifted her shirt, exposing her abdomen and a pair of long, thin welts. "Our *Space Quest* uniforms don't cover much so we've got these marks everywhere. And I mean everywhere."

"The cops made me strip and they photographed them," Kirk said. "Front and back."

"Standard procedure," Ray said. "And the ME will look for your DNA under Kristi's fingernails."

Kirk stared at him. "What if they find it?"

"Will they?" Ray asked.

Kirk shook his head. "I don't know. Kristi wasn't a scratcher if that's what your asking. She enjoyed sex but wasn't that wild."

"Doesn't matter anyway," Ray said. "You two had consensual sex, so that wouldn't mean too much in court." He opened his hands. "If you two had been strangers, then that's a different story. But as it is, your attorney can easily explain it away."

Kirk took a deep breath and let it out slowly. "This is a nightmare. It's like everything is spinning so fast and I can't get off the ride."

Another silence fell.

"Anything else you guys need right now?" Ebersole asked.

"Lots of things," Ray said. "But I don't think Kirk can help us with that. Not right now anyway."

"I'm sorry," Kirk said. "I wish I could remember more."

"That's okay. This gives us a little to work with."

"Like what?"

"We'll get to that another time," Ray said. "Right now, Pancake and I have to do some digging." He looked at me. "Jake and Nicole, too."

Did he really say that? He actually needed our help? Was Ray mellowing in his old age? Not likely, but still, it was nice to be on the team.

Ebersole stood. "It's been a long couple of days. And we shoot tomorrow. Early. We have some lost time to make up. Let's all get some rest."

CHAPTER SIXTEEN

I HADN'T GOTTEN much sleep last night. At least not in hours. Four or five. But those hours must have been deep and coma-like because by morning I felt refreshed. So much so that I woke ready to go—so to speak. I crept a hand toward Nicole but found an empty bed. Then I heard the hiss of the shower.

Last night, after our chat with Kirk, we swung by the Monteleone bar for a quick drink. Turned into four. I think. Could've been more. Probably was. We ran into a family from Chicago. Mom and dad and their twentysomething son. He gave Nicole the once-over—the son that is. Come to think if it, so did dad. But the son was more interested in me. Not that way, but in a Major League Baseball way. Turned out he was some sort of baseball savant. Knew everything about everything. He remembered things about my career I couldn't have pulled from my memory banks even if someone held a .357 to my head. Stats galore. And yes, I signed a napkin for him before Nicole and I said our good-byes and headed upstairs. It was after midnight.

I wanted to play, but Nicole stripped, crawled beneath the covers, and went facedown into a deep sleep. I cracked open my self-defense book. Before I flicked off the bedside lamp, I learned to control someone with their pinky, snapping it if need be, to rip the ligaments in a knee with a well-placed kick, and to collapse an instep with a stomp.

I was getting more dangerous every day.

Just as I decided to roll out of bed and join Nicole, the shower fell silent. Then she came out, wrapped in a towel, a swirl of steam following.

I patted the bed next to me. She glanced down at the now tented sheet.

"Put that away before you hurt someone."

See, I told you I was getting dangerous.

"Maybe I could hide it somewhere?" I smiled.

She shook her head while stepping into a pair of jeans. "As appealing as that sounds, crude but appealing, I don't have time. Got to meet the limo in about fifteen minutes."

"The limo?"

"Ebersole's ride. I'm going out to the shoot with Kirk and the twins."

"Oh. When did you decide that?"

She shook her head. "We discussed it last night."

"We did?"

"We did. Before we left Ebersole's suite. Then I told you again. In the bar. Twice."

"I don't remember."

"Of course you don't. You were playing baseball hero with that kid."

"Me? He started it."

She laughed. "I was amazed at all the stats and stuff he knew." She tugged on a black tee shirt. "Sorry to abandon you and your friend." She nodded toward my friend, who had apparently given up all hope. "But I have to run. Will you be okay on your own?" Another smile.

"Funny. I have important stuff to do anyway."

"Like what?"

"Ray, Pancake, and I are getting together with Detective Doucet later this morning. Then we'll come out your way."

She sat on the edge of the bed, tying her sneakers. "I'll call you later." She kissed my cheek, grabbed her purse, and was gone.

So much for fooling around.

Now what to do? I had a couple of hours to kill. Maybe a walk. Shirt, shorts, and my New Balance shoes, and I was out the door.

The Riverwalk, a major French Quarter tourist attraction, was a great place for an early morning stroll. As I headed downstream along the banks of the Mississippi, I passed a few other walkers, a couple of hard-core joggers, and a small group doing Tai Chi—an odd form of pretzel-like contortions that I suspected were the origins of yoga, Pilates, and probably Mummenschanz. They seemed happy so I guess it was working.

A barge piled with what looked more like junk than anything else motored north and another maneuvered toward the opposite shore—Algiers—with the aid of a tug, its props churning up the water. I always thought tugs were cool. They worked for a living. I stopped and watched for a few minutes, then turned and headed back upstream.

They don't call the Mississippi "The Big Muddy" for nothing. Even in the flat early morning light, the water looked like coffee.

Speaking of which.

I made my way back to Café du Monde and grabbed a cup from the take-out window. I saw Gloria, Kristi's friend, balancing a tray of beignets as she weaved through the tables. She saw me and nodded. After she delivered the powdered sugar bombs to a table of six, she walked my way, her elbow clamping the now empty tray to her side.

"What's new?"

"Kirk Ford got out of jail last night," I said.

"Already?"

"Bail."

"I'm sure he can afford it."

"He's not clear of the charges, if that's what you're thinking."

"I would hope not. But you just never know. Money talks. Loudly."

A busboy came by, and she handed him the empty tray, nodding a thanks.

"Can I ask you something?" I said.

"Sure."

"The cops found a half-smoked joint in the room. Where Kristi was . . ."

"Murdered."

"Yeah. Anyway, Kirk said it wasn't his. Said Kristi brought it."

"No way. Not a chance."

"It's what he said."

Her eyes flashed. "He's trying to blame this on Kristi?" She looked across the patio, unfocused, a slow shake of her head. "Just great."

"I didn't read it that way," I said. Her gaze returned to me. "And I didn't say I necessarily believed him."

"Don't. I told you, Kristi never touched that or anything else. And she damn sure wouldn't carry it around with her."

I nodded. "For the sake of argument, if she did have some, where would she have gotten it?"

"She didn't."

"But if she did?"

"She wouldn't." She sighed. "But it's not exactly a rare commodity around here. And just about anything else that stirs your gumbo."

I smiled. "Voice of experience?"

Now she smiled. "Maybe."

"So, if she, or anyone else, wanted to purchase some, who would be a likely source?"

"You're dense, aren't you?"

Was that an insult? She softened it with another smile.

"It's been said."

"I'm sure." She laughed. "This is New Orleans. There ain't nothing you can't purchase on just about any corner." She waved a hand toward the sidewalk where a couple of performers were already setting up for the day, while across the street, an artist was hanging his wares on the wrought-iron fence that hugged Jackson Square. Free enterprise started early around here. Gloria went on. "But, if Kristi did pick some up, and I'm not saying she did, it wouldn't have been from a stranger."

"Then who?"

"A couple of the cooks here always have some. And so do her brothers."

"Oh?"

"They were born stupid and I know they smoke, which doesn't make them any smarter. And I know they deal a bit. Small-time, but they do."

"Wonder what their uncle thinks of that."

"Shit. That's probably where they learned to deal. Drugs are part of Tony's domain." She looked around. "I didn't say that."

"I didn't hear it either."

"But if he found out those two clowns were feeding Kristi drugs, he'd kill them. Maybe literally."

"You did say he was protective of Kristi."

"No doubt." A couple seated near the sidewalk waved to her. She raised a "just a sec" finger. "I got to get to work."

"Thanks for chatting."

"Anytime." Then she was off.

I had forty-five minutes before I hooked up with Ray and Pancake, and needed to shower, shave, and look somewhat presentable, so I pointed myself toward the Monteleone. I passed the fortune-teller's shop. It was dark. Closed up tight. I guessed fortunes weren't available until after morning coffee. Maybe breakfast at Brennan's. She could afford it. I mean, forty bucks for fifteen minutes of mumbo jumbo.

As I turned up Royal, my cell chimed. Caller ID said Tammy. That's Tammy the Insane. My ex. My never-ending headache. Even though she tossed me out years ago—not without reason, mind you—and married dear old Walter Horton, her divorce attorney and the extractor of half my net worth, she still seemed to regard me as some sort of advisor, confessor, or something. Never could figure out my role in her little dramas. And they were dramas. Always. Tammy lived for drama. I could expect anywhere from two to twenty-seven calls from her on a weekly basis. I hadn't heard from her for a few days, so it was time.

I considered punching it over to voice mail but that was a fool's errand. It would only lead to a rapid series of calls and rants. With Tammy, everything was a war of attrition. Voice of experience here. I answered.

"Where are you?" she asked.

"New Orleans."

"Doing what?"

"Nicole." I did love pushing her buttons. It was a small reward for the crap I took from her.

"Asshole. What are you really doing?"

"Negotiating the Louisiana Purchase."

"Don't be an ass."

"I try not to, I really do."

"No, you don't." I waited her out. "You didn't tell me you were leaving."

"News flash—you're not my secretary."

"You know Walter and I are going through a tough time."

"Any time with you is tough."

"You can be so exasperating." Again, I waited her out, knowing Tammy didn't expect or need a response. "Jake, I need your help."

"About what this time?"

"Walter. He's really depressed. So much so it's scaring me."

"Don't you think that's a normal response given recent events?"

"But..."

"But nothing. His girlfriend was murdered, he was a suspect, his life was threatened by a Ukrainian mobster, and he's still stuck with you. Depression seems reasonable to me."

"Barbara wasn't his girlfriend." Was that her takeaway from all that? Apparently so. She continued. "She was a mistake. A distraction."

"Semantics."

"She was my friend, too. And I'm not depressed."

See? Everything in Tammy's world is about her.

"Walter's the sensitive type," I said.

"And I'm not?"

I almost laughed but mustered the good sense to reign it in. "Tammy, I'm not Walter's therapist. In fact, he doesn't like me very much. Maybe he should see a pro."

"But you have a knack for making everything seem unimportant. Light. Meaningless. Walter could use that."

"You have a charming way of asking for help."

I had reached the Monteleone, but rather than drag this conversation into the lobby, I loitered on the sidewalk. Kirk's protesters and supporters hadn't yet arrived, so the street was quiet. "Look, I have nothing to offer Walter. And I'm a bit busy right now."

"What's more important than Walter's mental health?"

"You want a complete list or just a thumbnail?"

"You're an ass." She disconnected the call.

Welcome to my world.

CHAPTER SEVENTEEN

RAY, PANCAKE, AND I hooked up with Doucet outside the court-house. The original plan was to meet at his office, but he had called Ray, saying he had to drop off some evidence materials at the court. An unrelated case. Rather than hassle with the parking area security, we met him out front near the steps where yesterday Kornblatt had done his song and dance for the media.

Ray and Doucet hit it off immediately. I knew they would. Both seemingly cut from similar cloth. After sharing a couple of who-do-you-know-that-I-know anecdotes, they dove into the Kirk Ford situation and the murder of Kristi Guidry. Doucet apparently considered Ray a comrade in arms and showed no reluctance to share what meager evidence he had in the case.

"Doesn't look good for Ford," Ray said.

Doucet shrugged.

"Any other suspects?"

"Not really." Doucet shoved his hands in his pockets and looked up the street. "I mean, locked room, two people, one ends up dead. Not sure where to go from there." He looked at Ray. "Don't see how anyone else could have."

"That's my take," Ray said.

"Unless it's one of those Agatha Christie stories," I said.

"I don't think old Agatha is in play here," Ray said. "I suspect Ford's best bet is a diminished-capacity defense."

"That'll be a tough sell," Pancake said. "Alcohol and marijuana might make you goofy and stupid, but it usually doesn't make folks violent."

"Nor completely erase memory as Ford has said," Ray added.

"Not even the new stuff?" I asked. "There's some pretty potent weed out there. I've seen it at my bar. Folks disoriented and confused."

"That's true of most of the riffraff that frequent your place," Ray said.

He can be so pleasant. But I had learned long ago to let Ray's jabs slide. Mostly. He hated Captain Rocky's. Hated that I owned it. That I chose that over "legitimate work." Legitimate in his eyes, anyway.

"We call them customers," I said.

Ray shrugged. "Regardless of the effects of marijuana, new or old, Ford will use that. And it seems he's already started down that road."

"Oh?" Doucet said.

"He's saying he doesn't remember anything—as in nothing."

"You saying he's faking that?" Doucet asked.

"I don't know what's in Ford's head. Or his attorney's noggin. Who I hear is pretty slick."

"Sure seems to be," Doucet said. "And, of course, we see the I-don't-know or I-don't-remember or it-wasn't-me-I-swear defense all the time."

"Kirk said Kristi brought the joint they smoked," I said.

Doucet nodded. "So he says."

"Nicole and I talked with Kristi's old boyfriend and a friend of hers over at Café du Monde. They both said she didn't move in those circles. That she never used anything."

"That's what I heard, too," Doucet said. "From everyone we talked to. Including her uncle Tony."

"Until she met Ford anyway," Ray said.

"What about the DNA?" I asked.

Doucet scratched one ear. "The ME did find some tissue beneath one of Kristi's fingernails. And Ford had scratches all over him. Some old, some new. He said they were from the swamp where they're shooting the movie. The ME told me his injuries were indeed consistent with that. Particularly given they're varying ages."

"The twins—Tara and Tegan—have the same scratches," I said.

"That's why I doubt DNA will play much of a role here. Even if it turns out to be Kirk Ford's. I mean, they had sex, after all."

"Scratching and all that," Pancake said. "My favorite kind."

Doucet smiled. "And since they were behind closed doors, who knows what kind of sex they had? Even if we find his DNA in those scrapings, you can bet his attorney will make Kristi into some kind of sex-starved wildcat."

"I'm sure that'd make her uncle Tony happy," I said.

"Oh yeah," Doucet said. "That could make courtroom history."

Doucet's phone buzzed. He pulled it from his pocket and walked a few feet away as he brought it to his ear.

"The deeper we get, the worse it looks for Kirk," I said.

Ray nodded. "Sure does. He better have a good attorney."

"My impression of Kornblatt is that he's a take-no-prisoners type."

"Yeah, but it's an away game for him. Ford, too."

Doucet ended his call and turned our way. "That was the coroner. He has the tox reports on Kirk and Kristi back and wants to go over it with me. In person."

"That sounds interesting," Ray said.

"That's the exact word he used. I'd better get over there."

"Mind if we tag along?" I asked.

Doucet hesitated, and then said, "Sure."

We followed his nondescript white department sedan to the coroner's office. It wasn't far to where it sat along Earhart Boulevard near Claiborne and in the shadows of I-10, only a couple of blocks from the Superdome. Very governmental—two-story tan brick with flattened windows and an American flag out front. The sign indicated it shared space with the Emergency Medical Service offices. I had read something about it in the *Times-Picayune*. I had found the latest issue abandoned in the Monteleone bar. The article, wedged between news of some French Quarter bar reopening after a restoration and a recipe for pecan pie, said the building was "state of the art" and had just opened in early 2016 at a cost of nearly $15 million. State of the art is always expensive.

Pancake parked next to Doucet in the mostly empty lot. Before we could get out, Doucet walked up and stood staring at Ray through the passenger's window. Ray lowered it.

"I think it's best if you guys wait here while I go see what the deal is. The coroner's a stickler for rules and I'd rather not try to explain you guys."

It crossed my mind that Ray and Pancake were unexplainable. Me? I'm easy. Really. Still, not riling the coroner made sense. So, we waited.

I told them of my conversation with Gloria earlier.

"Bottom line is she doesn't know where Kristi might've gotten the stuff?" Ray asked.

I nodded. "But she did remind me that this was New Orleans and almost anything is easily available. She mentioned a couple of the cooks at Café du Monde were sources. And Kristi's brothers, too."

"Interesting," Pancake said.

"Gloria said they even sold a little. Not much, as far as she knew, but some."

"Even more interesting."

"But she also said they would never have given any to Kristi. If they're anything, they're overly protective."

Pancake grunted. Meant he didn't really buy that. "I guess she could have clipped some from their stash. If they have one and if she knew where it was."

"True," Ray said. "But I think that's a lost leader. She was strangled, not poisoned."

"Unless the coroner found something else," I said.

And the coroner had. Big-time.

Doucet walked out and up to the truck. Stress lines creased his face.

"What is it?" Ray asked.

He leaned straight-armed on the window frame. He looked toward the building and then back to Ray. "This is not for public consumption. Got it?"

"No problem."

"What the toxicology guys found is a game changer. Ketamine."

"What?" I asked.

He looked past Ray at me. "In the joint remnant and both Kristi's and Ford's blood."

Ketamine, bump. Purple. Special K. Goes by a lot of names but it's one of the so-called date rape drugs. Started as a general anesthetic but made it's way into the rave culture and then into the hands of some really bad actors. I know because we had had a problem with it at Captain Rocky's once. Some asshole had slipped some into an unsuspecting girl's drink. Fortunately, Carla Martinez, my manager, recognized the girl was acting a little weird and prevented her from leaving with the guy. He protested that she was free to do as she wished, but Carla isn't someone you mess with. She said unless the guy wanted his head opened with a barstool, he'd step back and take a breath. She called the cops and the guy took off. The girl was taken to the ER and was fine, but it turned into a big mess. Nearly lost my liquor licenses over that one. Definitely got a bunch of bad press.

"That does change things," Ray said. "Ask Jake. Nearly lost his bar over that shit."

"Oh?" Doucet said.

"Long story," I said.

Doucet nodded. "Let me guess. Date rape situation?"

"Almost."

"We've had more than our share of that crap around here. Mostly GHB but we've seen a few ketamine cases."

"You said the lab found it in the joint remnant," I said. "What about the other two? The ones they didn't smoke?"

Doucet shook his head. "Those were clean."

"Hmm," I said. "That means the two Kirk had were cool and Kristi brought the laced one."

"If he's telling the truth."

"But if his plan was to drug her—which I simply don't believe—why only mess with one of them?" I asked. "Why not all three?"

Doucet shrugged. "Maybe he meant one for her and the others for him?"

"Yet the ketamine was found in both of them?" I said. "That doesn't make sense."

"Nothing in this case does."

That was an understatement. Why would Kirk need to drug someone he was having sex with? If that was his plan, why would he drug himself? For fun? Recreational so to speak? And things went sideways? I felt that most likely neither of them knew the joint was contaminated. I laid out those thoughts for Doucet.

"If so," he said, "it raises the question of who would've done that. And why? Was it all a coincidence? I mean Kristi buys a joint from someone and either they give her a doctored one by accident or did so purposefully. And if the latter, was it just for fun—to really fuck her up—or was her murder part of some grand plan?"

"It's always the who and why, isn't it?" Ray asked.

"True," Doucet said. "And the why usually points the finger right at the who. But here? I can't see a why."

"The drugs could explain why Kirk can't remember anything," I said.

"True that," Pancake said. "That shit'll fry your cortex for sure."

"The question is where did it come from?" Ray said.

"We have a few guys on our radar that could be sources," Doucet said. "I'll check them out."

"But how would Kristi have come across something like that?" I asked. "I mean, a nonuser stepping into that?"

"Like you suggested, maybe she didn't know," Pancake said. "You can't smell or taste that stuff. Maybe someone gave her a loaded joint and she didn't have a clue."

"Which brings us back to who," I said. "And why."

"Still can't rule out Ford," Doucet said. "We only have his word that Kristi brought the stuff to the room."

"I have trouble buying that," I said. "He and Kristi were having regular sex, so it wouldn't have been for compliance—for lack of a better word."

Doucet shrugged. "Maybe just for kicks."

"But would he have drugged himself?" I asked.

Doucet straightened. Shoved his hands in his pockets. "Unless he likes it." He rattled some keys in his pocket. "Guess we'll have to ask him."

"We can ask him," I said. "We're headed out that way."

"Where's that?" Doucet asked.

"The shooting location," I said. "Over off Highway 90, near Bayou Sauvage."

"You know the area?" Doucet asked.

"No, but Ebersole gave me a map."

Doucet rapped a knuckle on the window frame. "Maybe I'll follow you out there."

"Not a good idea," Ray said. "I don't think his attorneys would allow a chat without them present."

Doucet nodded. "But I need a sit-down with him."

"We'll talk with Kirk," I said. "And I'll call Kornblatt and see if we can set it up. How about that?"

Doucet glanced up the street, and then back toward me. "I guess that'll work. I can't force him to sit down—unless I arrest him again—but I don't think that'd be best."

"Probably not."

"Okay," Doucet said. "You guys go have a chat with Ford. I'll see what I can dig up on the drugs."

"Street sources," Ray said. "Always good to have in your pocket."

"Oh, yeah. I got a guy who knows everything about everything in that world."

"You mean like an informant?" I asked.

"Not exactly. More like a career criminal." Doucet rapped the window frame again. "Keep me in the loop."

CHAPTER EIGHTEEN

DETECTIVE MARLON DUGAN was one of Tony Guidry's most useful assets. An inside source. Good eyes and ears, kept a low profile. One of those smallish, disheveled guys that no one ever notices. And most importantly, he readily accepted the stuffed envelopes Tony winged his way. His info had always been right on, but Tony always had other sources. Redundancy being the word. There was McCredy and Pettway, both detectives, and if need be, he could climb the food chain all the way to the chief's office. He used those higher connections sparingly so they would be in his debt and not the other way around. Such an escalation wasn't needed here.

Tony Guidry held his cell to his ear. Based on the background traffic noise, Dugan was outside. Probably in the PD's rear lot, away from any interested ears. His scalp tingled. His jaw tightened so much his teeth hurt. He sat at one end of the bar at Belly Up. One of his French Quarter clubs, this one near the corner of Bourbon and St. Anne. Still an hour or so before opening, he had been going over the ledgers, the official ones, anyway, not the secret ones. Those stayed in his office vault at all times. Why give the IRS any help? They already held all the cards anyway.

Johnny Hebert and Reuben Prejean huddled at a nearby table, playing penny-ante poker and guzzling coffee. Robert and Kevin hung near the far end of the bar, chatting with one of the waitresses. One of the new ones. Normally Tony would have dragged them away, by their ears if need be, the brothers having offended and run off new employees more than once. But right now, Tony had a more pressing problem.

"What the fuck are you saying?" Tony said, his voice low, almost a hiss.

"Just what I said. They found ketamine in both Kristi and Ford. And in one of the joints found at the scene."

"Is this solid?"

"Right from the horse's mouth."

"Doucet?"

"Yep."

Tony closed the ledger and stood, the stool scraping the floor. Johnny and Reuben looked his way.

"You gotta be fucking kidding me. Where did this shit come from?"

"No clue," Dugan said. "Not yet, anyway."

"Okay. Keep your radar on and let me know what you hear."

"You got it."

"There'll be a little gift headed your way. Maybe not so little this time." He disconnected the call and walked to where his nephews stood. He waved away the girl.

"Did you clowns give Kristi any drugs?"

"What?" Kevin said. "No way."

"Don't lie to me."

"We're not," Robert said. "We would never."

Tony twisted his head one way and then the other, working out the gathering tightness. "If I find out you're lying, there will be no end to the grief I'll drop on you."

"Uncle Tony, we didn't," Kevin said. "We wouldn't. Never."

"But you're still selling some shit." It wasn't a question. "Even after I told you again and again not to."

"A little," Kevin said. "But only to friends."

At least they were smart enough not to lie about something Tony knew was true.

"And friends never turn on you? Get popped for something stupid? Buy their way out of a jam by giving the cops something they can use against me?"

Two blank faces stared at him. He wanted to rip them apart right now.

Johnny and Reuben pushed back their chairs and moved to Tony's side. "What is it, boss?"

Tony raised a finger and then punched a number into his phone. His secretary answered. "You know where they're filming that movie?"

"No, Mr. Guidry."

"Find out. Now." He hung up and looked at his nephews. "Besides weed and a few bags of meth, have you guys dabbled in anything else?"

Kevin shook his head. "No. Like what?"

"Like ketamine."

"No. We wouldn't even know where to get that."

Tony held their collective gaze, making sure they felt his anger. He looked at Johnny. "The call I got was from my guy at NOPD. He says the coroner found ketamine in Kristi. Kirk Ford, too. And a joint they found at the scene."

"Where the hell did that come from?" Johnny asked.

"That's what I want to know." He looked back at Kevin. "At the risk of being redundant, if you're lying to me it'll get very ugly, very quickly."

Kevin held up his hands, palms out. "We don't know anything about that. That's the truth."

Did he believe them? Could he? They were idiots and liars by nature. But looking at their bewildered and scared faces, he tended to believe they were telling the truth. For once.

Tony looked at his feet, trying to wrap his head around all this. Ketamine? He looked at Johnny. "If that pretty boy is telling the truth, Kristi brought that joint to the party. A joint laced with ketamine."

"Where would she get that?" Reuben asked.

"That's what I want you guys to find out. Scorched earth. Lean on whoever you have to, but I want to know anyone and everyone who could have."

"You got it."

"But first I want to go have a chat with Mr. Ford."

"You think he'll talk to you?" Johnny asked.

"He won't have a choice."

"I'm just saying I don't think his attorney will allow that."

"Walton Greene? You think I can't twist him into a knot?"

"Not him. That Kornblatt character. The one from LA."

"I don't give a flying fuck about some Jew fuck from Hollywood. He's not here anyway."

His cell chimed. His secretary. He answered. He listened and then, "Okay. Text me the exact directions. We're rolling." He disconnected the call and headed toward the door, Johnny and Reuben in tow.

"We're going with you," Kevin said.

Tony stopped and turned. "The hell you are. Stay here and do your fucking jobs for once."

"We're all caught up."

"Really? You got the bar restocked yet?"

Kevin stared at him.

"Didn't think so." Then he was out the door.

"Where to, boss?" Reuben asked as he held the limo door for Tony.

"Up off Highway 90 near Bayou Sauvage."

CHAPTER NINETEEN

KEVIN TOOK A hit from the joint and passed it to his brother. They were standing near Robert's eight-year-old black Jeep and a pair of trash bins that snuggled up against a cinder-block wall behind the Belly Up. He exhaled the smoke and waved it away.

"Haven't seen Uncle Tony that pissed in a while," Kevin said.

Robert nodded. "Sure was." Smoke leaked from his mouth as he spoke. "And you better hope the new girl doesn't screw up the bar or he'll have our asses."

"How hard can it fucking be? Lug a few bottles from the storage room and line them up behind the bar. Any moron could do it."

"She ain't exactly a genius."

"But she's hot."

Robert nodded. "She is that. But, I'm just saying you better hope she doesn't screw it up."

Kevin rolled his eyes. "You worry too much."

"And you not enough." Robert passed the joint back to Kevin. "You sure talking with Ju Ju is a good idea?"

"Uncle Tony wants to know where the ketamine came from. Ju Ju will know."

"For sure, he'll know. But don't you think Tony'll want to talk to him directly?"

"So we save him a couple of steps." Kevin took another hit.

"You know how he gets when we try to get into his business."

Kevin exhaled. "You mean other than moving whiskey bottles around?"

Robert shrugged.

"If we can find out where that shit came from, he'll be happy."

"Really? Not sure I've ever seen him happy."

Kevin extinguished the joint with a pinch and slipped the remnant into his jeans pocket. "Let's go."

It only took five minutes to reach Ju Ju's place. But as they approached, Kevin grabbed his brother's arm with one hand and pointed with the other. "Who's that?"

A man stood on Ju Ju's small front porch, rapping on the door frame. Robert kept driving.

"Is that who I think it is?" Kevin asked. He twisted and looked back through the rear window.

"Yes, it is."

"What the hell's he doing here?"

"Same as us. You don't think he knows what Uncle Tony knows?"

"What now?"

"Let's chill. Over by the park. Think this through."

"Maybe we should call Uncle Tony? Let him know?"

"He'll know soon enough. Besides, he might not be thrilled with us being here. Unless we can find out something he can use."

Kevin sighed. "We should talk to Ragman."

"Why?"

"Let him know the cops will be coming his way."

"You don't know that." Robert looked at him. "You think Ju Ju would hand over Ragman? Are you crazy?"

Robert settled the car against the curb along Dumaine near the intersection with Rampart. He switched off the engine. They crossed Rampart and entered Louis Armstrong Park, passing beneath the

entry arch and through the open iron gates. They walked to the water's edge. Kevin picked up a couple of loose rocks and began skim-
ming them over the water's flat surface.

"No, I don't think Ju Ju would roll on Ragman or anyone else,"
Kevin said. "The exact opposite. He protects those guys. But if
Detective Doucet is knocking on Ju Ju's door, how long you think
it'll be before he starts leaning on the dealers?"

Robert gazed out over the water as if pondering that idea.

Kevin hurled another pebble, this one getting four good bounces
before sinking from sight. "You know Ju Ju and the cops play games
with each other. Exchange information. It's what they do."

"I guess this is a big deal," Robert said. "Kristi. Uncle Tony. All the
media shit. And now with drugs like bump involved, it'll be an even
bigger deal."

"Exactly. Ju Ju can earn a lot of points by helping out here. With
the cops and with Uncle Tony."

"That makes sense." Now Robert skimmed a rock. Three skips.

"All I'm saying is that we could give Ragman a heads up," Kevin
said. "Let him know what's coming down."

Robert nodded. "He might like that."

"And we can impress on him once again that Tony, anyone else for
that matter, has no need to know we buy shit from him."

Robert sighed. "Tony finding out we're still using, not to mention
dealing, would not be pretty. That's for sure."

"He already knows."

Robert shook a pebble in his hand. "He suspects. He doesn't really
know."

"He knows. He knows everything, it seems."

Robert shrugged. "Let's go find Ragman."

"One thing—what if Ju Ju finds out we told Ragman all this shit?
Don't you think he'd be pissed?"

"He's going to tell him anyway. Don't you think? I mean, if Doucet is in there talking about bump, he's doing it so Ju Ju will get his ear to the ground. Find out who's dealing it."

"My point exactly. If Ragman blabs and the word gets out we stuck our noses in here, Ju Ju will go ballistic. You know what a control freak he is." Robert skimmed the stone. "I'm wondering if maybe we should just lay low on this. I mean, Ju Ju will ramp up big-time if we go behind his back."

"We wouldn't be. And if we get what Tony needs, find out where that shit came from, Tony will be impressed. Might even trust us more."

"Right? I don't think that's even possible. He's such a dick."

Kevin tossed the pebbles he held on the ground and rubbed his hands together. "Look, we can grab some more weed from Ragman and then casually bring up bump. See if he sells that shit. Or knows who does."

"Casual huh?"

"Casual."

CHAPTER TWENTY

Ju Ju. Real name Junior Makin, Junior. Made him Junior, Jr. Where the Ju Ju came from. No stranger to law enforcement, Doucet had had his run-ins with him. But he also had leaned on Ju Ju for help, giving him a little rhythm in return. Truth was Ju Ju kept a firm hand on the dealers in the Treme. Half the Quarter, too. Every time there was a territory dispute—one dealer stepping on another's perceived domain, stealing customers, undercutting prices—Ju Ju put a boot on their necks. Kept many a disagreement from escalating into a full-on range war. Kept the peace in a way the NOPD never could.

Doucet knew Ju Ju well. Including his rap sheet, which wasn't as long as most people might imagine. He lived in the Treme, a block from Louis Armstrong Park, and only three blocks from where he was born. He was forty-eight and looked nothing like a drug boss. More like a high school football coach. Twenty years earlier, he had dabbled in the drug trade, got popped for possession a couple of times, once for intent to distribute. But other than a six-day stretch in county, he had never been inside.

His house was a small, two-story, yellow with white trim affair. Red door all shiny, bright flowers in the windows. Well kept. The kind of place a family would live. Harmless. An asset to the community.

Besides his rap sheet, Doucet knew other things about Ju Ju to be true. He was in the drug business, but he didn't sell drugs. You'd never find drugs around him. Never at his home or on his person. Maybe a little weed for personal use, a small party every now and then. But he didn't deal. He had moved on to greener pastures. To the business of protection. Protecting the real dealers and those involved in other criminal activities like prostitution and cigarette smuggling and untaxed whiskey and so on. No one messed with Ju Ju. Big, strong, and could take a man down with either hand. No questions asked. And he had a crew that held things tight. No one could go off the reservation in Ju Ju's world. If you were under Ju Ju's umbrella, no one touched you. No one ripped you off. No one stepped on your supply lines or hassled your street guys. No one. Ever. But if you stumbled over to his bad side, Ju Ju's response was swift and painful. Even deadly.

Ju Ju was smart. Didn't make mistakes. Do stupid stuff. He never used harder drugs and drank only a little. Always in control. He didn't rip folks off, so long as they paid what Ju Ju considered a fair price for his largess. Not like most criminals who couldn't keep their hands out of the till, or the candy jar, in the case of dealers. Nothing would get you busted faster than snorting or smoking your own product. Made you reckless and stupid. Ju Ju was neither.

And Ju Ju loved women. Always had them around. Three or four on any given day. All kinds. Black, brown, white. He loved them all.

The one that opened the door to Doucet's knock was white, blond dreds, blue eyes, big pink lips. She didn't say a word, only giving him a flat look before she turned and walked away, leaving the door standing open, her tight, slim hips rolling beneath pink shorts, "The Big Easy" in white block print across the back. She flopped on a sofa next to a trim black girl, similarly attired. The TV was on to some movie with a car chase in progress and the aroma of weed filled the air. Ju

Ju's muscle, two guys Doucet knew as Chapo and Stormy, slouched in nearby chairs.

Chapo, a short, stocky Hispanic, looked much like the real El Chapo, the ex-leader of the Sinaloa cartel. Probably where he got the handle. He had two teardrop tattoos beneath one eye, his announcement to the world that he had killed a couple of folks. Doucet never understood why some dirt balls liked to advertise they had killed before. Did give them a certain street cred, of course, at least among those that crawled through the underbelly of society. But to cops it said "no human involved." Handle with care, but also with aggression. Made cops a little more likely to use excessive force. Out of fear, if nothing else. Bottom line: a couple of tattoos just might get your ass shot.

Stormy was a thin, big-eyed black kid, a gold stud in each ear. He was more a criminal wannabe. Not too bright and not as tough as he wanted others to think. Doucet knew he always stood in Chapo's shadow, using Chapo's toughness to pump up his own chest.

Chapo and Stormy jumped up in unison as Doucet entered. Their collective gaze darted to the coffee table where a couple of joint remnants rested in a large yellow ashtray next to a water-filled bong. The girls picked up on their alarm and the black chick reached for the ashtray, probably hoping she could make it disappear.

Doucet waved a hand. "It's okay. I ain't here about that shit."

She froze. Doucet could see the confusion in her eyes.

"What you want?" Stormy asked.

"I need to see Ju Ju."

"He don't talk to no cops."

"Guess we'll see." Doucet moved past him, bumping Stormy's shoulder with his own, toward the kitchen and the back patio where he knew Ju Ju did most of his business. "You boys sit tight. Enjoy your movie."

"Hey, you can't go out there 'less he say so."

Doucet ignored him and stepped outside.

Ju Ju sat at a redwood picnic table, shirtless, phone to his ear. Thick, carrying a few extra pounds, but still muscular and fit, mahogany skin, thinning white fuzz on his head. He looked up as Doucet came through the kitchen door and motioned to the slat seat on the opposite side of the table.

"Let me get back at you," Ju Ju said into the phone. "Got me a cop here with something on his mind." He laid the phone on the table.

Stormy appeared. "Sorry, boss. He wouldn't listen."

Ju Ju waved him away. "I got this."

Stormy hesitated, obviously chastised, and then disappeared back inside.

"What brings you by?" Ju Ju asked. "Must be important for you to come here without notice."

It wasn't Doucet's first visit to Ju Ju's place, but there was a certain protocol that Ju Ju expected. A heads up. And mostly Doucet honored that arrangement.

Doucet shrugged. "I was in the neighborhood and thought I'd drop by."

Ju Ju smiled. "Right. Just sightseeing in the Treme? So, what is it? One of my guys do something stupid?"

Now Doucet smiled. "I'm sure they did. But that ain't why I'm here."

Ju Ju leaned back, the black matte Glock nestled beneath the waistband of his jeans exposed. Doucet ignored it.

"Need some information," Doucet said.

"About?"

"Ketamine."

That got a raised eyebrow. "What about it?"

"Need to know where someone might've gotten it."

"It's out there."

"I'm sure. But who sells it on the street? To strangers? Someone that ain't from around here?"

Ju Ju rubbed his graying stubble. "I see."

"It's a case I'm working."

"Figured. Maybe the murder of Tony's niece?"

"You know about that?" Of course he did. Doucet was merely playing the game.

Ju Ju smiled, gave a lazy shrug. "I do keep my ear to the ground."

"I know you do."

"But this? Everyone who has a pulse knows about it. I'd bet even them actors out there in the swamp are jawing about it." Ju Ju removed the Glock, laying it on the table, and leaned forward, elbows on the redwood. "I heard there was drugs involved. But my people tell me it was only weed."

Doucet shrugged. "This is new info. Probably hasn't filtered down the street yet."

"It will," Ju Ju said. "Always does." He smiled again.

Doucet knew Ju Ju had eyes and ears in the department. Even had a few names he was sure of. Nothing he could prove, but the truth was the truth. Meant Ju Ju would hear about the ketamine in short order. If he didn't already know and was simply playing coy.

"Need to keep this on the DL," Doucet said. More gamesmanship. Always let the informant think he's on the inside. Privy to private information. Pump up their perceived importance. With Ju Ju, importance was a given but it was still part of the dance.

"Cone of silence," Ju Ju said.

"As always, I appreciate that. It looks like Kristi and Kirk Ford were doing ketamine. Had a spiked joint. Not sure yet where it came from—whether it was Ford or Kristi—but it was there."

Ju Ju shook his head. "For the of life me, I don't see why anyone would want to use that shit. Fuck you up big-time. And it can kill you deader than dead."

"We don't run across it very often. At least now that all that rave shit has died out. But somehow it ended up in a suite at the Monteleone."

"That ain't what killed Kristi. So I hear."

"No, it wasn't"

"Yeah, I heard she was strangled. But you thinking maybe that shit twisted Ford's mind? Made him a crazy? Homicidal?"

"That's a possibility."

"Shit. That's a defense attorney's dream. Diminished capacity and all that."

"You can bet on it. But my problem is finding out where it came from." He raised a shoulder. "Any ideas?"

"I know a couple of guys who spread that shit around."

"Any names for me?" Doucet asked.

"Let me look at it. Don't want to get the tribe all sideways."

"Quick as you can."

"I'm on it." Ju Ju smiled. "You know me. Always want to help the police."

"I'll await your call."

CHAPTER TWENTY-ONE

A REMOTE MOVIE set is like a small village. Lot's of folks involved, each trying to make it all work smoothly. Mostly, as Nicole had often pointed out, it was slow and boring. People standing around, chatting in small groups, waiting for something to happen. Then urgency prevails as the "shot" is captured. To do this, all must be perfect—actors, setting, lighting, sound, photography.

And it's expensive. Travel, hotels, meals, audio and video equipment, security, leasing the site, not to mention the salaries of the actors and the others who make the magic happen, can explode a budget in short order.

This is particularly true when you're a long way from Hollywood and the script requires that you build a real village. Not just some facade, but actual buildings and roadways and protective walls. In this case the village was the home of the Yaktous, the peace-loving clan Kirk Ford and the James twins were charged with saving from a group of intergalactic marauders known as the Korvaths, who were hell bent on universal domination. And destruction of the Yaktous, for some vague reason. I mean they lived in huts. How could they possibly threaten the powerful Korvaths?

The Yaktou village was a series of grass-roofed huts surrounded by a low wall of sticks and stones and what looked like dried vines. It sat across a finger of swamp from the main production area, which consisted of several canvas-covered pavilions where the director, crew members, cameramen, script girls, grips, and extras hung out when not actually doing something.

Then there were a series of equipment trailers and a pair of luxurious ones to pamper the stars. In Hollywood speak—the talent. One for Kirk, one for the twins. Such pampering was common in Hollywood, but then again, no stars—no billion-dollar franchise.

I saw all this when we arrived.

Only took us about thirty minutes to get there from the Monteleone. The movie camp and the fake Yaktou homeland sat at the end of a dirt and gravel road that wound along elevated high ground in a world of swampland. Beautiful but a little spooky with Spanish moss–draped cypress trees and herds of cypress knees that looked like little soldiers marching through the dark water.

Finally, we reached an open area and a chain-link fence, with a gate guarded by two men. To the left, in a public parking area, several dozen fans gathered, obviously hoping for a glimpse of Kirk Ford and the twins. They had a big fan club, too. Among them were a couple of protesters, holding anti-Kirk signs. They seemed more subdued than they had been at the courthouse. Probably because they were outnumbered at least ten to one. Or so it seemed. There were, of course, several media types, cameras on shoulders, microphones in hands, one attractive female reporter staring at a camera and talking, the set as backdrop. I suspected I'd see her on the six o'clock news.

Our name was on the list, so we were waved through the gate and directed to another parking area near the collection of pavilions. Pancake parked. We climbed out. I saw Ebersole, standing with a guy next to a large camera mounted on a dolly that clung to a pair of tracks, which led to the swamp's edge.

Ebersole looked up as we approached. "Any trouble finding us?"

I shook my head. "Your directions were perfect."

"Good, good." He waved a hand. "Well, welcome to my world." He laughed. "Such as it is."

"Where's Nicole?"

He pointed across a swampy inlet to where she stood with a couple of crew members. Kirk Ford and the twins were waist deep in the swamp, Kirk shirtless, the twins in bra-like tops, dripping wet. Hollywood. Never miss a chance to show some skin. Even in a swamp. The trio pushed through the water, looking back as if being chased, Kirk turning and "firing" a weapon of some kind. Not really firing, the ray gun, or whatever it was, merely a prop. I was sure that later bright and noisy laser bullets would be added digitally by some geek in the basement of the production studio back in LA. As would whoever or whatever was chasing them. Right now, Kirk fired at a blue sky. No flying creatures or space craft in sight.

They scurried up the swamp's bank toward a cameraman, who knelt on the shore capturing their dramatic escape. I heard Kirk yell, "Run!" They did. Past the camera, before stopping, each bending over, hands on knees, as if catching their breaths. A young woman handed each of them a towel, and they began wiping away the swamp.

"They're just finishing up a scene," Ebersole said.

"Looks like fun."

"They might disagree about now. This was a—how shall I say it?—rather testy shoot. In this scene, they're being pursued by a group of Korvath warriors. The digital guys'll drop them in later."

See? Told you.

I saw two men on a swamp boat, one of those deals with the big fan blades on the back, maybe fifty years into the water. One sat at the helm, the other on the bow, a shotgun on his hip. "Who are those guys?"

"Snake and gator wranglers."

"What the hell?" Pancake said.

Ebersole shrugged. "It's a swamp. Snakes and alligators are expected."

Said the guy who didn't have to go in the water.

"In fact, they killed a big water moccasin about an hour ago."

"Really?" I asked.

"Sure did. Big one. About the size of Pancake's arm."

I hated water moccasins. Cottonmouths. Call them what you will, but they're nasty creatures. I knew there were only four types of poisonous snakes in the US. The shy and rarely seen coral snake was the most toxic, its red, yellow, and black stripes stacked like a roll of Life Savers. Looked a lot like the harmless milk snake. Led to the death of many of those innocent creatures. But, why take a chance? I mean, if it could remotely be a coral snake, the best course would be to avoid it, or kill it. The key to discriminating one from the other laid in the pattern of the bands, whether the red and yellow touch each other (coral snake) or the red band is adjacent to only black ones (milk snake). Every Southerner knows the rhyme: red touches yellow will kill a fellow; red touches black is safe for Jack. Ray had taught me that at a very early age.

Then there were copperheads, beautiful reddish snakes that aren't as deadly as rattlesnakes, which come in many varieties. But the cottonmouth is the scariest. Dark gray/brown/black with big fangs, an ugly, prehistoric face, a constantly searching tongue that whips around here and there, and a powerful venom. They can get you on land or in the water. Every year someone gets bit in some river, lake, pond, or watering hole where a summer swim is a southern staple. As kids, Pancake and I had scared away snakes to take a dip more than a few times.

With cottonmouths in the picture, the luxury trailers seemed a trivial reward.

"That's our last scene this morning," Ebersole said. "We'll break for lunch."

"Lunch?" Pancake said.

Of course.

Nicole, Kirk, and the twins walked around the water's edge and came to where we stood.

"I love my job, I love my job," Tara/Tegan, said. "I really do."

"Keep telling yourself that," her sister said. Then she looked at Ebersole. "Are we finished with the damn swamp scenes yet?"

"Two more."

She shook her head. "I want a raise."

"They aren't until tomorrow," Ebersole said. "You'll feel better then."

"No. I won't."

Nicole gave me a hug. "I thought you guys wouldn't be here until later."

"Pancake needed lunch."

She punched his arm. "You came to the right place. Breakfast was great, and I'm sure lunch will be better."

That got a grunt from Pancake.

"Then we need to sit down with Kirk." I looked at him. "Something's come up."

"What?" he asked.

The twins gave each other a worried look. "Yeah, what?"

"Let's get you cleaned up and have some lunch and then we'll tackle it," Ray said.

Tara/Tegan twisted one shoulder toward me. She had several healing scratches and a new one that was red and angry. "I need to get this cleaned up."

Kirk nodded. "I got a couple of new ones, too. I swear, this swamp is going to kill us."

"Where's the doc?" one of the twins asked.

"You have a doc on set?" I asked.

"Not really," Ebersole said. "He was a medic in the Army. But he can handle a few scratches."

Kirk headed to his trailer and the twins to theirs. Nicole, Ray, and I followed Pancake toward a group of canvas-shaded picnic tables and a buffet counter piled with sandwiches, seafood, sides, and an array of desserts. Pancake could always sniff out food. And attack it. Which is what he did.

Nicole stuck with salad; Ray and I, salad and some grilled shrimp. Pancake had shrimp but no salad. Not that he didn't like greens, he just considered them filler food when something better was around. The fact was I had never seen Pancake filled, so it seemed a moot point. He had seconds, and thirds, of crawfish étouffée, red beans and rice, blackened fish, grilled chicken, and, of course, bread pudding with whiskey sauce. It would have been amazing if it weren't so common. The big guy could pack away the groceries.

Had to admit though, the studio made sure cast and crew were well fed. Even out here on the edge of civilization.

CHAPTER TWENTY-TWO

AFTER KIRK AND the twins had lunch, Pancake having another dose of bread pudding, so they wouldn't have to eat by themselves, or so he said, we settled in Kirk's trailer. It was plush and then some. The living area had two sofas and a couple of leather captain's chairs. Hardwood paneling, drapes, canister lighting. Better than my place. The kitchen seemed to have all the conveniences, also better than my home. The door beyond was closed and I guessed it led to a sleeping area.

Kirk, now wearing tan cotton drawstring pants and a light green tee shirt, sat on one sofa, flanked by the twins. They wore identical black shorts and white tees. Fortunately, Tara's shirt had "Tara" in black block letters across the front, Tegan's "Tegan." Sure helped to have a roster. Ray and Pancake faced them from the other sofa, Nicole and I taking the chairs. I swirled mine back and forth a few times. Nicole gave me a look. One that said quit acting like a kid in a toy store. I never get to have fun.

Ray began. "You and Kristi only had wine and half a joint. Right?"

Kirk nodded.

"How many joints were in the room? Total?"

Kirk looked at him. "I told you. Three. The two I had, and the one Kristi brought."

"That's what the cops found. And they agree that only one was smoked. And only partially."

"That's right. Why?"

"Bear with me," Ray said. "The one you fired up? One of yours?"

"No. The one she brought."

"You sure?"

"Why does it matter?"

"It does." Ray locked that Ray gaze on him. "Again, you sure?"

"Yes. I'm sure."

"How? If you had three, how did you know which one?"

Kirk shook his head, smiling. "I'm terrible at rolling those things. Never ever got the hang of it. Mine are always loose and tend to fall apart. The one she brought was much tighter."

Ray nodded.

"Besides, Kristi pulled it out of her purse and said we should try it. Supposed to be good." Kirk looked at me and then back to Ray. "Why is that important?"

"The one you guys smoked was the only one that had been laced."

"What does that mean? With what?"

"Ketamine."

"What?" Kirk asked.

The twins stiffened in unison, looked at each other, and then to Ray.

"Are you sure?" Tegan asked.

"It's what the crime lab found." Then to Kirk, he said, "And the drug was present in both yours and Kristi's blood."

Kirk stared at him, jaw slack. Confused would be the word. "You're telling me Kristi brought a joint that had drugs in it?"

"Looks that way." Ray gazed at the floor, then cut his eyes up toward Kirk. "You ever use anything like that?"

"No. Never."

Again, in unison, the twins each laid a hand on Kirk's shoulder. "No wonder you don't remember anything," Tara said.

Kirk dropped his head. "God, I wish I did."

"But you don't," Tegan said. "Nothing. Right?"

"It's a total blank."

Tara asked, "Isn't that one of those date rape drugs?"

"Sure is," I said.

"So the cops are going to think Kirk drugged Kristi?" Tegan asked.

"Not if she brought the joint."

Tears welled in her eyes. "But it's only his word. Won't they twist that around?"

I nodded. "I'm sure they will."

Tegan squeezed Kirk's shoulder. "This is not good. Definitely not good."

"Except," I said. "Why would he do that to someone who was a willing partner?" I glanced at Nicole. "So to speak."

A small smile lifted one corner of Nicole's mouth but quickly disappeared. "And why would he also drug himself? Does that make any sense?"

"Sure don't," Pancake offered. "Killers usually like to stay awake and focused."

"You guys sound like you think I'm guilty," Kirk said.

"No," Ray said. "Just looking at it the way Doucet and the cops will."

"And the jury?" Kirk said.

Ray shrugged.

"Well, I didn't. I didn't know there was anything in that joint, and if I had, I damn sure wouldn't have smoked it."

"I suspect that's true," I said.

"And the truth is, I don't think Kristi would have either. She wasn't very experienced. I can't see her jumping up to the big leagues all of a sudden." His shoulders slumped. "I mean, she had never done anything. I introduced her to marijuana. That's on me. And I feel guilty about that. But this?" He shook his head. "I'm totally fucked."

"Maybe not," Ray said.

"I sure don't see it any other way."

"If the drug was only found in Kristi, it'd be a different story," Ray said. "But that isn't the case. Which means that whoever gave her that joint wanted both of you drugged."

"Why would anyone do that?" Tara asked.

"Only thing that makes sense," Pancake said, "is someone wanted both Kirk and Kristi out of it."

"Who?" Kirk asked. "And why?"

Pancake shrugged. "The *who* is the mystery. The *why* might be someone wanted to kill Kristi and frame you for it."

Bewildered. That was the look on Kirk's face. "That doesn't make any sense," he said.

"It does to someone. If you didn't do it, someone did." Pancake raised an eyebrow. "Didn't happen all by itself."

A moment of quiet followed.

"Will the cops try to find out where Kristi bought that joint?" Tegan asked.

"I assume so," I said. "If they believe Kirk."

"In a place like this, I don't see how they'll ever be able to do that," Tara said. "This is New Orleans. I suspect that kind of thing is easy to come by."

"Probably not," Ray said.

"Definitely not," Pancake added. "Ketamine isn't common. Not easy to get and not much of a market for it. I suspect the number of street sources aren't all that great."

Tara looked at her sister, Kirk, and then Pancake. "If they find the seller, maybe they can solve this."

"And get Kirk off the hook," Tegan added.

"That would help," I said.

"So, this is like one of those true-crime TV shows," Tara said. "They'll take a picture of Kristi around to all the dealers they know and see if any of them recognize her? Something like that?"

"I don't think a dealer would talk to the cops," Tegan added.

"You might be surprised," Pancake said. "Cops and dealers often have an uneasy but mutually beneficial relationship. One gets info and the other gets a little less heat."

The twins exchanged a glance and in unison hugged Kirk.

"It'll be all right," Tegan said.

A knock on the door. It swung open. A crew member stuck his head inside. "Mr. Ebersole wants to talk with you," he said to Kirk.

"We're a little busy."

"He said it was important. Some dude named Tony is making noise at the gate. Wants to talk to you."

CHAPTER TWENTY-THREE

NOBODY COULD REMEMBER where Ragman got his name. For sure Robert didn't. Probably from high school, maybe before, definitely before he got tossed from school for selling dope. Ragman never gave a doo-wa-diddy about school anyway. From what Robert could see, he didn't care about much else either. Except selling shit on the street.

Which was fine. That's all they needed him for. But he did appreciate Ragman's closed mouth. He could be trusted. As well as any other street thug, that is. But he had at least kept all their dealings off the radar. And away from Tony's ears.

They found him walking Decatur Street, his usual haunt. He was chatting with a couple of dudes. Looked like college kids. They ducked around the corner, a minute later reappearing and going their separate ways. Deal done.

"Ragman," Robert said.

Ragman turned, sauntering toward them. "What you two up to? Need a little sumpin, sumpin?"

"Yeah. And some information."

Ragman stopped. "I ain't got no information."

"It's cool," Kevin said.

"Usually ain't. But you want to do business, then okay. You want to jaw about things I don't know nothing about, then have a nice day."

"What you got?"

Ragman scanned the street. "Got a bundle in my sock."

"The usual? Fifty?"

"Yeah, man."

Ragman jerked his head. "Follow me."

They did. They headed up Decatur and ducked into the alley Ragman used for most of his sales. Robert never felt comfortable there, the alley being right next to the fire station. Closed up and quiet now, the firemen probably inside napping, watching TV, playing cards, whatever they did while waiting for the next catastrophe. He wondered if the guys inside knew what Ragman did right in their face. Ragman seemed unconcerned. In the alley, they made the exchange.

"That's some good shit," Ragman said. "From my best supplier."

He always said that so Robert simply nodded. "I'd expect nothing less."

"But we do have a question for you," Kevin said.

"Told you. I ain't got no answers."

"Know where someone might get some bump?" Kevin asked. "You know. Special K? Ketamine?"

"What the fuck you think this is? Amateur hour? I know what the fuck you talking about." He leaned against the wall, his shirt riding up above his frayed jeans, exposing a nickel-plated .38 stuffed in the waistband.

"So?" Robert asked. He could see curiosity rise in Ragman's face.

"What's this about?"

"Our sister."

Ragman shook his head. "I heard about that. Her getting killed and all. Some cold shit there, I'm telling you."

"Someone sold her, or that pretty boy who killed her, some bump-soaked joints."

Ragman came off the wall, stretched his neck one way and then the other. "I don't sell that shit, so I don't see why you getting on me about that."

"We ain't," Kevin said. "We just know you know everything about everything and thought you might be able to help us."

"Help you?"

"Yeah. Find out where it might've come from."

Ragman stared at him, a film of suspicion settling over his face. "Who'm I talking to here?"

"What do you mean?"

"Am I talking to you two, or Tony?"

"Does it matter?"

"Fuck yeah. If you ain't here on Tony's business, we got nothing to jaw about."

"It's about our sister."

"You still ain't said nothing. Is this for Tony?"

Robert glanced at Kevin. "Yeah."

"If Tony wants to know this, why don't he call or come by hisself?"

"Yeah, right. I'm sure Uncle Tony will rush right down here and chat with you. On the street. Besides, he's looking into something else. We're helping out."

Ragman nodded slowly as if considering whether Robert was telling the truth. "Like I done said, I don't deal that shit. But, I'll see what I can find out."

"That would help."

"Ain't promising nothing."

CHAPTER TWENTY-FOUR

FROM WHAT I had heard and what little I had seen, I sensed one thing was true—Tony Guidry was a man who expected to get his way. In business, with law enforcement and the courts, and definitely on the street. Whether he leveraged money, muscle, or information, he seemed to be able to put a full Nelson on anyone. I mean, every time his name came up—whether from his nephews, Kristi's ex Owen Vaughn, her friend and coworker Gloria, even Detective Doucet—it was laced with a bit of caution. As if the mere mention of his name was dangerous. He seemed to cast an aura that made everyone's radar go on high alert as if they feared Tony might have them triangulated. I suspected that he did have ample eyes and ears on most of New Orleans. If you spoke of him, you had to assume it just might ping Tony's network.

My heart rate kicked up and my stomach felt queasy as Ray, Pancake, and I walked the hundred yards to where Tony's limo sat, he and his two thugs facing the gate guards. You could almost feel the tension and it seemed to increase as we neared.

Ray insisted that Kirk and the twins hang back, inside, out of sight, while we assessed the terrain—his word. Kirk protested but not too strongly. Like he didn't really want to see Tony. A sentiment I shared.

Nicole was another story. When I suggested she stay behind she would have none of it, saying she wasn't about to hide from some punk. Gotta love her grit. But Ray sided with me. So did Pancake and it was him that calmed her down, saying we needed to focus on Tony and his guys, make sure all this didn't turn into the OK Corral or some such, and that he didn't want to have to worry about her. She countered that he didn't need to worry over her, but he said he would anyway and that that might be distracting. That got a smile and an okay from her.

Anger creased Tony's face as he squared off with the studio guards. Ray stepped between them and offered his hand.

"Mr. Guidry," Ray said. "Ray Longly."

Tony ignored the hand. "That supposed to mean something to me?"

"Probably not. But then, until a couple of days ago, I'd never heard of you either."

I thought Tony might explode. Literally. His face reddened and seemed to swell. "Listen, asshole, I don't give rat shit who you are, but you're in my domain now."

"Oh," Ray said. "You make movies, too?"

That knocked Tony back a step. Like he wasn't sure how to respond. Confusion will do that. I had seen it many times. Ray had a knack for moving any conversation off-center. For making folks lose their focus.

Tony, obviously not able to process the question, simply stared at him.

"So, what can I do for you?" Ray asked.

"You in charge here?"

"Depends on what you mean by in charge. If you mean am I part of this production crew, then no."

"Who are you?" Tony asked.

"Ray Longly. Longly Investigations. Private firm."

"A PI looking into what, if I might ask?"

"The murder of your niece."

"All due respect, but I think I have that covered."

"You? Or the police?"

Tony's eyes narrowed. Then, he shrugged. As if to say—is there a difference?

"Mr. Guidry," Ray said, "I know who you are. I know your position in the community." He emphasized the word "position." Ray jerked his head toward the camp. "And I understand that you'd want to talk with Kirk Ford. But I don't think his attorney would agree to that."

"Like I care what his attorney thinks."

Tony's guys—Johnny Hebert and Reuben Prejean—flanked him, as Pancake and I did Ray. Johnny was tall and wiry with long arms roped with veins; Reuben short and thick with arms that had seen the weight room. I faced Johnny. I smiled. He didn't but rather gave me a flat-faced glare. At least I think he did. Hard to tell through his wraparound sunglasses. He had his hands folded before him, relaxed, confident. Since I couldn't see his eyes, I glanced at his knees and his feet. Wondering which one I could most easily take out if I had to. Neither looked promising. Ray's book made it seem so easy, but here, standing on a gravel road, not so much.

"Tony," Ray said. "May I call you Tony?" Not waiting for a response, he pressed on. "Kirk is on private property. Property leased by the studio. And these gentlemen"—he nodded toward the two guards—"are here to protect that property and Mr. Ford's rights."

"So, Ray. May I call you Ray?" He smiled. More a smirk than a smile. "Maybe you should tell these two clowns who I am, since you seem to know."

"They're from Hollywood. I wouldn't think they'd know you."

Tony hesitated. "But you think you do?"

"We're an investigative firm. We look into things."

That got a derisive chuckle from Tony. "Then you know I'm not the guy you want to fuck with."

"That's my impression. But, let me add there is no way you are going to sit down with Kirk. Not here, not now."

Tony glanced at Reuben. "Get a load of this guy?"

"There's no reason we can't talk this through like gentlemen," Ray said. "If that's what you prefer. If you want things to go another way, then that can be arranged, too."

"You threatening me? You know what happens to guys who do that?"

"I imagine some of them end up floating down to the Gulf."

Tony's face hardened.

"Can I say something?" I asked. Everyone looked at me. "Aren't we on the same side here?"

"How you figure that?" Tony asked.

"We're trying to find out what happened. Why your niece was murdered. And by whom."

"That's an easy one," Tony said. "Ford drugged, raped, and strangled my Kristi."

"Did he?"

"What the hell else could have happened?"

"Maybe it was someone else?" I said.

Tony looked at me like I was an idiot. "Two people in a room. Drugs and alcohol. One ends up dead. It's an old story."

"But do killers usually drug themselves?" I asked.

Tony stared at me but said nothing.

"Look, like it or not, Kristi and Kirk were having an affair. Truth is, he liked her. A lot, it seems."

"Funny way of showing all that love," Tony said.

"The facts are that he was drugged, too. He remembers nothing about what happened."

"Convenient, don't you think?"

"Maybe," I said. "But there are a lot of holes in what might seem obvious. Both Kirk and Kristi had ketamine in their systems. Kirk, regardless of what you might believe about him or Hollywood actors in general, didn't use anything harder than alcohol and a little weed. The laced joint came from Kristi."

"Not a chance."

I hesitated, deciding whether to push this or not, ultimately choosing to press on. Ray and Pancake were there, after all. "You sure? People always think they know their children. Or their nieces and nephews. But in situations like this, things that are unexpected pop up. I'm sure you've seen it before."

Again, Tony had no response. But he did seem to be listening, thinking. Progress is often measured in small steps.

"All I'm saying is that this might be an Agatha Christie locked-room case. There might be someone else involved."

"I doubt it."

"But it's possible?" I asked. "Right?"

Tony sighed. "I guess."

"So, let's work this out. Let us sniff around. You, too. I'm sure you have folks out there who can trace exactly where this drug came from."

Tony gave a half shrug.

"What if someone did give Kristi a loaded joint and neither she nor Kirk knew that was the case? And, according to Kirk, had they known they would have tossed it. Neither would have used it on purpose. So, if someone did give her a drugged joint, you have to ask who? And why?"

"It's always the who and why, isn't it?" Tony said.

"That's my point. If Kirk did this, he should pay and pay big-time. But if he didn't, there's someone out there who took your niece from you. And just might get away with it. Would that sit well with you?"

Another sigh. "I still want to talk with him. I want to look him in the eye. Is that asking too much?"

"No," Ray said. "Let me see what we can work out. But not here. Okay?"

Tony nodded. He looked toward the production area, as if thinking. "Okay. When?"

"I'll let you know."

"Be sure you do."

Tony and his guys climbed in the limo and drove away. I watched the dust-trail behind the limo rise and ride away on the breeze.

Ray turned to me. "Good work. I like the way you brought the temperature down."

Did he really say that?

CHAPTER TWENTY-FIVE

AFTER TONY AND his boys drove away, Pancake decided it was time for more dessert, then maybe watch a little moviemaking. Jake, Ray, and Nicole passed and left for the hotel, after Pancake assured he could hook a ride back with Ebersole. No problem. Only a couple of hours shooting left, some close-ups, so it wouldn't be too long.

Pancake's return visit to the catering table led to a plate piled with bread pudding, bourbon sauce, of course, a slice of pecan pie, and two ramekins of creme brûlée. He sat at a table with Kirk and the twins.

"Wish I could eat like that," Kirk said.

"No one's stopping you," Pancake said.

Kirk patted his belly. "Don't think it would go well on camera."

"Camera adds ten pounds," Tegan, according to her tee shirt, said. "I hate them." She munched on a bowl of strawberries, licking the juice off her fingers.

Pancake spooned in some creme brûlée. "Glad I don't have to worry about what I eat. Much as I love food and being a growing boy and all."

"You ever done any acting?" Kirk asked.

"Every day. PI work requires a bit of role playing."

"You mean like undercover work?" Tara asked.

"Sure. But mostly day-to-day stuff. Getting folks to say things they don't really want to talk about."

Kirk nodded. "You'd make a good villain. In a James Bond sort of way."

"I am a villain," Pancake said. He smiled. "It's what I do best."

"We might want to use you in the next episode."

"Do I get to eat like this every day?"

Kirk laughed. "They do feed us well."

"Then I'm all over it."

"Have you met Nicole's uncle yet? Charles Balfour?"

"Nope." Pancake shook his head and dug into the bread pudding. Damn, it was good.

"You should. I'll have a chat with him about you."

Pancake pointed his spoon at him. "Do I get to punch a few folks? Break some stuff?"

"Absolutely."

"Sounds like an Oscar's in my future."

The twins laughed.

A girl walked up. Small, maybe five-two, no bigger than a minute. Lean and tight with dark red hair, pinned to one side with a clip, falling in a wavy cascade over her shoulder. She spoke to Kirk and the twins. "I think Mr. Ebersole wants to do the closeups in about forty-five. You guys ready to get your war paint on?"

"This is Sophie," Kirk said. "She's does our makeup. Makes us look good."

Sophie shrugged. "Not always easy."

Kirk rolled his eyes. "And this is Pancake."

"Nice to meet you," Sophie said, extending a hand toward him.

Pancake shook it, her hand disappearing inside his. Soft and warm. And electric. "Pleasure's mine."

"Oh, a gentleman."

"That's me."

"And a redhead. We reds have to stick together."

"Ain't that the truth."

Tegan stood. "We need to go wash our faces then we'll see you in the trailer." She tapped Kirk on the shoulder. "You coming?"

"See you guys in a few," Sophie said. "I'm going get to know the big guy for a minute."

Kirk gave her a wink, stood, and followed the twins.

"So, who are you?" Sophie asked.

"I work with Ray and Jake and Nicole."

"A PI? How mysterious."

"It can be. Mostly it's tedious."

"I doubt that."

Pancake shrugged. "So you do the makeup?"

"Sure do. Have on every *Space Quest* episode. You mind?" She nodded toward the mountain of bread pudding before him.

"Knock yourself out."

She ran her finger through the bourbon sauce and sucked it off her finger. "I love this stuff. Fact is, I haven't found much about New Orleans I don't like."

"Never been here before?" Pancake asked.

She shook her head, her red hair swaying. "Seems I never get to leave Hollywood. Unless it's a remote shoot. And most of those aren't to places like New Orleans."

"Well, don't be a stranger. We need all the pretty women we can get down here."

"I'd say there are plenty of those around. I've seen quite a few in the past couple of weeks."

"True. But pretty redheads are special."

She laughed. "Aren't you the charmer?"

He smiled.

She reached up and mussed his hair. "You could use a trim."

"Didn't have time before we left. To come over here."

"From where?"

"Alabama. Gulf Shores."

"Never been there either. What's it like?"

"Beachy."

She laughed. "My favorite kind of place. Good food there, too?"

"Jake's place has great ribs. Then there's a ton of seafood joints."

"What do you think? Maybe a trim after I get them all painted?"

"You do that?"

"I do everything." She gave him a look and a smile.

Pancake felt a current run through him. Parts of him anyway. "Sounds like a plan."

"Cool."

After slamming down the pecan pie, Pancake followed Sophie into a trailer, where Tegan sat in a makeup chair facing a large mirror. He took an empty stool and watched as she worked. After applying all the makeup, giving Tegan that camera-perfect look, she began applying splotches of brown powder, smudging it on one cheek and her chin.

"Why're you doing that?" Pancake asked.

She turned to him. "The closeups will be cut into the scene they just shot. Them being chased out of the swamp. Swamp means mud."

"Makes sense."

Thirty minutes later, Kirk and the twins left. Sophie patted the chair. Pancake climbed in. It creaked under his weight. She pulled a comb through his hair, working out a few tangles, and then began snipping away.

After a couple of minutes, she asked, "How do you see this? This thing with Kirk and that girl?"

"Doesn't look good for him. Hard to explain away a dead girl in your bed."

"I find it hard to believe. I've known him for years. Sure, he loves women. He seems to find one or two in every port as they say. But this? I don't see it."

"Not sure I do either," Pancake said.

"Really? Why?"

"Can't say. But there are some things that don't add up."

She stepped around to face him, scissors in one hand, comb in the other. "Like what?"

"I can't talk about an investigation."

She nodded and went back to work. "I bet you're a good PI."

"I am."

"Tell me about you," she said. "Other than snoop around on people, what do you do?"

"Eat and drink. Harass Jake when I can." He smiled. "'Course, he's an easy target."

"And I bet chase women."

"I'm too shy for that."

She laughed. "Yeah, I believe that." Another couple of snips. "Girlfriend?"

"Nope. You?"

"No girlfriend. No boyfriend."

"That's what I meant."

"I know. Just messing with you." She walked around him, examining her work. "I think that'll do it. Now you look positively handsome."

"That I do." He turned his head side to side, inspecting the results in the mirror. "You do good work."

She smiled. "I do a lot of things well."

"That I do not doubt."

"Plans tonight?"

"Sure do." He stood and looked down at her. "Having drinks with you."

"Sounds like a deal." She poked his stomach with a finger. "I'm buying."

"How do you figure that?"

"I don't want you to feel guilty about getting me drunk."

He laughed. "What about you?"

"I'm not big on guilt."

CHAPTER TWENTY-SIX

TONY RARELY VISITED Ju Ju's place. Most of their communication went through intermediaries. On Tony's side, Johnny and Reuben. Guys he trusted. Too many eyes and ears out there and Tony wanted little direct connection with Ju Ju. Their mutual business dealings weren't for public, or cop, consumption. The rare occasions face time was needed, it took place in the back room of the Belly Up. Late at night. Not after closing. That would be way too suspicious. But late, while the night crowd was in full swing. When Ju Ju was just another customer, drinking, listening to the music, checking out the girls. When a visit to the head, or the door just beyond that led to Tony's office, would go unnoticed.

Plausible deniability was always a good thing.

But now he felt an urgency. Didn't want to wait until midnight to scratch the itch he felt worming around inside. It was what Jake Longly had said. He hated to admit it, preferring this case have a simple and complete courtroom resolution, but the truth was he had no answer that sat well in his gut. Why would Ford drug himself? He definitely would not if he had something truly evil on his mind. Not if his plan was to assault, or kill, Kristi.

And that pained him. The fact that Kristi had of her own free will taken up with this guy. That she had willingly been with him. That wasn't the image he wanted of her. She was a good girl. Very good. Never did wrong. Wasn't starstruck or the kind to be overly impressed with anyone. She got that from her mother, Tony's late sister-in-law. Kristi's infatuation with Ford seemed out of character.

The other thing that caused his chest to hurt was the drugs. His sources told him that she and Ford had been using marijuana regularly. That Ford had admitted he had made the introduction but that Kristi had welcomed it. Had fallen right into smoking dope and having sex with him on a nightly basis.

Maybe it was Ford's pretty face, his A-list star quality, his money, his suite at the Monteleone, his world, that had turned her head. Made her stupid. Or maybe, just maybe, he didn't know Kristi as well as he thought.

But what really niggled at him was that if they, both of them, had taken the drug on purpose, it offered Ford a diminished-capacity defense. And that could get him off. Tony couldn't abide that. No way her killer would walk on this. Couldn't happen. But if the courts didn't take him down, he would have to. And that was an exposure he wanted to avoid. The dots would be difficult, if not impossible, to disconnect.

Shit.

And the person who sold the bump to either Ford, or God forbid, Kristi, would suffer. Grievously. His death would be epic.

So here he sat. At Ju Ju's backyard picnic table, his de facto office, and looked across at Ju Ju and Ragman. He liked Ju Ju, but Ragman was a punk. He did good business but he was a pain. A jive-ass Tony couldn't warm to. Or trust.

"Since I guessed what the topic would be, I took the liberty of asking my man Ragman to sit in," Ju Ju said. "Figured he could offer some intel."

Tony shrugged, waving a hand. Giving his blessing.

"Thanks for letting me sit down with you, Mr. Guidry," Ragman said.

Tony ignored him, fell silent.

"That cop was here a little while ago," Ju Ju said. "Detective Doucet."

"I figured he would get around here sooner or later," Tony said. "What'd he have to say?"

"He don't know shit. But he ain't stupid. He knows tracking the source of the bump might be the key to all this."

"And he wants your help finding the source?"

Ju Ju shrugged. "I suspect that's why you're here."

"It is. What are you going to give him?"

"As little as possible. But enough to keep my relationship with him intact. That's good for both of us."

Tony nodded.

"I'll give him a couple of leads that don't go nowhere. Be the concerned citizen."

"Tell me," Tony began. "How did bump end up in the room where my niece was murdered?"

"I don't know," Ju Ju said. "But I got guys, including Ragman, on it."

Tony hated uncertainty. He looked at Ragman. "Please tell me you don't sell this shit."

Ragman had that deer-in-the-headlights look. He glanced at Ju Ju and then back to Tony.

Tony leaned his elbows on the edge of the table, giving Ragman the look. The one that said be careful. "The only thing you could do wrong here is lie to me."

"I swear, I didn't. I wouldn't. Know what I'm saying? I know her. She come around, I'm gonna walk the other way. Truth is, she never come around. Not once. Ever."

Tony held his gaze, searching for some sign he was lying. He saw only fear. Good. Always a good motivator.

"But you do sell bump?"

Ragman hesitated, obviously weighing his options. Then he said, "A little. Not often. Ain't much of a market for it."

"But if someone wanted it, you could hook them up?"

"Customer service is important on the street, Mr Guidry. You know? But I swear, I didn't and I never would pass anything, anything at all, to your niece."

"What about Kirk Ford? He ever come around?"

"Know him, too. I mean I know of him. I'd've recognized him right off. Anyone would. Never saw him neither."

"What about your crew? Maybe one of your crew sold this shit to one of them?"

"I been all over them," Ragman said. "Got a big negative everywhere."

"I put the word out," Ju Ju said. "Not just to Ragman but to all my guys. Here, Metairie, Algiers, everywhere. If someone sold to her, I'll know."

"When you do, that's for my ears only. Right?"

"If you mean am I going to pass that along to Doucet, you hurt my feelings by asking." Ju Ju smiled.

"And I appreciate that," Tony said. He started to stand, but Ragman spoke.

"Mr. Guidry, did you send your nephews by to talk with me?"

Tony felt his blood pressure spike. He settled back onto the bench seat. "Why do you ask?"

"They came by my spot this morning. Asking about all this." He waved a hand. "Said you asked them to."

"What did you tell them?"

"Nothing. Don't know nothing to tell."

Tony spread his hands on the tabletop. "You did good. Don't tell them shit." He looked at Ragman. "Clear?"

"Yes, sir."

"They don't work for me. Not in this world anyway. If they come by again, you let me know."

"Absolutely."

CHAPTER TWENTY-SEVEN

I WAS LYING in bed, on my back, tossing a baseball up and catching it. Seeing how close I could get to the ceiling without hitting it. Nicole was in the shower. The news murmured from the TV, but I wasn't paying attention. The shower fell silent, and in a couple of minutes, Nicole came out, towel draped over her shoulder. She stood there in all her glory and looked at me.

"What are you doing?"

"Playing ball."

She stepped into her thong. This one white. Oh, yeah.

"You brought a baseball with you?"

"Sure. Why not?"

"Don't tell me it's one of the ones Detective Morgan grabbed from Barkov's boat."

"It is." I examined it. "The Willie Mays one."

She tugged on her jeans, doing a series of little jumps to get them settled. "Is that the one that took down Joe Zuma?"

"Yes, it is."

"Good. He was very creepy."

She slipped on a gray silk blouse and began buttoning it. "Wish I had been there to see it. But if memory serves, I was bobbing in the water trying not to swallow half the Gulf."

"True. And then there were all those gunshots."

"I'm glad Ray's guys could shoot better than Barkov's could."

She sat on the edge of the bed, tying her sneakers. Pink and black. Girly. Nicole might be feminine, very much so, but girly is not the word that comes to mind.

"I like your sneakers," I said.

"No, you don't. You probably think they're too girly."

How the hell does she do that? Know what I'm thinking?

"Maybe. But they're cool anyway."

She stood. "I'm out of here."

"Where are you going?"

"Do you ever listen to me?"

Uh oh. I must have missed something.

"I told you. I have a nail appointment."

"Where?"

"It's called Nail Artiste. Over off Chartres near Dumaine." She cocked her head. "Want to go?"

"I think not."

"Okay. You stay here and play ball. Just don't break anything with that bat Pancake gave you."

"I'd rather play with you."

She laughed. "Later."

"I'll read my self-defense book then."

"Sounds like a good idea. Unless you want to carry that baseball everywhere."

Now I laughed. "Those were a couple of pretty good fastballs."

"Yes, they were. And they saved our asses." She leaned over, gave me a kiss, and then she was gone.

* * *

Nicole stepped off the elevator into the Monteleone's lobby. As she passed the entry to the Carousel Bar, she saw the twins huddled at one of the tables just inside. She veered that way. They looked up.

"How're you guys doing?" Nicole asked.

"Okay, I guess," one of them said. They weren't dressed alike today—both in jeans, but one in a white shirt and the other a red checked one.

"Tegan, right?"

The white-shirted one nodded.

"You guys need to wear name tags."

Tara nodded toward an empty chair. "Join us."

Nicole glanced at her watch. "I have a nail appointment but I have a few minutes." She sat.

"What are we going to do?" Tara asked. "About Kirk?"

"I'm not sure. I do know the guys are working on some things."

"Pancake isn't," Tegan said.

"He's working on Sophie," Tara added.

"Sophie?" Nicole asked.

Tara laughed. "She's our makeup guru. Makes us look good. She and Pancake really hit it off."

"Yeah," Tegan said. "I think they're at some bar down the street."

Tara nodded. "Sophie will take good care of him." She laughed.

That's when Nicole saw it. The difference. The twins were identical, scarily so, but Nicole had always felt that there was something about them that was different. That they looked alike, yet didn't. She could never put a finger on what it was. But at that moment, the light slanting through the door from the lobby caught Tara's face just right and there it was. The deep blue of her eyes matched her sister's, but a single brown fleck seemed to jump out. Left eye, about eleven o'clock. She looked at Tegan. Nope, not a blemish in the blue.

She smiled to herself. This was going to drive Jake crazy. She could now tell them apart and he couldn't. Sharing this bit of info with him never crossed her mind. Not even close. This would be fun.

"Pancake can take care of himself," Nicole said.

"We'll see," Tegan said. "Sophie has an aggressive streak."

They both laughed.

"What are Jake and Ray looking into?" Tegan asked.

"The drugs. Ketamine is pretty rare. Ray thinks that if we can find out where Kristi got a dusted joint, that might lead to someone other than Kirk."

The twins exchanged a glance and then Tara said, "I hope so. This is tearing Kirk up. I think part of him isn't sure he didn't do it."

"Really? He said that?"

Tegan shook her head. "Not in those words. But we know him. Know what he's like. We can tell when he's stressed."

"When I look at him I can see it," Tara said. "He's scared."

"And guilty," Tegan said. "That he can't remember anything. I know he's racking his brain for a memory. For anything. But he's come up with nothing. And it's killing him."

Nicole nodded. "For sure there isn't any evidence someone broke in and she did end up dead in his bed, so I guess the not knowing what went down in that room could make him wonder what really happened."

Tara wiped a tear away. "Do you really think they'll be able to find out who sold that stuff to Kristi? I mean, with her not able to tell where she got it?"

Nicole shrugged. "I don't know. But I do know Ray. Pancake, too. They have ways of getting information. They're pretty relentless when they get focused."

"I hope so," Tegan said. She clutched her sister's hand, squeezing it. "Is there anything we can do to help?"

"I'm sure if there is, Ray will ask." She stood. "I've got to run but I'll see you guys later."

CHAPTER TWENTY-EIGHT

"WHAT THE FUCK do you two think you're doing? Talking to Ragman? On the street?"

Robert looked at his uncle. He and Kevin sat across from him in his office at the Belly Up. Tony had called and told them to get their asses back there. Like now. Tony's face was red and his neck veins looked like two ropes. His knuckles white as he gripped the edge of his desk.

"We—"

Tony waved a hand. "You what? Thought you'd stick your nose into my business?"

"We were trying to help," Kevin said.

"Don't you think if I needed your help, which for the life of me I can't imagine how that thought would ever enter my head, that I'd ask?"

"But we thought—" Robert began.

"That's your problem. You try to think." He shook his head. "I don't ever want you two to think. I don't want you to eat, breathe, or take a shit unless I say so. Am I clear?"

"She was our sister," Robert said.

"And I don't know that? Am I not working on it?" He twisted his neck. "You never see the big picture. You see a slice of your little world and think that's all that matters."

"What did we do wrong?" Kevin asked. "Didn't you say you wanted to know where those drugs came from?"

"I have guys on that. Guys who know how to find out without blasting a fucking hey-look-at-me horn."

"I don't understand," Robert said. "We talked with Ragman on the DL."

"The DL? Is this a fucking movie?" He stood and walked to the window, the one that looked out over the rear parking lot.

Kevin started to say something, but Robert grabbed his arm, looked at him, and shook his head. Better to stay DL about now.

Tony turned. "You want to be the heroes? Sniff out the drug trail? Make a name for yourselves? Something you can brag about? Run your fucking mouths about?" He returned to the desk, leaning on it, staring at them. Giving them that Tony look. "You don't see a problem with what you did?"

Robert looked at Kevin, and then back to Tony. "We simply asked Ragman if he knew where the bump came from."

"On the street. Broad daylight."

"So?"

"You don't think the cops have eyes and ears over there? They know deals go down over on Decatur. They know who the hell Ragman is. They see you two, my nephews, chatting up a known dealer. On his turf. You don't see a problem there?"

"Not really."

"Jesus." Tony dropped into his chair. "I have layers, multiple layers, in place to keep people like Ragman out of my sphere. At least on the surface."

"We buy shit from—" Robert froze.

"You buy drugs from him?"

Robert looked at him but said nothing.

"Answer me. You buy shit from Ragman? On the street?"

"Not often."

Tony massaged his temples. "My nephews buy drugs from a known dealer on a public street. In the middle of the day. What part of that don't you get?"

"Lots of people do."

"Lots of people aren't my relatives. Lots of people, if they get popped, couldn't be twisted in the wind and create blowback on me."

"You mean like rat on you?" Kevin asked. "We would never do that."

"Unless you were looking at jail time. Time that could run a decade or more."

"But we would never—"

"Know how many guys've said that? Guys much tougher than you two?" Tony took a deep breath and let it out slowly. "The fact that you better not be doing drugs at all, the fact that you told me you weren't, aside, even a hint that someone close to me is buying on the street can be a problem. That could be the loose thread that unravels things and dumps shit in my lap."

"We only wanted to help," Robert said.

"You can do that by doing your job here. By keeping a low profile on the street. By not using your feeble brains to try to help me. Can I make that any clearer?"

"No, sir," Kevin said. "We're sorry."

Tony pulled up his shirtsleeve and examined his watch. "I got an appointment." He looked at Robert, then Kevin. "You two do your fucking jobs. And that doesn't include talking with Ragman. Or anyone else."

CHAPTER TWENTY-NINE

NICOLE KNEW SHE was beautiful. How could she not? She'd been told that all her life. As far back as she could remember, anyway. Her parents, friends, even complete strangers. But she had learned it could also be a curse. She knew that sounded like a cliché. An almost arrogant thought. But those who weren't burdened—God, she hated that word—with beauty didn't know that it was—speaking of clichés—a double-edged sword. It had caused her more than a few problems. Everything from being labeled stereotypically "unbright"—some dude actually said that to her once—through jealous, bitchy classmates and colleagues, right on to stalkers. Those were the worst. She had had three in her life. More than enough.

But she also knew her looks could be a tool. Help open doors. Defuse some dicey situations and even put her in charge.

Like now.

After finishing her nail painting, Nicole headed back toward the Monteleone. She called Jake, asking him if he wanted to meet in the bar for a drink. He did.

"On my way," she said. "I'll meet you in the Carousel Bar."

"Sounds like a plan. I need to jump in the shower and give Ray a call. I'll drag him down, too."

"Did you fall asleep or something?"

"Been reading my self-defense book."

"Learn anything new?"

"Lots of stuff. Never knew there were so many ways to do harm."

"You're getting dangerous."

"That I am."

She laughed. "Lord, help me."

"Oh, Pancake called. Said he and some girl named Sophie were at Pat O'Brien's."

"That's Sophie the makeup artist," Nicole said. "The twins told me they were an item now."

"Item?"

"Well, spending quality time together."

"Speaking of dangerous. Pancake on the prowl."

"From what I heard, Sophie can handle herself," Nicole said.

"I hope so. I'll give him a call and tell him where we'll be."

"It'll be a party. Now get your ass in the shower and I'll see you in a few."

As she turned the corner onto Royal, she ran into, almost literally, Robert and Kevin Guidry.

"Well, well, our paths seem to keep crossing," Robert said.

Nicole gave a start but recovered. "So it seems."

"And here you are without your bodyguards," Kevin said.

Her brain went into overdrive weighing the situation. And her options. Would she need Jake, or Pancake, or Ray? Here on a busy street in broad daylight? Were these guys as dangerous as they acted? Part of her said run, but there was something about these guys that didn't seem all that dangerous. As if they were trying too hard to convince everyone that they were. Maybe even themselves. She wasn't sure where this impression came from. Maybe it was their almost sad faces. Expressions that even their scowling couldn't hide. Maybe it was how their uncle Tony had cowed them over at the courthouse. They had looked like a pair of abused puppies. Fearful of their master.

Were they? Had Tony railed on them all their lives? Since he took over as their surrogate father? No doubt, Tony Guidry seemed the type.

If so, could she use that to garner information on Kristi? Or the drugs that ended up in Kirk's and Kristi's bloodstream? On Tony and his intentions?

She didn't run, or scream. Instead she smiled and said, "Don't think I'll need them."

"How's that?" Robert asked.

"Because I have a better idea." That seemed to confuse them. "Why don't I buy you guys a drink?"

"A drink?" A look of shock came over Robert's face. Definitely not what he expected.

"Of course." She laid a hand on Robert's arm. "Can't a girl buy two handsome guys a drink?"

That really confused them.

"Come on," she said. "It'll be fun."

Robert looked at Kevin and then back to her. "Okay. Where?"

"The Monteleone," she said. "I'm headed that way."

She stepped between them and took their arms and off they went. Beauty had its advantages.

The slowly spinning Carousel Bar was packed and drinkers stood three-deep around it. Happy hour in the Big Easy. They pushed through the crowd and found a sofa and chair arrangement around a coffee table. Nicole sat in a chair, offering the sofa to the brothers. A waitress must have followed them as she appeared immediately. Nicole ordered wine, the brothers a pair of Coronas. Robert reached for his wallet, but Nicole waved him away.

"I invited you. These are on me," she said. Robert hesitated. "Besides, the studio is covering all my expenses."

"That because they hired you to get that actor dude off?"

She shrugged. "That's not how we do things."

Kevin smirked. "Yeah, right."

"Let's just say we don't have any agenda here. Or any real loyalty."

"Don't seem that way to me," Kevin said. "Ain't you and he friends?"

"Not really. I did date him once."

Robert shook his head. "Just great."

"Only a couple of times. He's not my type."

"I thought he was everyone's type," Robert said. "Being a big star."

She laughed. "He'd probably agree with you." She shrugged. "But he's not my type. I like guys who are a bit more rugged. More muscular." She smiled at him. She could almost feel his face getting warm. Bingo.

The waitress returned and placed the drinks on the table. "Anything else?"

"Not right now," Nicole said. She took a sip as the brothers grabbed their beer bottles. "Why don't we be friends?" she asked.

"Don't see how," Kevin said.

"We can try." She fingered the collar of her shirt. Slipping her fingers just beneath the lapel. A practiced move all women know. "Tell me about you guys. Are you from here? New Orleans?"

"All our lives," Robert said.

"Did you play football? In high school?"

"We did."

"That explains all the muscles."

Now a little color appeared in Robert's face.

"We were pretty good," Kevin said.

"I bet you were. Linemen? Linebackers?"

"Line. Defensive." Robert took a slug of beer. "We like hitting folks."

"What about Kristi? What was she like?"

Robert settled back into the cushions. Beginning to relax. "Pretty. Nice. Smart. A great sister."

Nicole nodded. "You were close?"

He tipped his beer bottle toward her. "Sure were."

"I know you lost your parents. Bet that was hard."

Kevin leaned forward, elbows on his knees, and worked the edge of the label of his Corona with a thumbnail. "It was hard. Unexpected."

"And your uncle took you in?"

"Don't know what we'd've done otherwise," Robert said. "Uncle Tony really stepped up."

"And now you guys work for him? Doing what?"

"This and that. Mainly making sure the Belly Up runs smoothly."

"Belly Up?"

"A club he owns."

"Sounds like a lot of responsibility. He must trust you." She ran a finger around the rim of her glass. Another move.

Kevin smirked again. "Sometimes." A slug of beer. "Uncle Tony can be a demanding boss."

"Most bosses are. Ray's the same way. Perfectionist at heart."

"Ray?" Robert asked. "He the older guy?"

She nodded. "He owns the firm. We all work for him."

"He looked like he could be tough," Robert said.

"He is. But also okay. Most times. What about you? Do you get along with your uncle?"

Robert shrugged.

"Not so much?" she asked.

"We have our moments."

Nicole laughed. She made it as light and musical as possible. "I hear you. Ray has his moments, too." She caught Robert's gaze and held it. He broke away before she did, casting a glance at Kevin.

"Truth is, Uncle Tony ain't too happy with us right now."

"Oh?"

"We did some stuff he wasn't thrilled about."

She waited but he didn't say more. But she sensed he wanted to. Wanted to ventilate his anger with his uncle.

"Let me guess," she said. "You took some initiative? Did something you thought would help? But he didn't see it that way?"

Both looked at her like she was clairvoyant. She wished Jake were here to see it. She smiled inside, but kept her face flat, stoic. But she knew she had grabbed a slice of trust here.

"Exactly," Kevin said. For the first time beginning to warm to her.

"Guys in charge are always that way," she said. "The alpha types. The macho ones. They always want to think everything starts and ends with them. And if someone comes up with a better idea, they feel threatened. Seen it before."

"You're pretty smart," Robert said.

"You mean for a blond?"

That got a smile from him. "For anyone."

"Thanks." Again, she held his gaze. "Women have to deal with that all the time. Guys who think they're smarter. Or tougher, Or whatever."

"I guess that's true," Robert said.

"It is. And it can be frustrating. Angering." She took a sip of wine and placed the glass on the coffee table. "What about Kristi? Did she and Tony get along?"

"Oh, yeah," he said. "She was his pride and joy. Even when Mom and Dad were around. He always doted on her."

Nicole nodded. "That's what little girls do. They always wrap daddies and uncles around their fingers. It's the norm."

"I bet you did," Kevin said.

She laughed again. "I am my daddy's girl." She sipped her wine. "Any sibling rivalry? Between you guys and Kristi?"

"Not really," Robert said.

"She did get her way a lot," Kevin said. "But then she was never in trouble like we were. And she made good grades." He tapped Robert's leg. "We weren't the best students."

Nicole nodded, letting the silence run for a couple of beats and then said, "I know you guys think we're the enemy here. That we're trying to get Kirk off." Robert looked at her but said nothing. "The fact is we want to find the truth. I'm sure you do, too?"

"We already know that. He killed her."

"Sure looks that way."

Robert couldn't hide his surprise. "Really? You believe that?"

"Let's say it doesn't look good. There were only two of them in that room."

"And one of them ended up dead."

"That's a fact," Nicole said. "But there are a couple of questions."

Robert's eyes narrowed. "Like what?"

"Let me ask you something. If you were going to drug a girl and take advantage of her—and I'm not saying you would—but if that was your plan, would you also drug yourself?"

"What do you mean?"

"Ketamine was found in both Kristi and Kirk. Enough to knock them both out, it seems."

"Or make him crazy," Kevin said. "Make him kill her."

"That's possible. But what if neither of them knew the drug was in that joint they smoked?"

They didn't have an answer for that.

She went on. "I mean, what if someone else did that? Then broke into their room. Someone who wanted to harm Kristi or frame Kirk?"

Still no answer.

"Look, I'm from Hollywood. Grew up in that world. I even write screenplays. I see stories and plots everywhere. I'm not saying that's what happened. But I do believe it's possible."

"I don't believe that's what happened," Robert said. "I believe he did it."

"You're probably right. But if not him, do you know of anyone who would want to hurt Kristi?"

"Everybody loved her."

"From what I've learned, I believe that. What about Owen? Would he do something like this?"

Kevin shook his head. "I don't see how. Owen's a good guy. And he loved her."

"Love makes folks do some awful things."

"Not Owen," Robert said.

"I agree," Nicole said. "We talked to him. He seemed like a broken man. Not angry or anything like that."

"He isn't," Kevin said. "If he was going to do anything to anyone, it'd be himself. For cheating on her. For breaking her heart."

"That's what I saw," Nicole said.

CHAPTER THIRTY

MAISON MARALEE, A high-class boutique hotel, sat deep in the Quarter on a quiet, tree-shaded corner lot. Three stories, thirty mini-suites, a small dining room where breakfast was served, and a price tag that ran several hundred bills a night. Most people didn't know it existed, its sole advertising word of mouth. Tony Guidry owned 70 percent. Through one of his shell corporations, of course. Gave him special privileges. Like decisions over who got a room and who didn't, like who paid and who were Tony's guests. But the perk he enjoyed the most was a private room, for his use only. Top floor, corner, back of the building, facing a willow- and flower-embraced pond. With its own gated stairs. Private and then some. Perfect for Tony's needs.

He lay in the king-sized bed, staring at the ceiling, the sheet pulled to his waist, sex sweat frosting his chest. He was content. Good sex always relieved the pressure. For a while anyway. But he wasn't happy. His mind raced over the day's events. His inability to see Kirk Ford, his visit to Ju Ju, something he always hated—too risky—and his moronic nephews. Those two could fuck up a one-car parade. He wondered what dumb-ass thing they'd do next. He had no doubts they would, and trying to anticipate exactly what seemed to be a full-time job. That's why he had Reuben shadowing them.

Waste of manpower. He needed Reuben on the street, tracking down the source of the bump. Not babysitting those two. He felt the beginning of a headache in his left temple.

He heard the toilet flush and then the bathroom door swung open. Melissa Mooring stepped out. She had slipped her panties back on but was otherwise nude. Lord, he loved her body. Tight and firm. Sex with her was always an event. They had been meeting here three times a week for the past six months. Ever since they hooked up at that fund-raiser for the mayor. What a night that had been. Her initial reservations about getting involved with him—she was an Assistant DA, after all—evaporated quickly once they shed their clothing and climbed into this very bed.

"The best-looking Assistant DA in the parish," he said.

"You always say that."

"Because it's true."

She wormed beneath the sheet and nestled against his chest. "Can you stay awhile?" she asked.

"Sure can. I have a dinner deal at nine, but until then, I'm all yours."

"I like the sound of that."

Her fingers played across his chest, moved lower. Then she was on top. A true cowgirl. Twenty minutes later, they again lay nestled against each other catching their collective breath.

"You really don't see this as a problem?" he asked.

"A minor one. But nothing I can't overcome."

"You are the best. But I still have a bad feeling. It gives the jury an out. Think the drugs made him all crazy."

She propped up on one elbow and looked at him. "Maybe. The defense will use a diminished-capacity defense. Say he was whacked out of his mind. So much so that he doesn't even remember doing it."

"You trying to make me feel better about all this?"

She laughed and kissed his cheek.

"If so, it ain't working," he said.

"It's the way it is." She brushed his hair back from his forehead. "And I suspect they'll say it was accidental. They were playing some sex game. Asphyxia stuff. And it all went sideways."

"Jesus."

"I know. It'll be tough to sit through, but you know they'll use it."

"It might work, too," Tony said.

"Possible. But it's my job to make sure it doesn't."

"How?"

"Don't know the dance moves until I see the dance."

"True."

"The best thing Mr. Ford has going for him is his celebrity. Folks don't like convicting superstars for anything. Football players, actors, politicos, anyone with big-time name recognition."

"At the risk of being redundant, you trying to make me feel better?"

"Let me finish. All that celebrity crap aside, anytime anyone, regardless of social position and celebrity, wakes up with a dead girl in their bed, in a locked room, things don't usually go well. Add to that that he drugged Kristi and things can get ugly in the jury's mind pretty quickly."

"But if he took it, too, and if he says neither of them knew the joint was stepped on, he has an out."

"Except he still killed her."

"But is that premeditated?"

"That's a different story. I'll grant you that. He might end up with murder two, even aggravated man, but he will go down."

"I wish I had your confidence."

"Look, he seduced a local girl. Your niece. The celebrity card swings both ways." Tony shrugged. She continued. "It's true. Folks know you. You're a successful business owner."

"Not with the best rep though."

She shook her head. "I didn't say you were a saint." She poked his ribs. "What I said is people know you. Many of them knew Kristi. She was the homecoming queen, for Christ's sake. That all counts."

"I guess."

"Bank on it. Add to that, Ford is all Hollywood. Privileged. There's celebrity and then there's celebrity. Folks around here think anyone from La La Land is a spoiled brat. Ford is that. And that's how I'll present him. Besides, he's done this before."

"What? Killed someone?"

"No. But he has a reputation for despoiling local girls wherever he goes."

Tony laughed. "Despoiling? I like that word. Be sure to use it."

"We've uncovered a couple of girls that he screwed, dumped, and humiliated. We can bring them in."

"Unless Judge Booth says you can't."

"He might. Prior bad acts aren't always allowed. But I think I can get it in to show a pattern of behavior. That Kristi was simply another throwaway to him."

"Were drugs involved in any of those?"

"I know wine and marijuana was in one. I've talked to the girl and she's willing to fly in and say so."

"From where?"

"Utah. He was there on a ski vacation. Picked her up in a bar. Sound familiar? Played with her a couple of days and then disappeared. She's pissed. Thinks he took advantage."

"Maybe it was her? Star fucking?"

"She probably was. But that's not how it'll go down."

"You hope. I hear that Kornblatt guy is good."

"And I'm not?"

He held up a hand. "You know I'm not saying that. You're the best. That's why I wanted you on this case."

"And I truly appreciate it." She kissed his cheek. "They'll throw out all kinds of stuff. Diminished capacity. An accident during kinky sex. Even try to blame Kristi for being there in the first place."

"Not sure I can sit through that."

"You can. And you will. You know that's how the game's played."

"From the conversation I just had with Ray Longly and his boy Jake, they are also trying to suggest it could have been someone else. Someone who had it in for Kristi, or Kirk, even me."

"I don't see that flying at all. First of all, who? Who would—or could—do that? And why? Secondly, Kirk and Kristi were alone. Behind a locked door. I don't see how the defense can maneuver around that."

"So, we're back to diminished capacity or a drug-induced freak-out? Or a sex game gone wrong?"

"That's how I see it."

Tony massaged his throbbing temple. "I just hope you can make it all stick. I damn sure don't want to have to take care of it."

"Don't talk that way. I'm still an officer of the court. I have no need to know anything about your plans."

"Point taken." He pulled her against him. "Now, where were we?"

She giggled.

His cell buzzed, vibrating against the bedside table. He rolled over and answered. It was Reuben.

"Tell me," Tony said.

"Robert and Kevin are holed up at the Monteleone bar with that PI chick. Nicole Jamison."

"What?"

"They hooked up on the street and I followed them there. Been trying to find a way to listen in, but there's no way without exposing myself. Figured it was better not to take that chance."

"Good move."

"But you know how they are," Reuben said. "Girl that looks like that can make those two swallow their tongues."

"Or wag them."

"That, too."

"Sit tight. I'm on the way." He disconnected the call.

"What is it?" Melissa asked.

"My nephews. What else?"

CHAPTER THIRTY-ONE

RAY AND I walked into the Carousel Bar, the crowd noisy and deeply into happy hour. Looked like it had been going on since lunch. Not unusual for New Orleans. Any hour was happy hour. I scanned the bar but didn't see Nicole. Then, as we moved past the carousel itself, I did. She sat on a sofa, facing me, with two guys. Robert and Kevin. What the hell?

I started that way, but she caught my gaze and gave me look that said, sit tight. I stopped, grabbing Ray's arm. I nodded toward Nicole.

"What's that about?" he asked.

"Don't know. But she wants us to hang back."

She leaned forward, said something to the pair, laughed, stood, and headed our way. We melted back into the crowd so the brothers wouldn't see us if they turned and looked at Nicole's magnificent ass. They did. Perverts.

"What is that about?" I asked when she reached us.

"I just made a couple of friends."

"How do you figure that?" Ray asked.

She told us she had run into them on the street and brought them back for drinks. That she had gotten them to relax, especially Robert, who seemed to be the dominant brother.

"How did you do that?" I asked.

"The same way I control you?"

Ray laughed. I shook my head.

"Relax, big boy," she said. "It's what us girls do."

"Where's Pancake?" I asked.

"He and Sophie ran into some folks and are entrenched—his word—at Pat O'Brien's. They'll meet us for dinner."

She then told us that she was getting a vibe that there was a bit of sibling rivalry between the brothers and Kristi, not a lot, but some. Mostly centered on Tony's favoritism. And that Tony wasn't exactly their biggest fan and that feeling was mutual.

"Maybe we can use that," Ray said.

"Why do you think I invited them for a drink?"

Ray smiled. "Clever."

Yes, she was. And downright manipulative. Control me? Not a chance. She seemed to sense my thoughts and smiled at me. I hate it when she does that. Not smile. Read my mind.

"What's the play?" Ray asked.

"I told them I was headed to the little girl's room and that they should order more drinks."

"And?"

"I'll bring you guys back. Say I ran into you in the lobby."

"Might spook them," I said.

"I don't think so. I get the impression they want to talk. About Kristi. About Tony. I've already told them about the ketamine and the concerns there as far as Kirk drugging himself."

"What did they say to that?"

"Nothing. But I think the wheels are turning."

Ray nodded. "Sounds like a plan."

And that's how it went down.

"Look who I found wandering around in the lobby," Nicole said as we walked up.

Robert and Kevin looked more than a little surprised. Or was it discomfort I saw? Like they had been caught doing something wrong.

"Mind if we join you?" I said. They didn't respond so I continued, extending a hand toward Robert. "I know we got off on the wrong foot the other day, but Nicole tells me you guys are cool." Robert shook my hand. "And her judgment is always right on."

"We are cool," Kevin said. He didn't sound very convincing.

Ray shook with them and we settled in chairs flanking them.

The waitress appeared. Good timing. Gave the brothers time to sort out their thoughts and hopefully get comfortable with our unexpected intrusion. We ordered drinks.

"I really am sorry about your sister," I said. "Must be tough dealing with that."

Robert still carried a dose of suspicion and discomfort on his face, but said, "Worse thing I've ever had to endure." He looked at his brother. "Kevin, too." Kevin nodded.

"We were just talking about her," Nicole said. "I was telling them that we weren't really on opposite sides here."

"We aren't," Ray said.

"That's what Nicole said," Robert responded. "But we are. On some level."

That was progress. Sounded like he was at least considering the possibility that we weren't Satan's spawn.

"I think you guys might be able to help us," Ray said.

"Help you do what?"

"I'm sure Nicole told you that we agree with you. All things point to Kirk Ford. But there are things that don't feel right. Like why would Kirk drug himself."

"Yeah, she told us that bump was found in both of them," Robert said. "'Course, he might just like it. Took it himself for the high."

Ray nodded. "That's possible. But from what I've learned about him, that would seem out of character. Everyone who knows him says he doesn't use crazy drugs. Just marijuana. And all agree he's actually a normal guy." Ray shrugged. "But I don't really know him. Fact is, we just met him. I don't know whether those impressions are correct or not."

Robert looked at him but said nothing.

Ray leaned forward, shoulders hunched; he looked around, as if getting ready to share a secret. He was good.

"We aren't from here," he said. "You guys are. And I'm sure you know everyone who's anyone here in the Quarter. I was hoping you might be able to help us find the source of the ketamine. Or bump, as you say."

"We aren't dealers," Kevin said. "What makes you think we'd know anything about that?"

Ray smiled. "I know who your uncle is." Robert started to say something, but Ray raised a hand. "I know he has his fingers in a lot of things. So, I can appreciate your reluctance to even talk with us."

Again, the brothers stared at him, neither offering a response.

"I know that you guys are well known around here. Know all the players. So, I thought maybe you'd know where we could look."

Robert hesitated. I could almost see the wheels turning. I knew Tony treated them like crap. Didn't care much for them. Probably pissed them off regularly. And here was Ray offering them a chance to play hero. Maybe even poke Uncle Tony in the eye.

"Maybe," Robert said. He looked at Kevin. "We do know a couple of guys that are rumored to sell stuff."

"Then there you go," Ray said.

"But I'm not sure we'll be telling you."

"Tony? I get it." Ray shrugged, hesitated, then said, "I see no reason he has to know about this conversation. Not now. Not ever."

"I don't think we should tell you shit," Kevin said.

Robert nudged his brother's leg. "Let me handle this."

Kevin scowled.

Robert glanced around as if making sure no eavesdroppers were around, then leaned forward. "All I want is for whoever killed Kristi to pay for it. I think it's the movie star." He sighed. "But if it ain't, I don't want the real killer to walk away because he goes down for it."

"That's all we want," I said.

Robert stared at his shoes for a beat. "Okay. There's this guy. His name's Ragman. He deals all sorts of stuff."

"Robert?" Kevin said. "Maybe you shouldn't be talking about this."

"Look, if he sold this stuff to Kristi, or that actor dude, I want his hide on a wall."

"He said he didn't," Kevin said. "What's wrong with you?"

"You've talked with this Ragman?" I asked.

"Yeah," Robert said. "This morning. He said he didn't sell that stuff and didn't sell Kristi anything for sure."

"I get the impression you might not believe him," I said.

"I do. And I don't. With him you just never know."

"Where might we find him?" I asked.

Robert hesitated.

"I meant what I said," Ray jumped in. "No one will ever know what's said here."

"He works an alley over off Decatur," Robert said. "Sells mostly to tourists. And his regulars, of course."

I nodded. "We'll look into it."

"You can't say anything about me and Kevin."

"Of course not." I caught his gaze. "We aren't here to turn your world upside down. We're trying to solve a puzzle."

"What about your uncle?" Ray asked.

"What about him?" Kevin said.

"I understand he's a guy who takes care of his own problems. Doesn't wait for others to intervene, so to speak."

Robert's eyes narrowed. "We ain't talking about him. You want to know about his business, go ask him."

No other answer needed. But then the answer walked into the bar. Tony Guidry.

CHAPTER THIRTY-TWO

As soon as Tony disconnected Reuben, he rolled out of bed and called Johnny Hebert, telling him to swing by, pick him up. He needed to get over to the Monteleone. Then he jumped in the shower for a quick rinse and dressed.

"What about you?" he asked Melissa. "You want to stay for a while?"

"Depends. Will you be able to come back?"

"Not till after my dinner deal. Probably eleven."

"That's fine. I have my laptop and a few briefs to work on."

He kissed her cheek. "I'll have Johnny pick up something at NOLA's for you."

"Hmm. Trying to ply me with food, I see." She laughed.

"There's wine here for that."

"Go take care of your nephews. I'll be here when you get back."

Fifteen minutes later, he walked into the Monteleone and turned toward the bar. He left Johnny with the car and ran into Reuben just inside.

"They're that way." Reuben jerked his head toward the area beyond the Carousel Bar.

Tony moved that way, but what he saw wasn't what he expected. There were Robert and Kevin and the chick, all right. But, also, Ray and Jake Longly. What the fuck? That changed the game. How to handle this? Definitely not go off on Robert and Kevin. Not in public. In front of the blond, okay, but not with Ray Longly as a witness. Might set off too many alarms. Like Tony just might have something to hide. Better to play it casual. Friendly. Low key. Turn on the charm. He was good at that. Then after he gracefully extracted Robert and Kevin, he could tell them what was what.

"You wait here," Tony said. "Stay out of sight."

Reuben nodded.

Showtime.

"How's it going?" Tony asked as he approached the group. Everyone looked up. Robert's and Kevin's expressions said it all. Riddled with surprise, and fear. At least they had the good sense to keep their mouths shut.

"Mr. Guidry," Jake said. "Want to join us?"

"I don't want to intrude."

"You're not."

Tony nodded and took the remaining empty chair.

"Buy you a drink?" Ray asked.

"That would be nice." He laughed. "That's why we're here after all."

Their waitress appeared. Tony ordered a Cajun martini.

"I have a dinner meeting down the street in a little while," Tony said, answering the question he saw in Ray's eyes. "Always good to have a drink before one of those."

Ray nodded. "Must be a business thing."

"You got that right."

"I don't think you've met Nicole," Jake said. "Nicole, this is Mr. Guidry."

Tony leaned forward and shook her hand across the low coffee table. "Tony. Please."

Nicole smiled. "Nice to meet you."

"Trust me, the pleasure is all mine." He had seen her in the courtroom. And just outside after the bail hearing. From a distance. Up close, she was breathtaking. Her hand was soft, yet her shake firm. He liked that. Not to mention the way she looked into his eyes as they shook.

"We were just chatting with your nephews," Jake said.

Tony reluctantly let go of Nicole's hand and yanked his gaze away. "About what?"

"Mostly football. And where the best restaurants are."

Tony nodded, eyeing his nephews. "They know them all."

"They suggested a visit to K-Paul's."

"Can't go wrong there. A Big Easy classic."

Tony's martini arrived. He took a sip.

"Of course, Paul's no longer with us, but his restaurant hasn't missed a beat as far as I can tell."

"We'll check it out," Ray said.

"Let me know when you want to go and I'll call them. Get you a good table."

"That's very kind," Ray said.

Tony waved a hand, indicating it was nothing. Truth was he could get the best table at any restaurant in the Quarter on a moment's notice. A perk he had used many times. He looked around. "Where's Mr. Ford?"

"I think he's resting and cleaning up," Nicole said. "The shoot today was pretty strenuous, I understand."

"Moviemaking," Tony said. "I don't really understand how it all works. Seems there are a lot of moving parts."

"Speaking parts, too," Nicole said.

Her smile seemed relaxed. Was she flirting with him? Of course she was. Women always did. Like moths, they wanted to be close to the flame. Even after a couple of rounds with Melissa, he felt the heat rise inside.

"I don't see how they remember their lines," Tony said. "I'm afraid I wasn't very good at memorization when I was at school."

She laughed. Her gaze never leaving him. Her hand going to her lapel. Definitely flirting. An interesting turn of events.

"Most actors have the same problem," she said. "But they have script girls there. To help them when they get stuck."

"I could use a script girl," Tony said. "I tend to ramble too much." He raised his glass. "Especially after a couple of these."

That got a laugh from everyone. Good. Charm always worked.

Tony turned to Ray. "Did you talk with Ford about sitting down with me?"

"His schedule's pretty tight. But we'll find a time."

"Maybe an evening at K-Paul's?"

"Maybe."

He examined Ray. His research on him left no doubt that this was a guy you couldn't push around. But buy? Maybe. Anyone could be bought.

Tony drained his glass. "Thanks for the drink. I owe you one."

Ray shrugged.

Tony stood. "We better get going." He looked at his nephews. "You guys coming?"

"To dinner?" Robert asked.

"Absolutely. You two are going to be part of this deal." He looked at Ray. "A couple of investors. Want to open a new club. Robert and Kevin will likely have to run it."

"Here in the Quarter?" Ray asked.

"Yeah. Over near one of my existing clubs. The Belly Up. At least that's these guys' plan. We'll see." He looked at Robert and Kevin. "Let's get going." He caught Nicole's gaze again, and smiled. "Nice meeting you."

Tony led his nephews through the bar, picking up Reuben along the way, and out onto the street. They climbed in the limo and Johnny spun from the curb.

"Want to tell me what the fuck that was all about?" Tony asked.

"Nothing. We ran into her on the street, and she asked us to join her."

"How convenient. What did she ask you?"

"Nothing."

"And the Longly duo? They didn't ask any questions either?"

Robert stared at him. "Like we said. Football. Restaurants. Small talk."

"My name come up?" When Robert hesitated, Tony instantly knew the answer to that question. "How? What?"

"That Nicole chick was very sympathetic," Kevin said. "She said she knew about our parents and how you took care of us and Kristi. How you must trust us if you let us work for you." He shook his head. "Don't seem that way to me right now."

"Do I trust you guys? Why should I? You two manage to make a mess of just about everything you touch."

"We do our best for you, Uncle Tony," Robert said. "We always have."

Tony waved a dismissive hand. "Really? My business never came up? No questions about what I do?"

"No," Robert said. "We wouldn't've said nothing anyway. We ain't stupid."

They were lying. Tony saw it on their faces and felt it in his bones. About what he wasn't sure, but their little chat had not been solely about fluff. He glanced at his Rolex. He didn't have time for this shit right now.

"You two get back over to the Belly Up. Do your fucking jobs."

"You going to take us there?"

"Jesus. It isn't that far. The walk will do you good. Maybe you can think of some way not to fuck everything up."

Tony turned and spoke to Johnny. "Pull over here."

He did. Robert and Kevin climbed out.

"Now, where's that fucking meeting?" Tony asked.

CHAPTER THIRTY-THREE

ROBERT SENSED HIS brother's tension. They walked a few blocks in silence before Robert asked, "What do you think?"

"About what?"

"About what they said. About someone else being the killer?"

"I don't think much of it."

"Not sure I do either, but what if it is someone else? I mean the fact that Kirk Ford was fucked up, too, does make you think."

Kevin said nothing and they covered another block.

Robert went on. "And another thing—what about Owen?"

Kevin stopped and stared at him. "What are you saying?"

"You know how crazy he was about her."

"Which is why he wouldn't do nothing to her."

"I don't think so either, but hear me out. He knew, hell everyone knew, he and Kristi would end up together. Even after the breakup, didn't you think that would all blow over and they'd be back together?"

Kevin nodded. "Sure."

"I bet Owen did, too. But then this guy comes along. An actor. A pretty boy. He might see that as a real threat."

"So what? He gives Kristi a bumped joint? They get fucked up and he breaks in the room and kills her? How?"

"Owen's pretty good with tools."

Kevin walked a few steps away, before turning and walking back to where Robert stood. "Listen to yourself. Are you insane? Even if he did all that, why would he kill Kristi? Not Ford?"

"I don't know." Robert looked up the street. Not really focusing on anything. "But I think we should at least talk to him."

"Why?"

"For one thing, we haven't since all this happened. We should have but we haven't."

"I agree with that. But I don't think for a minute he had anything to do with this."

"I don't either. But let's go see him. See where his head's at."

"Now?"

"Why not? They'll be closing up about now. Good time for a chat."

Kevin sighed. "I guess."

"Only take ten, fifteen minutes to walk over. Let's go."

"Uncle Tony wants us at the bar."

"Fuck him."

"Ooh, big man," Kevin said.

"I think it's about time we went away. Away from him. Away from here."

"And go where? Do what?"

"Biloxi. You know Aunt Clara said we could come over and stay with her anytime we wanted. Said she could get us work."

Aunt Clara. Their mother's sister. No love lost between her and Tony.

"You think Tony's fingers don't reach into Mississippi?"

Robert shrugged. "What I think is he wouldn't be all that sad if we took off."

Kevin had no comeback for that. Probably because he knew it was true.

When they reached Vaughn's Motor Works, Carl Vaughn was in the office, closing out the register and the books.

"Is Owen still here?" Robert asked.

"I was wondering when you guys might come by."

"Haven't felt much like it," Robert said. "Not that we weren't worried about Owen, just that we're tired of talking about and thinking about Kristi."

Carl nodded. "We all are. I'm truly sorry for the both of you. Owen, too."

"He doing okay?"

Carl shrugged. "Doesn't say much. Seems to be diving into his work. I think that's because, like you, he don't want to think or talk about it."

"You think he'd want to see us?"

"I think he'd like that." He jerked his head toward the back. "He's out there. Putting stuff away for the night."

That's where they found him.

"How's it going, Owen?" Robert asked.

He turned. "Oh, hey." He wiped his hands on a stained orange shop towel. "Okay, I guess."

"Sorry we haven't come by sooner."

Owen shrugged. "I understand. I ain't been up for talking about it either."

"It's been tough."

Owen nodded. "Still don't seem real."

Robert sighed. "Let me ask you something. Did you know Kristi was doing drugs?"

"Not before she met that guy. That's for sure." Owen continued wiping his hands, concentrating on cleaning the grime that stained his cuticles. "But I heard they found some stuff in the room. A joint."

"Three, from what we hear," Robert said. "But that ain't all. It seems the coroner found bump—you know—ketamine—in her. And in Kirk Ford."

"What?" Owen tossed the towel into a large white plastic bucket. "There ain't no way she would've done that. He must've done it to her." He looked up toward the sky, his eyes glistened. "And I'd bet a whole pile of cash that she didn't know it."

"That's what we think. The cops, too."

"They'd be right."

"But it also seems they might be looking at another theory."

"Like what?"

"Since Ford has that shit inside himself, they're thinking he wouldn't have drugged himself if his intention was to harm Kristi."

Owen stared at him, his mouth open slightly. "I don't understand."

"They think, maybe considering would be a better word, that maybe someone else did it. Drugged them both. Broke in and killed Kristi."

"You get all this from Tony?"

Robert glanced at his brother. "Sure did."

Owen shook his head. "That don't make no sense."

"Sure don't. But I wouldn't be surprised if they came back around to talk to you."

"Me? I didn't do nothing."

"I know. But since you are the ex, and she dumped you, they just might think you had it in for her."

He shook his head. "Unbelievable."

"Where were you that night?"

"What are you saying?"

"It's what they'll ask."

"Them? Or you?"

Robert stared at him.

Kevin jumped in. "Of course we ain't saying nothing about you, Owen. Right, Robert?"

"Don't sound that way to me." Owen's jaw tightened. "Maybe I should ask you where you were that night?"

"Us? She was our sister," Robert said.

"Yeah, she was. And she was Tony's favorite. And I know that pissed you both off."

"You're crazy."

"Really? She got everything. She was Tony's darling. You think I don't know that? You think I don't know you two were full of all kinds of resentment?"

"Just so you know, we were at the Belly Up. Until nearly three in the morning. With a bunch of people. You?"

"I think you should leave."

"Or what?"

Owen walked to an open tool box and grabbed a large wrench. "Or I just might put this upside your head."

"Come on, Owen," Robert said. "We ain't accusing you or nothing."

"Like I said. I think you two should leave."

Carl came out the back door. "You about finished out here?"

"Just about," Owen said.

"Okay. I'll get to locking up." He disappeared back inside.

"Look," Robert said. "We ain't here to give you grief. There's enough of that to go around already."

Owen nodded. He tossed the wrench back into the tool box. "I'm sorry I reacted that way. I'm just all torn up inside."

"As are we," Kevin said.

Robert nodded his agreement. "We just wanted to know if you had any ideas about where that shit might've come from."

Owen gazed up toward the sky. "I don't. God knows I wish I did."

"We'll get out of here and let you finish up your day." Robert tapped his brother on the shoulder. "Let's go."

CHAPTER THIRTY-FOUR

I WAS PAYING for last night. Not that the price wasn't worth it, but still, settling the debt was painful.

I stood in the shower, head bowed, letting the hot water wash over my head, down my back. Trying to loosen the stiffness in my shoulders and neck.

Last night, as Nicole and I waited in the hotel lobby for Ray and Pancake to show for dinner, a curious thing happened. One of the twins walked by, apparently heading to the bar to meet her sister. Nothing odd there. But after she greeted us with hugs, Nicole had called her Tegan. Just like that. Like she knew which twin she was. And she was right. After Tegan walked away, I asked, "How did you know that was Tegan?"

Nicole slapped my butt. "Wouldn't you like to know."

"Yes, I would."

She smiled. "My secret."

"Come on."

"Nope."

"Not even a hint?"

"Not even. I like having the upper hand."

Woman was evil.

Before I could twist her arm—like that would work—Ray showed, telling us he had called Pancake and that he and Sophie would meet us there. There being GW Fins, around the corner on Bienville. Five minutes later we were seated, and a couple of minutes after that Pancake arrived. With a cute, feisty redhead he introduced as Sophie the Makeup Queen. To which they both laughed hysterically. Inside joke, I suspected. Obviously, their time at Pat O'Brien's had been spent getting blown away by their famous Hurricanes. Which was fine except they didn't stop there. Through dinner they had more whiskey, wine, whatever, and unfortunately Nicole and I boarded the same train. Ray, less so. By the time we returned to our room, we were both hammered. Nicole fell twice trying to get out of her clothes. Me, only once. I'm a professional athlete, after all. Or was, anyway.

I foolishly thought we would crash, slip into a coma, and that would be that. Not Nicole. She was on fire. The next two hours were an exercise in Mummenschanz. She was like a gold-medal gymnast. She threw in a few back flips, walkovers, and a handstand or two, if memory serves. Me? I could only manage a layout. Afterward my legs were jelly, my back torqued, and I had no idea what happened with my neck. Only that twisting to my left wasn't an option.

The hot water helped.

"How long are you going to stay in there?" Nicole asked as she pushed the door open. The room was foggy with steam.

"Still trying to recover from last night."

"Wimp."

Did I say she was evil?

"Better get a move on. We have to meet Ray and Pancake in about five."

"Is he alive?"

"He texted an hour ago. While you were still sleeping. Asked if we wanted breakfast. After texting a no, I checked you for a pulse."

"Funny."

"Said he and Sophie were going to grab a bite before she headed to the set."

"Sophie? That dog."

"He is that. Now get your ass in gear."

I did and off we went.

Last night, before it turned into a blur, we had talked with Kornblatt, who green-lighted a chat between Kirk and Doucet. As long as it was done with Kornblatt on speakerphone and as long as it was early so Kirk could get out to the set without upsetting the day's shooting schedule too much.

Ebersole's limo ferried us over to Doucet's office. He had set up a speakerphone and recording device in a conference room and we gathered around the table. Ray, Pancake, Nicole, and I on one side, Doucet on the other, Kirk at the end. Once Kornblatt was on the line, Doucet turned on the recorder and began. After stating the date and time, he listed who was present. That went smoothly until he got to Pancake. Apparently, he realized he didn't know Pancake's real name.

"What's your name?" he asked.

"Pancake."

"No, your given name?"

"I like Pancake."

Good grief.

"But for the official record I need your true name."

"Oh. Tommy Jeffers."

With that out of the way, Doucet went on to explain that the three of us were from Longly Investigations and were there at the request of Kirk Ford and his counsel. Then the questions began.

"Mr. Ford, I don't want to rehash all the events of that night as you've already given a statement and I don't want to waste your time. But I have a few specifics I want to go over."

"Fine," Kirk replied.

"You said that you and Kristi Guidry had dinner that evening. Where?"

"At NOLA."

"With Tara and Tegan James?"

"That's right."

"What time did you leave?"

"Nine thirty."

"Can anyone corroborate that? Besides the James twins?"

"The restaurant was packed. And I signed a half dozen autographs for people. Maybe some of them would remember the time."

"Anyone specifically that you can recall?"

"The hostess. I don't know her name but I signed one for her as we left. And Kristi took a picture of me and her on the girl's phone. I imagine that would have a time stamp."

Doucet nodded. "You returned to your room at the Monteleone. Immediately? Or did you go anywhere else?"

"No, we walked back. Took about five minutes."

"Okay. And in the room you drank more wine and smoked some marijuana?"

"We drank wine with Tara and Tegan. Maybe a half hour. Then they left and we smoked after that."

"To hide it from them? The marijuana."

Kirk shook his head. "No. They just don't use it, so we waited."

"Okay, so after they left, you and Kristi smoked a joint?"

"Half a joint," Kornblatt inserted, his voice metallic through the speaker.

"Yes," Kirk said. "Half a joint."

"And that joint was the one Kristi brought? Not one of the ones you had?"

"That's correct."

"You're sure of that?"

"Yes."

"How can you be sure?"

Kirk smiled. "I could never get the hang of rolling joints. Mine are always too loose and fall apart."

"You are absolutely sure it was the one you say she brought?"

"Asked and answered," Kornblatt said.

"Did she say where she got it?" Doucet asked.

"A friend."

"Any idea who that was?"

"I'll object to that," Kornblatt said. "Calls for speculation. Unless she said who."

"She didn't," Kirk said. "She only said 'a friend.'"

"Did she say it was given to her or did she say she bought it?"

"I don't recall her saying either. It wasn't a big topic of discussion."

Doucet nodded and consulted the notes he had before him. "Then the two of you had sex? True?"

Kornblatt interrupted again. "If you add consensual to your question, I'll allow an answer."

"Okay, consensual sex?"

"Yes."

"And what happened after that?"

"That's where things get fuzzy."

"Fuzzy?"

"Don't guess," Kornblatt said. "If you recall anything clearly and specifically, then okay. But don't assume."

"We were lying there, holding each other. Catching our breath. And that's the last thing I remember."

"Until the next morning?"

"That's correct. I woke up. She was laying there. I thought she was asleep. Until I tried to wake her."

"That's when you discovered she was dead?"

"Yes, sir."

"That's when you called Mr. Ebersole?"

"That's correct."

"Not the medics? Or the police?"

"I knew she was dead. I mean, she was cold. And I freaked out."

"In what way?"

"I think I'll stop this line of questioning," Kornblatt said. "It calls for him to say things that might or might not be true. Given his state of mind."

I smiled. The defense at work.

Doucet continued. "But after Mr. Ebersole arrived, you did call the police. Correct?"

"Mr. Ebersole did."

"The night before," Doucet said, "did anyone else drop by the room? After the James twins left?"

"No."

"Did either of you at any time after that leave the room? After the James twins left?"

"No."

"You're sure?"

"Asked and answered," Kornblatt said.

"If Mr. Kornblatt will allow, let me ask it this way," Doucet said. "Do you have a clear recollection of either of you leaving the room later that night?"

"Don't speculate," Kornblatt chimed in.

"Like I told you, I was out. Gone. I don't remember anything after that."

"And you didn't give a room key to anyone?"

"No. Why would I?"

"Not to Kristi? For convenience?"

"No. I only had one and it was in the dresser drawer with my wallet."

Doucet nodded. "That's where we found it."

Doucet shuffled the pages before him. "Okay, I think that's all I need for now. Thanks for coming down and talking with me."

Kirk nodded.

The meeting broke up. Kirk needed to get to the set so we turned him and Ebersole loose, saying we'd grab a cab. Ray wanted to chat with Doucet for a few minutes, and Doucet said he'd take us back to the hotel. Kirk and Ebersole left.

"I think tracking down where the drugs came from might be important here," Ray said.

"You mean like someone who might have it in for Kristi, or for Ford?" Doucet asked. "Maybe an attempt to frame him?"

Ray nodded.

"The questions are who? And why?"

"Don't have those answers. Yet. But pulling on that string might turn up something."

Doucet shrugged. "Maybe. Probably not, but maybe."

"What about some payback for Tony?" I asked. "Would that seem reasonable?"

"Nothing is reasonable as far as Tony Guidry's concerned," Doucet said. "But, I suppose that's possible. Not sure I could come up with many names with the balls to do that though."

"The ketamine?" Ray asked. "Any sources you can think of?"

"Several. We're beginning to root around in that world. Hopefully something will shake loose."

"What about this dude Ragman?" Pancake asked. "He someone on your radar?"

Doucet raised an eyebrow. "You know about him?"

"We do know what we're doing," Ray said.

"Ragman," Doucet said. "Jimmy Walker's the name his mother gave him. He's a local punk. Deals. Under the umbrella of Junior Makin. Ju Ju to his friends. And the cops."

"And he is?" I asked.

"A bad guy. Doesn't deal drugs. He found a different niche. Sells protection to most of the dealers in the Quarter. Metairie and Algiers, too."

"Sounds like a citizen," Ray said.

"All that and then some. I had a chat with him. We scratch each other's back from time to time. Said he'd look into it."

"You believe him?" I asked.

"No. He's just jerking us around. He ain't going to dig up shit on his own guys."

"Mind if we take a run at Ragman?" Ray asked.

Doucet smiled. "Sure, I'd love that. Anything that makes him uncomfortable is fine with me. He hangs in an alley over on Decatur. Between Bienville and Conti." He shook his head. "Get this. Right next to the fire station."

"Really?" I asked.

"He's either clever or stupid. Probably both. But truth is the firemen, if they aren't washing their gear, are usually on a call or resting up for the next one. The alley next door ain't a big priority for them."

"What about Tony Guidry?" I asked. "Do you think he's a threat here? To Kirk?"

"Wouldn't put anything past Tony. But that would be a stretch. I mean, would he whack someone? You bet. But this would be a shade too high profile for Tony. He likes to stay in the weeds."

"Hoping the courts will take care of things?" I asked.

"Yep. And he's tight with the DA." Doucet looked at me. "Especially Assistant DA Melissa Mooring. Rumor is they're an item."

"Really?" Nicole asked. "How convenient."

"And cozy," I said.

"Not to mention a big old fat conflict," Pancake added.

Doucet nodded. "Tony rarely worries about conflicts. At least not those kind."

CHAPTER THIRTY-FIVE

WE HAD DOUCET drop us at Mother's Kitchen, just off Poydras at Tchoupitoulas. Home of the world's best ham. Said so on the sign right over the entry door. Also said it was founded in 1930. Nicole had never been; Pancake and I never missed it when we were in New Orleans. Busy as always but the line at the order counter was shorter than usual. Nicole, Ray, and I ordered egg and ham biscuits, one each; Pancake, four—with a double order of grits. We grabbed a table and the food appeared in minutes.

Afterward we waddled back to the Monteleone where we left Nicole. We were heading over to Decatur Street to track down Ragman, and I didn't want her around something that could go sideways. She protested. Ray took my side and didn't budge. So, she decided to hit the spa and get a massage.

"Why?" I asked. "Did I wear you out last night?"

She slugged my arm.

I've got to learn to keep my mouth shut. But sometimes things just tumble out.

Decatur was only two blocks from Royal, toward the river. Ragman's hangout, according to Doucet, was just around the corner. On the way, I thought about what we might accomplish by chatting with him. Probably not much. In my gut, I still felt that Kirk just might be the bad guy here. I hoped not, but the feeling was there. Trailing the drug's path from the street to Kristi's corpse and Kirk's blood would only be useful if someone else had actually procured it and passed it along. I mean, if Kirk bought the drug that would only solidify his guilt in my mind. But if it were Kristi, that opened other doors. It was one of those doors we were hoping for.

Door number one would be Kristi paying some miscreant like Ragman for it. That would be way out of character for her. At least everything I had learned about her screamed that.

Door number two would be if she got it unknowingly. Bought it, but didn't know what she was getting. Maybe some dealer simply handed her the wrong joint? That sort of thing. Or maybe it was supposed to be some sort of prank? Some dealer or a friend trying to fuck with her and Kirk. Really? Prank Tony Guidry's niece? I figured any dealer, or friend for that matter, that did that had a death wish.

Door number three would be a friend giving it to her for some darker reason. Who? Why? It could only be if that someone had it in for her or Kirk and was planning to kill her and frame Kirk. Seemed convoluted and not likely, but it was that door we were trying to pry open. It seemed to be Kirk's only path to freedom.

Jimmy Walker, aka Ragman, was a piece of work. A piece of something, anyway. The alley he did business from, as Doucet had said, was wedged between the fire station and an industrial-looking building that had seen better days. The sidewalk was veined with cracks and the alley narrow and littered with refuse. As we reached the alley entrance, we saw him. Thin, black, baggy pants, a New Orleans Saints jersey, three sizes too large, almost reaching his knees, cigarette hanging from his lips, slouching against the building. He looked up from the phone he was working with his thumbs and came off the wall, moving toward us. He didn't seem alarmed. Probably thought we were customers.

"Good day, gentlemen," he said, smiling. A true salesman. Probably would do well with aluminum siding. Or as a midway barker.

We introduced ourselves, Ray saying we were PIs and needed to ask a few questions to which Ragman said, "I don't got to talk to you." His head swiveled up and down the street. Like he didn't want to be seen talking to us.

"No, you don't," I said. "But we'd appreciate it."

"Go appreciate something else," he said.

"It's about your business," Ray said.

"I ain't got no business." Another glance up the street. "I suggest you move along. Get out of my face. Might not be healthy for you white boys to hang around here. Know what I'm saying?"

I love watching Pancake work. It's a true art form. Mostly he's a gentle giant, wouldn't hurt anyone. Even go out of his way to avoid trouble. Then there were times he did stuff that made you stare in disbelief. Even if you'd seen it before.

This time, he simply grabbed Ragman's arm and tossed him into the alley. Just like that. Like a kid having a tantrum and tossing a doll across the room. Ragman rolled and bounced a couple of times, but to his credit, quickly scrambled to his feet. Pancake was on him. He poked his chest with a finger. "No, I don't know what you're saying."

"Hey, dude, you can't do that."

"I'm just getting started." Pancake palmed Ragman's chest, pressing him against the wall.

I had to give it to Ragman. He was scared, no doubt, but not exactly terrified. Not yet. "You guys don't know who you're dealing with."

Ray tapped Pancake's shoulder. Pancake lowered his brace and stepped back. A half step.

"Listen up, Jimmy, Mr. Walker, Ragman, whoever the fuck you are, you're going to talk with us. One way or the other."

"I don't think so," Ragman said, still trying to sound tough. "I got my guys watching."

"Really?" Ray looked up and down the alley. "I don't see them."

"They be here if I need them."

"You mean Ju Ju? Tony Guidry?"

His fear ramped up a bit. Trying to figure how we knew so much about him, I suspected. I mean, we had known him all of a minute and yet we knew all his names and his associations. I could almost hear the hamster wheel whirring in his head.

Ray was just getting warmed up. "If you think they can protect you, you couldn't be more wrong. If you want to escalate this into a little range war, I can have a half dozen guys here before the sun sets. Guys who love war. Got a PhD in it. Over in that shit hole they call the Middle East. Guys who actually love it. And have no compunction whatsoever about waging a scorched-earth campaign. Am I clear?"

Ragman stared at him. He had run out of clever comebacks and bluster.

Ray wasn't done. "But that ain't going to help you right here, right now. Whether you walk out of this alley or are carried out by the medics is your call. If you want, I can turn my man here"—he nodded toward Pancake—"loose on your sorry ass. And if he don't want to, I will."

"I want to," Pancake said. "I really, really want to."

"What's it going to be? Answer a couple of questions or get a lung punctured?"

Ray was on a roll. It was a beautiful thing to witness.

"I don't know what you want, man," Ragman said. His voice had risen an octave. "Why you come here getting in my grill about shit I probably don't know nothing about."

"What kind of shit do you sell? Marijuana? Crank? Oxy?"

"I don't sell nothing. If you heard something else, you be listening to the wrong people."

Ray twisted his neck one way and then the other. "We're beyond all that, Ragman. I know you do. Everyone knows. What I want to chat about is ketamine. You know, bump? Purple? Special K?"

"I know what it is. What I don't know is how come everyone come around here asking me about that shit? The cops. Tony's nephews."

"We aren't the only ones that know you supply it." Ray smiled.

"Okay. So what?"

"The question of the day is, did you sell any to Kristi Guidry?"

His head wagged back and forth. "You think I'm crazy? Think I'd sell anything to Tony's niece? Shit, man, that'd be suicide."

That was a very good answer. And it seemed truthful to me. Even Ragman wasn't that stupid.

"What about Kirk Ford?" I asked.

"Who's that?"

"Don't get stupid on me, Ragman," Ray said. "Everybody knows who he is."

Ragman shook his head. "Yeah, I know. But I never seen him. Not in person."

"Okay, now we're getting somewhere. What about someone that isn't your usual customer? Say the last week or so?"

Finally getting a grip on his situation, he said, "Maybe a couple of folks."

"Tell me."

"There was two dudes. About your age. Too old for that shit. But they had cash, so, there it is."

"What'd they look like?"

"Two white dudes. Looked like tourists. Shorts, new tee shirts that said some shit. I don't remember what but some tourist shit. One had a baseball cap. New. Turned backwards like he was some badass."

"You only saw them the one time?" I asked.

"Yeah. Like I said, they weren't local."

"Who else?"

"A couple of college girls. Not from around here either. Good-looking bitches's all I remember."

"Two hot chicks and that's all you remember?" I asked.

"They was in jeans, halter tops. Short dark hair." He looked up as if remembering. "Both had on red lipstick. I remember that."

"Eye color?"

"They had on sunglasses. They was scared, too. Kept looking around. But I see that a lot."

"I bet," Ray said. "Selling on the street has its disadvantages."

Ragman shrugged. "What you gonna do?" Like that justified his entire existence.

"Anyone else?" I asked.

"Yeah. They was this couple. Maybe thirties, forties, I don't know. Looked like they was from Ohio or some such shit. Tourists for sure. Don't know what the hell they wanted with bump. Looked like schoolteachers or something. The dude's hair was already getting gray."

"You have a big tourist trade?" I asked.

He shrugged. "Some. You asked about folks I didn't know. Not local or usual buyers. I got my regulars. Lots of them. Most of the rest are tourist types. Seems like this place is infested with them. Like a fucking plague."

"But they do come see you?" Ray said. "For their party favors?"

Ragman laughed. "You might say I do community service. Promote tourism. Shit, the mayor should give me a fucking recommendation."

"Commendation," I said.

"What?"

"It's called a commendation."

"Well whatever it is they should give me one."

Somehow, I didn't think a mayoral proclamation was in Ragman's future.

"What did you sell these people?" I asked.

Ragman looked at me like I was insane. "What we been talking about, man?"

"What I mean is did you sell them laced joints or what?"

"Don't do that, man. Too hard to carry and hide. Liquid's the way to go. They can do what they want after that."

"Is that it?" Ray asked. "All the onetime customers you can think of?"

"Yeah."

"Anything else you want to tell us?" Ray asked.

"Ain't I said enough?"

"You did good," Ray said. "But I need a favor from you."

"Shit. You climb in my face and now you want my good graces?"

Ray handed him a card. "If you think of anyone else, or if one of the people you told us about shows up, can you give me a call?"

"Probably not."

"Well, that's fine. But if we need to have another chat, we know where to find you."

CHAPTER THIRTY-SIX

"THAT WAS FUN," Pancake said.

We had left Ragman in his alley and were now standing a half block away, on the corner of Decatur and Conti, discussing our next move. Ray was of the opinion that we might want to go shake Ju Ju's tree. See what fell out. Pancake had other ideas.

"I'm hungry," he said.

"I'm shocked," I said. "What's it been? An hour since your last feeding?"

"Wasn't much."

Pancake's idea of "much" and mine were different things altogether. I only had one biscuit at Mother's Kitchen and I was stuffed. But I knew not to argue with him when he was hungry. Sort of like poking a bear with a stick. A big, angry, hypoglycemic bear.

"Okay," I said. "Let's head down to Café du Monde. Maybe Gloria's working. We can see if she's heard anything."

"I love their beignets," Pancake said.

"Of course you do."

We found a table more or less in the middle of the covered patio. Still messy, as the couple who had been there were just leaving as we walked up. A busboy appeared and the clutter of dishes and the tabletop's frosting of powdered sugar disappeared. We sat. I saw Gloria coming from the kitchen and waved her over. She nodded, and after delivering the order she carried, weaved through the tables toward us.

"How you doing?" she asked.

"Fine." I introduced her to Ray and Pancake.

"Pancake?" she said. "I love pancakes. Especially big old strawberry ones."

He smiled. "That's me."

Charming. Always charming.

Once Pancake and Gloria finished their banter, we ordered. Ray and I, coffee; Pancake, coffee and two plates of beignets. Took only a few minutes for our order to return and then Gloria was off serving other tables, but before Pancake finished the first plate she was back.

"Anything new?" she asked. "About Kristi?"

"I was going to ask you the same thing," I said.

She glanced around. "The cops were here."

"A Detective Doucet?"

"Yeah." She looked at me. "Did you tell him about me?"

"No. But I'm sure he knows you and Kristi were friends. Makes sense he'd come by."

She shrugged. "Guess that's true."

"And?"

"He talked to me and a couple of the guys in back. Wanted to know about Kristi and where she might have gotten the smoke." Again, she scanned the area, then squatted, placing her tray on the table. Her voice dropped low. "And he asked about ketamine. What's that all about?"

"Looks like that was involved."

"What? Kristi?"

"Looks that way."

"Jesus Christ on a bicycle." She shook her head. "I asked that detective dude why he was interested in that shit. He wouldn't say. I thought maybe it was that actor dude. Never crossed my mind that he meant Kristi." Then her eyes widened. "Did he drug her? Please tell me he didn't."

"Wish we could. It's possible, but the truth is it looks like both of them were drugged."

"That don't make no sense." She shook her head for emphasis. "I know for damn sure Kristi wouldn't use any of that. Shit, smoking a joint is a stretch."

"Did you talk to the guys that work here?" I asked. "The ones you mentioned. About them giving anything to Kristi?"

"I sure as hell did. Police did, too. They both swore to me that that would never happen. Said only an insane person would feed drugs to Tony Guidry's niece."

I smiled. "That seems to be the consensus."

"You can bet on it."

"What about a friend at college? Could Kristi have gotten it there?" She thought for a minute. "Possible, I suspect. But she lived at home and commuted to school. Didn't hang out there or do any of that sorority stuff. I don't think she had a lot of friends there."

"Really?" I asked. "She seemed to be the friendly type. From what we hear."

"She was. But she wasn't into all that college campus stuff. Her friends were her friends way before that. She hung close to home. Except for her classes, anyway."

I nodded.

"There was one girl. She came by here a couple of times with Kristi." She shook her head. "But I don't think she would've. Far as I know, anyway. She seems like a carbon copy of Kristi. Nice and all."

"What's her name?"

"Betty Smithson."

"Know how we might reach her?" I asked.

"Hattiesburg. She only did one semester. Had some family deal. Someone, I think her mother, got the cancer. Had to leave and handle all that, so she ain't been around for a few months."

A dead end.

She stood. "I better get back to work."

"Thanks. If anything comes up, call me. You still have my number?"

"Sure do." And she was gone.

My cell chimed and I answered. It was Owen Vaughn. He wanted to talk.

Took twenty minutes for us to walk back to the Monteleone, grab Pancake's truck, and drive over to Vaughn's Motor Works. Carl greeted us as we entered. I introduced him to Ray and Pancake.

"You the PI guys?" he asked.

"We are," Ray said.

"What can I do for you?"

"Owen called me," I said. "Wants to talk."

"I see." He didn't look happy, but he jerked his head toward the back. "He's out back cleaning up a couple of carburetors."

That's where we found him.

"Thanks for coming," Owen said. He stood next to a metal table, a pair of disassembled carburetors before him. He wiped his greasy hands on an orange shop towel.

I introduced Ray and Pancake.

"You have some questions," I said.

"Robert and Kevin dropped by yesterday. They as much as accused me of being the one that killed Kristi."

"They did?"

"More or less."

"Why would they do that?"

"Because they're idiots. Maybe because they're confused, probably hurting and wanting answers."

That was an excellent take on things. Owen continued to impress me. He seemed smarter than he first appeared.

"They also told me some disturbing stuff." He looked at each of us in turn. "Told me about ketamine. That true?"

I nodded. "Looks that way."

"They said the police were looking at maybe someone else being the killer. Someone who had it in for either Kristi or Kirk Ford. That true?"

"Yes."

"And so folks like Robert and Kevin think it might've been me? Of course, the truth is that right about now I don't give two shits what they think. But what about the cops?"

I could sense the anger—fear?—in his voice.

"I'm not sure you're where the cops are focused," I said. "But the idea that it might've been someone else is at least part of the discussion."

"I'm here to tell you that I ain't had nothing to do with it. I wouldn't do that. Couldn't. I loved her." He looked up toward the sky. "Still do."

"I believe you," I said.

He looked at me. "But do the police?"

"I can't tell you that for sure, but my impression is that they aren't looking real hard in your direction. Have they talked to you again?"

"No."

"They probably will be back."

"Shit." He looked lost. Almost like an abandoned puppy.

"Just tell them exactly what you just told us," I said.

"I wish it was that simple."

"Oh?"

"Cops don't always believe the truth,"

"That's what they do," Ray said. "That's their job. To suspect everyone."

"Well they can suspect somewhere else." He shook his head. "Please tell me they're looking elsewhere, too."

"They are."

"You mean they have someone else in mind? Who?"

"That we don't know," I said.

He said nothing for a moment. "This ain't ever going to be over, is it?"

"Not until it is," Ray said. "Not until the killer is uncovered."

"They don't think Ford did it?" Owen asked.

"Actually, they do," I said. "They're just doing their jobs. That's all. Don't take it any other way."

"Hard not to feel under the gun here."

"Do you know Betty Smithson?" I asked.

"Sure. Why?"

"I hear she was Kristi's friend from college."

Owen nodded. "She is. But she wouldn't have anything to do with this. She's a good girl. Very nice and definitely not a drug user. Big in her church." He kicked at the gravel. "Besides, she had to leave school. Her mom's sick. She ain't been around for a while."

"That's what we heard."

"Let me ask you," Ray said. "What about Robert and Kevin? Would they do this?"

"I don't much see how."

"Correct me if I'm wrong, but wasn't Kristi treated a little better by Tony than her brothers were?"

"No doubt there."

"So, could sibling rivalry be at work here?" Ray asked.

Owen sighed. "Could be. But I don't think so."

"Why's that?" I asked.

"My impression is that she protected her brothers. From Tony's wrath. They were always screwing up, but Kristi stood up for them.

Over and over. Calmed Tony down. I've seen it a few times over the years."

"I suspect that's true."

"Fact is, now that Kristi's gone, wouldn't surprise me none if Tony cut them loose. He only tolerated them for her sake. At least that was my take."

"I think you're in the majority there," I said. "But just so we're on the same page here, you don't think they would've done anything to harm her."

"I don't see that as possible." He took a deep breath and let it out slowly. "But I guess I could be wrong. My brain isn't exactly working well about now."

CHAPTER THIRTY-SEVEN

As SOON AS we entered the front door of the Monteleone, a dude stepped into our path. Stocky, Hispanic, dark menacing eyes, a scowl on his face.

"You the guys that leaned on Ragman this morning?" he asked.

"Who are you?" Ray asked

"Chapo. I work for Ju Ju."

"Congratulations."

Chapo's eyes narrowed. "I know you're the dudes." He jerked his head toward Pancake. "Couldn't be no one else like him around here."

Ray nodded. "Pancake is one of a kind."

Pancake took a step toward him. Chapo took a half a step back, tensing. Fists loose at his side.

"What are you?" Pancake asked. "The engraved invitation?"

Chapo stared at him for a beat. "Consider me your escort."

"To where?" I asked.

"Boss man wants a sit-down."

It's good to be popular. Most times. Not always. Suddenly it seemed that everybody wanted to talk to us.

"Why does Ju Ju want to chat with us?" I asked.

"He don't like folks making waves in his world."

"Where exactly is his world?" Ray asked.

"You're standing in it."

Ray smiled. "Truth is, we'd love to see your boss."

"Ain't far. Over in the Treme. Near Armstrong Park. Ten-minute walk."

"We'll drive."

Not waiting for a response, Ray exited through the front door to the sidewalk. We followed. Around the corner to the parking garage. The valet we had handed off Pancake's truck to was shuffling down the ramp.

Pancake raised a hand. "Sorry. Need my truck."

The young man stopped, jingled the keys in his hand. "No problem. Be right back."

He was and we climbed in. Chapo in back with me. He rubbed a hand over the leather.

"Nice ride."

"It functions," Pancake said. He spun left out of the entrance, stopping at the Royal Street intersection. "Where to?"

"Up here a few blocks." Chapo pointed to his right. "Then left on Saint Ann."

Five minutes later, we pulled up in front of Ju Ju's place. Looked nice. Yellow, white trim, flowers. Not exactly what I expected.

Inside, three girls lounged on a sofa, watching TV. Looked like a *Lucy* rerun. White, black, Hispanic. One of each. Attractive in a trashy sort of way. They paid little attention to us.

"Ju Ju likes pretty things," Chapo said, explaining the three young ladies.

Speaking of young, I wondered if any of them were street legal. "Looks like he has an entire charm bracelet," I said.

Chapo actually smiled at that.

In the kitchen, we picked up a skinny black dude, Stormy, according to Chapo, and then we were outside. Nice yard. Tree-shaded, lots of flowers. The kind of place where you expected kids to play. No kids, just a large black guy, white hair, sitting at a picnic table. Ju Ju, no doubt.

He closed the laptop before him and looked up. "Thanks for dropping by." He waved a hand toward the bench seat across from him. Ray and I sat. Pancake stood at the end of the table, arms folded over his chest. Chapo and Stormy loitered behind Ju Ju, trying to look serious and scary.

"So, what can we do for you?" Ray asked.

"A better question might be what I can do for you, Mr. Longly?"

"What might that be, Mr. Makin?"

I thought I caught a moment of surprise in Ju Ju's face. As if he hadn't expected Ray to know his real name. He covered it quickly and smiled.

"I know a bit about you," Ju Ju said. "Longly Investigations. Over in Gulf Shores. And this is your boy Jake, and he's your road grader. Pancake. Tommy Jeffers."

"You've done your homework," Ray said.

"Always do."

"So do we. Junior Makin, Junior. Aka Ju Ju. Smart enough to stay out of the drug trade, but you've carved yourself another niche in that world."

"Sounds like you've had a sit-down with Detective Doucet."

Ray shrugged, opening both palms toward him.

Ju Ju spread his own hands on the table. "Now that we got all the rooks, knights, and bishops positioned on the board, let's talk business."

Ray gave a quick nod. "Let's."

"I'm interested in your visit to Ragman. I think you can see why I can't have folks knocking my people around. Wouldn't look good."

"Actually, tossing," Pancake said. "I didn't really knock him any. Maybe a little love tap."

Ju Ju gave him a slight smile. Didn't look very sincere. More menacing, in fact.

"Ragman tells me you guys threatened him. Said you had some kind of badass hitters you could bring in."

"Not hitters," Ray said. "Ex-military. Special forces."

"I got my own soldiers," Ju Ju said. "Bunch of them."

"I'm sure you do."

Ju Ju smiled. Gave a slight nod as if to say, "you can bet on it."

"Truth is," Ray said. "Sure, I could bring folks in, but mostly I wanted to rattle Ragman's cage. He had a bit of an attitude and needed a jolt."

"A little attitude adjustment never hurts." Another smile. "But I don't think either of us wants to stroll down that bloody road."

Ray nodded. "You'd be right."

"Good. Good. Glad we got that settled." Ju Ju leaned back. The butt of a weapon appeared. Beneath his shirt, shoved down into the waist of his jeans. "I know you guys were hired by Kirk Ford, or the studios, whoever, to try to extract that boy from the mess he got hisself into."

"It is a mess," I said.

"And I assume you're trying to find someone else to pin it on?"

"If someone else did it," Ray said.

"You have doubts, I take it?"

"Everyone does. Doesn't look good for Ford. But we wouldn't be doing our job if we didn't look under all the rocks."

"And that's where our worlds collide, so to speak," Ju Ju said.

"How's that?" I asked.

"You're thinking that if you can connect the dots between the bump and Ford and Kristi Guidry, you just might stumble on someone who can supply that reasonable doubt you need to pull your boy's bacon out of the fire? Something like that?"

"If that's where it leads," Ray said.

"But to do that you've got to shake things up on the streets. My streets. That makes people nervous. Gives me headaches I got to deal with."

"Not to mention getting Tony Guidry's nose out of joint."

"That's never good for anyone," Ju Ju said.

"I take it you and Tony have some mutual interests?" Ray asked.

Ju Ju hesitated. "Tony and I go way back. Been friends a long time. As for any interest, that's between me and him."

"I understand. And those arrangements aren't my concern or interest."

"That's good. Better for everyone that way."

Ray nodded. "I take it you have a proposal?"

"I do."

"I'm listening."

"Let me do the sniffing. I have better contacts and can make fewer troubles."

"I suppose that's true."

"I'll do that. As a courtesy," Ju Ju said. "Sort of a welcome to my city."

"All we want is to find out where that shit came from," I said. "See if that trail leads us to someone who had a reason to drug a couple of people. And kill one them."

"And frame the other?" Ju Ju asked.

"Something like that," Ray said.

"Consider it done. I'll be in touch."

We had been dismissed. We left.

As we drove away, I asked Ray, "What do you think?"

"I think we just got warned away from snooping around."

"Ain't going to happen," Pancake offered.

"But do you think Ju Ju will help us?" I asked.

Ray shook his head. "Not a chance. It's just a smoke screen. I think the ketamine came from Ju Ju's world. Had to have. And he don't want any spotlights shined on his operation."

CHAPTER THIRTY-EIGHT

NICOLE AND I slept in the next morning. It had been a late night. Before heading over to K-Paul's for dinner, we had gathered in the Monteleone bar with Pancake, Sophie, and the twins. Ray had declined, opting for room service and doing some computer work. Kirk had also begged off, saying he was going to crash early.

Nicole did it again. As soon as the twins walked into the Carousel Bar and sat on the sofa opposite us, Nicole knew which was which. What really pissed me off is she wouldn't tell me how she knew. She can be such a bitch sometimes. All through drinks, lots of drinks, and dinner, I examined them. What did she see? Nose, ears, eyes? I even looked for freckles. Being so perfect, neither had any. What the hell was it? Made me crazy.

I woke before she did, flicked on the bedside lamp, and began reading my self-defense book. Got most of the next chapter covered before she rolled over, rubbed her eyes, and asked what time it was.

"Eight thirty."

She stretched. "My head feels like the Red Army marched through."

"They did."

She looked at me and blinked.

"You and the twins did a few Stoli shooters for dessert."

"I forgot. But I'm starting to remember." She suppressed a yawn. "I wonder how many brain cells I sacrificed last night."

"An army."

"Why didn't you stop me?"

"I'm only one man. How could I stop an entire army?"

She laughed. "Isn't there a chapter on that in your book?"

"I haven't gotten there yet."

"Read faster."

I closed the book and laid it on the bedside table. "So, tell me."

She propped up on her elbow. The covers fell way, revealing one breast. "Tell you what?"

"How you know which twin is which?"

"Not that again." She fell back on the pillow, pulling the covers up to her chin. "You asked me that a hundred times last night."

"And you wouldn't tell me."

"Still won't."

"Why?"

She rolled toward me. "Because I like messing with you."

"You are evil. You know that?"

"I work at it." She sat up. "Let's jump in the shower, and I'll show you evil."

How could I argue with that?

We did. She did. Wow.

Afterwards, I slipped on jeans, a tee shirt, and sandals, and while Nicole blow-dried her hair, I walked down the hall and rapped on Ray's door. He was on the computer. A room service tray sat beside the TV. Looked like the remnants of breakfast—eggs, bacon, and toast. Oh, and two empty Mountain Dew cans. Ray's usual breakfast.

"What's on the agenda today?" I asked.

"On the Kirk Ford situation? Not much. Pancake and I are going to sort through all the material we have on the fraud case over in Pensacola. Ton of papers to go through."

"Sounds like fun."

"I'm sure."

"What's your take on Kirk's ordeal?"

Ray shook his head. "The truth is that we don't have much. Unless something else pops up, I'm not sure we have a lot to offer."

I sighed. "Looks that way. And you don't see Ragman or Ju Ju being any help?"

"Doubt they'll even try. Why would they? I don't see them exposing any of their dealers or customers to outsiders. Why ask for trouble?"

I nodded.

"And if we can't find someone who has a connection to Ford or Kristi, someone who bought ketamine off the street, that'll be a dead end anyway."

"My take is that the folks Ragman told us about will be a big zero."

Ray rubbed his neck. "True. And they were likely all tourists, like he said, and his descriptions were so generic that there aren't any trails to follow."

"Frustrating."

"Some cases are just that way. Pancake is sniffing around Ju Ju's world. Trying to see if there is anyone else we should look at. But so far, nothing of interest there."

"Nicole and I are going out to the set. Unless you need us to do anything."

"Have fun." He pulled open the small fridge beneath the TV and grabbed another Dew. I left.

* * *

Nicole and I stood along the banks of the swamp and watched the scene unfold. Across the water where earlier the Yaktous' village had stood. It was more rubble than village now, the Korvath onslaught having done its damage. I felt sorry for the Yaktous. They seemed like nice people.

Kirk, shirtless, and the twins in their skimpy "uniforms," were scurrying among the flattened, shredded, and tilted huts, exchanging imaginary laser weapon fire with imaginary attackers. Looked pretty silly. I mean, adults in goofy outfits, firing plastic ray guns at, well, nothing. Moviemaking at its finest. The attackers and the red and green laser blasts would of course be digitally added back in LA and the whole thing would come to life. I was sure it would thrill every *Space Quest* fan.

"What the hell's going on over there?"

I turned to see Detective Doucet.

"Major battle," Nicole said. "Life and death stuff." She laughed.

"Sort of takes all the magic away when you see how it's done," he said.

"What brings you by?" I asked.

"Need to chat with Kirk Ford."

"Did something come up?" I asked.

"Oh, yeah."

"What?"

"I'll wait until I can sit with him."

"Sounds intriguing," Nicole said.

Doucet shrugged. "You might say that."

"Can you at least give us a hint?" I asked.

"Rather not." He looked across at the action. "How long until the battle's over?"

"Twenty minutes or so," Nicole said. "According to the schedule, anyway."

He nodded.

"Coffee?" I asked.

"Sure."

The caterers had just brewed a fresh pot so we grabbed cups and sat at one of the picnic tables. Small talk followed, but Doucet offered nothing. He kept glancing toward the ongoing battle, antsy written all over him. Like he wanted to get on with something that was eating at him. What could it be? Had to be important for him to drive out here and be so secretive. The suspense was much thicker than the intergalactic war Kirk was waging.

Thirty minutes later the crew and extras appeared, followed by Kirk and the twins. When Kirk saw Doucet, he slowed, surprise on his face. Or was it fear? Maybe that was too strong a word, but a healthy dose of concern for sure.

"Detective," he said. "What brings you out here?"

Doucet stood. "We need to talk."

"About what?"

Doucet looked around. "Somewhere else."

"My trailer."

We moved that way. Doucet stopped. "Alone."

"We need to hear this," I said.

"Not yet."

"I'd feel better if they did," Kirk said.

Doucet hesitated. "Okay. But no one else."

Once we settled inside the trailer, Doucet jumped right in.

"I need to ask you about the women on the set."

"What about them?"

"You have an issue with any of them?"

Kirk look perplexed. I was, too.

"What do you mean?" Kirk asked.

"Any problems. Any bad blood, as it were."

"No."

"Think carefully. Anyone you had a disagreement with? Anyone you slept with? Or dumped? Or pissed off? Or anything?"

Kirk now looked scared. "No one. This has been a very relaxed and friendly shoot."

"What about before? Any of them have a history with you?"

"No." He looked at me, Nicole, back to Doucet. "What are you asking?"

Doucet rubbed his chin. "From the beginning, I didn't think DNA would be part of this case. Even if your DNA was found under Kristi's fingernails, there could be several innocent explanations." He shrugged. "I was wrong."

"What are you talking about?" I asked.

"Got a call from the ME. There was tissue and DNA found under Kristi's nails. Under one, anyway." He looked at Kirk. "And it isn't yours."

"That's good? Right?" Kirk said.

Doucet shrugged.

"What does that mean?" Nicole asked.

"It means Kristi scratched someone else," Doucet said.

"Who? When?"

"The when is easy. The tissue was fresh. ME is sure of that. But the who is unknown."

"But it's not mine?" Kirk said.

"No. In fact, it's from a female."

"What?" I said.

"Yeah. That was more or less my reaction."

"At the risk of being redundant, what does that mean?" Nicole asked.

"It means that some unknown female was scratched by Kristi. Sometime that night."

My head was spinning. This was not what I expected. And from Doucet's expression, he hadn't either.

"So I must ask, you guys didn't have a threesome or anything like that?" Doucet asked.

"No. It was just the two of us."

Doucet nodded. "Apparently not." He straightened. "But as best as you can remember, no one else came in the room. Before you guys passed out? Room service? Housekeeping? Anything like that?"

"Like I said, after dinner we walked back to the hotel. Kristi and I, and Tara and Tegan. We had a glass of wine in the room, the twins left."

"Did you lock the door?"

"It does that automatically."

"I mean the dead bolt. Or the chain thing."

Kirk hesitated. He looked toward the ceiling, as if trying to recall the scene. "I can't remember." He shook his head. "I usually do, but I can't be sure."

"And no one else dropped by?" Doucet asked.

Kirk shook his head. "No one."

"Well someone did," Doucet said.

"I don't understand," I said. "What're you saying?"

"Someone accessed your room. Right about midnight."

"How do you know that?" Kirk asked.

"I didn't mention this before, but the computers log every entry into the rooms."

"And someone came in? While we were out cold?"

"Looks that way."

"Who?"

"That's the question, isn't it?" Doucet said.

"Housekeeping or maybe security?" I asked.

Doucet shook his head. "They also log what key was used. Wasn't the hotel staff. It was Kirk's key."

Kirk now looked confused. I completely understood that feeling.

"That doesn't make any sense," Kirk said. "My key was in the drawer. Where you found it. With my wallet."

Doucet sighed. "Guess it could've been cloned. Something like that."

"Not hard to do," I said. "If someone had the right tools and the know-how."

"This is good, right?" Nicole asked. "For Kirk?"

"Maybe. Juries decide what evidence means."

"But if someone else was involved, even possibly involved," I said, "that injects a certain degree of reasonable doubt. Right?"

"So it would seem."

"What now?" Kirk asked.

"We'll have to take DNA from any females with access to you and Kristi and your room. That kind of thing."

"That's why you asked about the women on the set?"

"And I'll ask again. Anyone we should look at?"

Kirk's gaze again lifted toward the ceiling, wheels turning for sure. He slowly shook his head. "I can't even imagine who." He looked at Doucet. "It had to be someone from the hotel."

"What's the next step?" I asked.

"I have a search warrant request before the judge right now. One that will cover every female on the crew and as yet unknown members of the hotel staff. But it would be much easier if all the cast and crew agreed up front."

"I'm sure they will," Kirk said. "Why wouldn't they?"

Doucet offered a grim smile. "Someone might have something to hide."

CHAPTER THIRTY-NINE

I HAD TO admit, Detective Troy Doucet was a pretty bright guy. And efficient. Several things happened that proved exactly that. He sat with Ebersole and generated a list of all the women involved in the production. He excluded the extras, mostly comprised of locals looking for a fleeting chance at stardom, since they had no access to Kirk's room. At least not any reasonable access. Not that he couldn't revisit that decision if things pointed that way, but right now he said it was best to narrow the focus. He did get a list of all the hired extras from Ebersole. Just in case.

That left nine, including the twins and Pancake's new friend Sophie the makeup artist, that were present the day of the murder. Eight were still on set, the ninth having headed back to LA the morning after the murder. Normally that would be suspicious, but the woman, an associate producer, was seventy-six and had had a hip replacement just six months earlier. Still not overly mobile, according to Ebersole. Not a good candidate for a strangulation murder. Still, Doucet said he'd ask her to submit a sample to the LAPD crime lab. Ebersole assured him she would gladly agree.

Doucet then arranged for a couple of techs from the crime lab to come to the set and gather the samples. Easier than having the women traipse over to the lab at the end of the shooting day.

While we waited, I called Ray, brought him up to date.

His response: "You've got to be kidding."

I heard Pancake mumble something in the background. Ray told him about the DNA. Pancake's response was loud and clear. "Well fuck me."

Seemed to be the consensus.

"Nicole and I'll hang around until the lab guys finish and then head your way," I said.

"Sounds good. Meanwhile, I'll call Kornblatt. Bring him up to speed. And maybe I'll reach out to Tony Guidry."

"Really? Why?"

"The DNA results might change his attitude. Take Kirk off the table. Maybe he'll be more forthcoming about where the ketamine might've come from."

"If he knows."

"I think what Tony doesn't know could dance on the head of a pin. And what he couldn't find out is even less."

"Makes sense."

"Later." Ray disconnected the call.

Took another forty-five minutes for the lab crew to arrive, so Ebersole used the time to film a couple of what he called "establishing shots" for the upcoming scenes. Then he shut things down and rounded up the women while the techs set up in one of the mostly empty equipment trailers. They laid out their gadgets and evidence bags on a metal table while one of the crew set up a director's chair for the women to sit on.

More proof of Doucet's smarts. The techs had arrived in an unmarked sedan, no crime scene truck, and they wore jeans and tee shirts, no lab coats or marked windbreakers or anything like that. They each carried black tackle boxes and looked like a pair of normal citizens, maybe repairmen. With the media and the gawkers gathered beyond the fence, the appearance of anything official would have headlined the evening news and erupted in the social media world. A headache Doucet didn't need.

Setting up in the trailer accomplished the same thing. Everything out of sight. Even from those huge lenses the media photographers lugged around.

The plan was to take photos, electronic fingerprints, and cheek swabs for DNA from each of the women. Nicole offered to go first, but Doucet pointed out she wasn't a suspect since she was in Alabama when the murder took place. She countered that she could send the sample to one of those ancestry outfits and check out her roots. He smiled, but declined, saying this was official business and if she wanted to shake her family tree she'd have to use one of the online services.

I didn't need DNA to know Nicole's family tree. I mean, just look at her. Her planet of origin was Venus. The goddess of love and beauty. Aphrodite to the Greeks. See, my education wasn't a total waste.

Tara went first. I knew it was her because she had changed into jeans and a green tee shirt that sported "Tara" in white script across the front. I loved it when they wore name tags. Kept the playing field level. Nicole still wouldn't tell me how she could tell one from the other. When I mentioned that she wasn't playing fair, she mussed my hair and said, "It's what we girls do."

Tara sat in the director's chair, smiled for the camera, pressed her finger pads to the electronic recorder, and opened her mouth for the gloved tech to gather the DNA swab. When she finished, Sophie took her place.

"Where's Tegan?" I asked.

"In our trailer. Changing. Probably redoing her makeup. I swear, she can primp more than anyone I know." A shake of her head. "I'll go get her."

Nicole checked her watch, said she needed to call her uncle, let him know the news on the DNA.

"That'll make his day."

"Sure will." She stepped down from the trailer and looked back up at me. "Want me to grab some coffee after I finish?"

"That would be great," I said.

"Mind getting some for me?" Doucet said.

"Will do."

I watched as she walked toward the catering area, punching numbers into her cell phone.

Venus. Definitely Venus.

By the time the other women had been photographed and sampled, the twins returned. Tegan jumped in the chair. She wore a blue tee shirt with her name in identical white script as her sister on the front. Her photo was snapped, DNA taken, and then the tech pulled out the handheld fingerprint device.

"Let's get this and we're done," the tech said.

Tegan looked at her hands. "I'm so stupid. I put on some moisturizer and my hands are all greasy. I don't want to gunk up your gadget. Let me go wash them." She started to get up.

The tech smiled. "No problem. I have some wipes that'll clean off anything."

"It's no problem," Tegan said.

"Here you go." He produced a flat white pack from his tackle box and tore it open. "This'll do it."

He wiped off each of her fingers and took the prints. "See? Easy."

While the lab techs packed up the samples and their equipment, Ebersole and the twins left, heading toward the canopy where Kirk sat looking over script pages.

Nicole returned with the coffees.

"How did Uncle Charles take the news?" I asked.

"How do you think? I thought he might cry." She smiled. "Well, maybe not cry. But thrilled didn't exactly cover it."

We, and Doucet, walked the techs to their car, Doucet thanking them, and we watched as they drove through the guard gate.

"Now we wait," Doucet said.

"How long?" I asked.

"The lab's going to rush it. We should have preliminary reports sometime tomorrow."

"And then?" Nicole asked.

"Depends on what's found, of course." He glanced back toward the set where things were returning to normal and Ebersole was busy setting up the afternoon's takes. "But I'm not optimistic."

"Why?" I asked.

"I watched each of the women carefully. While they were tested. I didn't see a guilty face in the bunch." He shrugged. "Of course, they're all in the movie business. Probably good at acting. So who knows? Maybe, we'll get lucky."

Kirk Ford could use some luck.

CHAPTER FORTY

Tony Guidry sat on the edge of the bed in his room at Maison Maralee. Mostly, anyway. He couldn't stay still, repeatedly jumping up, pacing, only to sit again, one foot tapping the carpet in time with his elevated heart rate. He couldn't get his head around what his guy at the ME's office had said. An hour ago. Called him on his cell. Spoke quietly, quickly, his voice muffled as if he had one hand shielding his words from any eavesdroppers.

What he had said made no sense. DNA from some chick? Who? And why not Kirk Ford? What did it really mean?

Tony had immediately texted Melissa Mooring. On the iPhone he had given her. His private line to her. The way they kept everything between them off the radar. Told her to meet him here. She had texted back she'd break free in a half hour.

So he waited.

He walked to the window, pulled back the curtain, and gazed at the pond and the flowers—and nothing. He couldn't focus on anything. Except the fact that the crime lab hadn't found Kirk Ford's DNA beneath Kristi's nails. He was sure they would. Sure that would be the evidence that sealed Ford's fate once and for all. Hard to discount DNA in the little bits of tissue Kristi had managed to rip from her attacker as she died. Her last chance to point her finger, so to speak, at the animal who strangled her life away. At least he knew that's how Melissa would spin it.

But now the tissue, the DNA, didn't come from Kirk Ford. How was that even possible? He glanced at his watch. Where was Melissa? She understood all this DNA stuff.

He began to pace back and forth between the window and the entry door. Was he overreacting? Making too much of this unexpected news? Maybe the case against Ford was still solid. Could this be explained away? Perhaps excluded from the trial? Melissa Mooring was tough and smart. She knew the rhythm of the court. It wasn't like she hadn't suppressed damaging evidence before. He could think of several offhand. Just last year she had gotten one of Ju Ju's guys off by showing that the cops had seized two kilos of coke from his car trunk illegally. That wasn't actually true, but she managed to contort the facts in such a way that the judge finally agreed with her and disallowed the evidence. The case evaporated.

Could she do that here?

And if she did, what would that mean? Kirk would take the fall for something he just might not have done. Was that what he really wanted? The case closed? No, that would mean Kristi's killer was out there, something he simply couldn't abide.

More to the point, if Ford hadn't killed Kristi, that would mean he'd been looking in the wrong direction. That he had been duped. Made the fool. Damn it, he hated this shit. To read things the wrong way, be so sure, and then have things spin off in some new direction. Didn't happen often. He prided himself on being the guy who knew all, who had the inside track. He'd built his entire empire on exactly that. Knowledge. Facts that others didn't have.

Things like that a certain area was being examined for development, so he could quietly buy parcels through one of his shell companies. That the city nabobs were planning some new laws, or rules and regs, so he could alter his businesses before anyone else. Take advantage. That the cops were focusing on a certain street or corner, so he could have Ju Ju move his dealers to new locations. Temporarily, of course. Such focus never lasted more than a few days, a week tops. Then all could return to normal.

But this? Shit.

And worse, hadn't he already put the machine in motion? The one that would take Ford off the board if the courts didn't? And now, if Ford came out of this innocent, truly innocent, where would he be? What would it look like? He knew the answer. Tony Guidry wasn't infallible, no longer on top of his game. Old Tony's reach into the cops and courts was defective. He would be seen as vulnerable.

Vulnerable.

Such a dirty and dangerous word. Not a good position in his world. It made people ambitious. Made people talk, and plan, and scheme.

He dropped back down on the bed, hunched forward, elbows on his knees, fingers trying to massage away the throbbing headache that rose in his temples. The door swung open. He looked up.

"I got here as fast as I could," Melissa said.

"Is this as bad as it seems?"

She dropped her purse in the chair and then sat next to him on the bed. "Maybe."

Maybe was better than yes. Maybe meant she might have a trick or two in mind.

"Maybe? Doesn't this blow the entire case?"

"I admit it complicates things. Definitely introduces reasonable doubt. But Ford was in the room. As far as we know, it was only he and Kristi in that room."

"Except someone opened the door around midnight."

"True. My plan was to write that off as one of them going to get ice."

"Did they?"

"No way to prove if they did or didn't. Kirk remembers nothing and Kristi—"

"Kristi's dead."

She sighed. "But there was water in the ice bucket. Like it had had ice in it that had melted. And it's reasonable to assume that if Kirk had gone down the hall to the ice machine, he would have taken his room key with him."

"Or someone else had a key."

"Only one was issued."

"The staff would have access," Tony said.

"Yes, but those are different keys. Different codes."

"The hotel tracks all that?"

"Sure do. The computers log every entry and register what key was used. The midnight entry was with Ford's key. And his key was found by the cops in his room, exactly where he said it would be."

"So no one stole it?"

"Possible. But that would require getting into the room without a key card in the first place. If that was doable, why would the killer need Kirk Ford's card?"

Tony nodded slowly. "My problem is that I think this takes a lot of the spotlight off Ford and casts it somewhere else." She started to speak but he stopped her with a wave of his hand. "I was so sure the killer was Ford. I wanted him up the river for life. But what if he didn't do it? What if you convict him, but he's not the right person?"

"We prosecutors don't think that way. Our job is to present the evidence for the state and attempt to get a conviction."

"I know how the game works. But for me, if you nail the wrong person, Kristi's killer is still out there. Breathing the same air I breathe." He took her hand. "That simply cannot happen."

"So, what? You want me to drop the charges?"

"No. That's not what I'm saying. In fact, it's best if everything stays as is. The focus on him." He looked at her. "I assume this new evidence won't be made public?"

"Not officially. But things like this do leak."

"Hopefully not for a few days. Not until I get my people sniffing around and uncover who really did this."

"Tony, don't you think you should lay low on this? Let Detective Doucet do the sniffing?"

"Probably." He offered a weak smile. "But I can't."

"I know. And I understand." She rubbed his thigh with one hand. "But as long as we're here, I imagine you could use a little stress release." She smiled.

"As could you."

"No doubt." She stood and began unbuttoning her blouse.

"Let me make a call first." Tony picked up his cell from the bedside table and scrolled through his contacts, found what he wanted, and pressed the number. Ray Longly answered after only one ring.

"This is Tony Guidry. We need to talk."

"You must be reading my mind," Ray said. "I was just getting ready to call you and say the same thing."

"Seven thirty. Dickie Brennan's over on Iberville. I'll grab a private room there. The Champagne Room."

"Will do."

When he hung up, Melissa, now down to only panties, walked over and pressed her tight abdomen against his face, her fingers sliding through his hair.

CHAPTER FORTY-ONE

"Tony Guidry?" Nicole asked. "He wants to have a chat?"

"Actually, dinner."

"You're kidding."

"It's what Ray said."

We were in our room at the Monteleone, lying on the bed. Ray had just called and told me about the meet and greet that evening. I had been reading from my self-defense book, getting more dangerous by the day. This chapter definitely so. Dealt with how to kill or severely incapacitate someone with various blows to the throat. Even the diagrams were gruesome. I had told Nicole that, showed her the line drawings. She said I was a wimp and went back to watching HGTV where a couple was remodeling a house.

She muted the TV. "Why would he want to talk with us?"

She rolled toward me and propped up on one elbow. I wore cotton drawstring pants, no shirt; Nicole, one of my tee shirts that rode up as she turned, revealing a nearly nonexistent black thong.

Now, where was I? Oh yeah. Kirk, DNA, Tony.

"I guess the DNA results have him rattled," I said. "I mean, to me, it seemed he was dead-solid sure Kirk was the one that killed Kristi."

"He wasn't alone in that assumption."

"You?" I asked.

"I'd be lying if I said I didn't have some doubts, but no, not really. My gut tells me he didn't do it."

"Not to mention the gypsy woman," I said.

She punched my ribs. Hard.

"Hey, I was just—" I couldn't come up with the right words. Then I did. "Pulling your leg."

"I know what you were doing."

"And I do love doing that."

"What? Giving me shit?"

"No. Doing stuff with your legs."

"Stuff?"

"Maybe that's not the right word."

She laughed. "But it's the sentiment that counts." She nestled in the crook of my arm. "What time's the dinner meeting?"

"Seven thirty."

"That means we have some down time." She ran her hand across my abdomen, lower. "Or up time."

Lord, I love the way she thinks. The book outran gravity on its way to the floor. She rolled on top of me.

"Pancake didn't need to give you that bat," she said with a laugh. "You already have one."

"Shut up and do me."

"Do you?" She sat up, straddling me. "You are such a pig."

"Sorry."

"Don't be. It's cute on you."

Thirty minutes later, we lay there trying to catch our breath.

"You're kind of fun," Nicole said. "Maybe I'll keep you."

"Funny."

She rolled away from me and stretched, her body all naked and perfect. "Maybe I'll jump in the shower and then get dolled up."

"You're dolled up right now."

"I think if I went this way, I'd be a distraction."

"You will be anyway."

"Isn't that part of my job? Distract the bad guys while Ray fillets them?"

I gave her a look. "You're getting dangerous."

She slid off the bed, picked up my book from the floor, and handed it to me. "Here. Try to catch up."

"Bitch."

"Pig."

And with that she disappeared into the bathroom.

By six o'clock we were ready to go. I decided on tan slacks, white golf shirt, and a black sports coat. Nicole a plain black dress that was far from plain on her. Low-cut and short, only reaching mid-thigh, exposing those legs. Lean, mean, athletic, and perfect. Her hair was pulled back and bound into a ponytail by a polished gold clasp that matched her hoop earrings. Lipstick pink. To match her new nail color, she said.

We headed toward the bar. While we waited for the elevator, I called Ray and said we'd meet him and Pancake there.

I had hoped for a seat at the Carousel Bar, but, as usual, it was filled. I still hadn't ridden it. We moved past and saw the twins at one of the two-tops along the windows that looked out on Royal.

"How was the rest of the day?" Nicole asked as we approached.

"Good. We're back on schedule and have a short day tomorrow," one of them said.

Unfortunately, they weren't wearing their named tee shirts, both now in jeans and dark green silk blouses.

"Want to join us for a drink?" Nicole asked, motioning to the vacant sofa and chairs nearby.

"Sure," the other twin said. They grabbed their wine glasses, and we settled around the pair of thick glass coffee tables. Nicole and I on the sofa, the twins flanking us in chairs.

"That's Tara," Nicole said, nodding toward the twin to our left.

"You can tell?" Tara asked, glancing at her sister.

"Sometimes. Depends on the light."

"Wow," Tegan said. "You're like maybe the third or fourth person ever."

Nicole shrugged.

"She won't tell me how," I said.

Nicole laughed. "It's on a need-to-know basis."

Tara laughed, too. "Love a girl who can keep a secret." She raised her wine glass to Nicole.

"It's not fair," I said. "I want to join the club."

Nicole mussed my hair. "No boys allowed."

They all laughed. I didn't. But I did plaster on a fake pout.

The waitress appeared and we ordered. Me, a Blantons on the rocks; Nicole, red wine. The twins, another round of dirty martinis.

"That was pretty crazy today," Tegan said. "All that techie stuff."

"It wasn't bad, though," Tara said. "And maybe it'll help find the real killer." She looked at her sister. "And get Kirk off the hook."

"Will it do that?" Tegan asked. "Get him out of this mess?"

"Maybe," I said. "It does create reasonable doubt. But whether a jury sees it that way or not is anybody's guess."

"Let me ask you girls this," Nicole said. "You know Kirk about as well as anyone after all these years. Is there anyone out there you think would hold a grudge strong enough to do this? To set him up?"

"Or Kristi?" Tegan said. "Couldn't it be her that was the target?"

"I thought so," I said. "That she might be the one that brought all this down. But, the one thing I couldn't get around was, if that's the case, why do it in a hotel room? A movie star's room? Seems very risky to me. If she was the target, it seems that some other location would be easier. Such as at her apartment or on the street." I shrugged. "Not to mention I'm not sure anyone around these parts would have the *huevos* to kill Tony Guidry's niece. Seems to me that would be a suicide mission."

Nicole looked at me. "But if somebody gave her a loaded joint, doesn't that play into this?"

"Unless they thought she'd do it at home," I said. "Make sneaking in much easier if she was out of it and alone, rather than in a hotel room."

Nicole nodded. "That makes sense."

"Of course it does." I smiled. "I'm very clever that way."

"Jake, even a blind dog finds a bone every now and then."

I shook my head. "That sentiment aside, in the end, Kirk being the bad guy is still in play. I can suspect that Assistant DA Mooring is already working how to spin this. Maybe even get it tossed by the judge."

"True," Nicole said, "but back to my question. Anyone you can think of?"

The twins exchanged a glance, then Tara said, "We love Kirk to death. But we also know he's a player."

"Big-time," Tegan added.

"Meaning?" I asked.

"He hasn't always been the nicest guy," Tara said. "He picks up women all the time. And I mean all the time. He has a brief fling and then they're gone."

"And he's not the kindest person I know at breaking up," Tegan said. "More than once, it's been a text or a voice message."

"Or nothing," Tara said. "He just doesn't call. Or answer calls."

"You dated him once, didn't you?" Tegan asked Nicole. "What's your take on him?"

Nicole shrugged. "I wouldn't say we dated. We went out a couple of times." She glanced at me. "Nothing physical. We were friends who went to dinner a couple of times. A party once. That's it."

"You were lucky, I guess," Tegan said.

"Truth is he wasn't my type. I knew he was into hit and run. One-night stands. That sort of thing. And we had no real chemistry anyway." She smiled. "Besides, a girl doesn't want to go out with a guy that's prettier than she is."

"What?" Tara said. "You're beautiful."

Nicole laughed. "But he's more so."

"Not to me," I said.

"Are you trying to get in my pants?" Nicole asked.

"Again?"

That got a laugh from everyone.

"Wasn't there an old actor that had that rap? Big-name actresses wouldn't work with him because he was so good-looking?"

"John Derek," Nicole said. "That was the rumor anyway. He sure was hot as Joshua in *The Ten Commandments*."

"But he did marry Ursula Andress, Linda Evans, and Bo," I said. "So there is that."

"Look," Tara said. "Kirk has pissed off a lot of women over the years. I'm sure the list of those who wanted to strangle him is long."

"Are any of them here?" I asked. "In New Orleans? On this shoot?"

The twins looked at each other as if trying to recall.

Tegan shook her head. "No, I don't think he's hooked up with anyone on this set."

"And we would know," Tara added. "He never tried to hide his escapades. That's for sure."

"So just Kristi?" I said. "No one else?"

The twins nodded in unison.

CHAPTER FORTY-TWO

THERE ARE MANY great restaurants in New Orleans, and Dickie Brennan's is among the best. So I'd heard. Never been there. The hostess led us past the bar, through the main dining room, and into the Champagne Room. Nice. Classy. The far wall, where Tony Guidry stood, was an enclosed wine cabinet. He was examining a bottle when we entered. He replaced it in its bin and turned to greet us, walking around the table to shake hands. And, of course, peck a kiss on the back of Nicole's hand. A true gentleman.

Then we sat. Pancake, Nicole, and I along one side of the rectangular table; Tony's muscle, Reuben Prejean and Johnny Hebert, across from us. Tony sat at one end, Ray the other, facing each other. Sort of like an old west duel. I was sure Reuben and Johnny were armed and that Ray wasn't. Didn't know about Tony. Me? I had neither bat nor balls, but I had read a couple of more chapters in my self-defense book today. Didn't see anything about how to handle someone with a Glock.

Tony made it clear from the jump that this was his treat, his show. Total power play, but Ray nodded and thanked him for inviting us. A sommelier appeared and, with great flourish and expertise, opened two bottles of wine. Red, probably expensive.

"I took the liberty of ordering wine," Tony said. "I hope that's okay."

"It is," Ray said.

The meal that followed was magnificent, the talk carefully small. Tony proved to be an expert of sorts on New Orleans history and told tales of the founding of the city, Jean Lafitte, Andrew Jackson, the Battle of New Orleans, and even the Louisiana Purchase. He went into great detail on the effects of Yellow Fever on the city. According to Tony, it took over 40,000 lives in the 17th century, including nearly 8,000 in the great 1853 epidemic alone. He talked of the mob control of Bourbon Street and surroundings under Carlos Marcello who held sway from the 1940s until his grip was loosened in the 1970s. I noticed he avoided discussing the Dixie Mafia. But overall, I was impressed with his knowledge of essentially everything New Orleans. And he was a great storyteller. I wasn't sure who he was trying to impress the most, Ray or Nicole—that dress, that face did make her the center of attention—but the undercurrent was clear. This was Tony's town. He knew everything about, and by extension controlled, the Quarter.

When I first saw him at the courthouse, Tony looked almost bigger than life. Godfatherish. Was that a word? But here, with Pancake sitting just to his right, he seemed much smaller. Less intimidating. But then Pancake had that effect. Still, Tony was large and in charge.

After dessert and after a round of Louis the XIII cognac was poured—which I had never had because it runs well over $100 a shot—Tony got down to business.

He looked at Ray. "What do you make of this new DNA evidence?"

Ray shrugged. "Not sure what to think. Definitely not what I expected."

"Do you think Kirk Ford did this?"

"I did."

"*Did* sounds past tense," Tony said. He took a sip of cognac.

"Closed room. Two people. A logical conclusion to think he was the guy." Ray folded his hands before him. "But this might change things. Don't you think?"

"Maybe." He hesitated. "Could be the DNA had been there for a day or more."

"The ME doesn't think so," I said.

Tony opened his hands. "An opinion. Doesn't mean it wasn't."

"But you don't believe that," Ray said. "Otherwise I don't think we'd be here."

Tony took a deep breath and exhaled slowly, puffing out his cheeks. "I admit I was sure, absolutely sure, Ford was the killer. But now? I'm not so sure."

"That's refreshing to hear," Ray said. "I feared you might have tunnel vision on this."

Tony shrugged. "Hard not to under the circumstances. But with this new evidence, I must admit, it doesn't seem so clear now."

"What about the prosecutor?" I asked. "What does she think?"

"I don't know."

"You know her," Ray said. He let that sit for a beat. "Haven't you talked with her about it?"

"Not yet. But I will."

He was lying. I saw it in his eyes. I was sure that his first call after he learned of the DNA was to her. Hadn't she, with a single glance and his permissive nod in the courtroom, essentially secured his permission to allow Kirk's bail to go through? No way he hadn't contacted her.

This also showed Tony's reach. The only way he could have found out about the evidence so quickly would be if he had people inside the police, the crime lab, even the ME's office. No surprise. The surprise would be if he didn't. I did wonder if he had received the information from Assistant DA Melissa Mooring herself.

"I suspect she'll say it piles a bit of reasonable doubt on Kirk's side of the table," Pancake said.

Tony nodded. "True."

"Then who?" Ray asked. "If not Kirk, who?"

"That I'd like to know," Tony said. "Let's say this evidence does indeed point to someone else. To a woman. Is there anyone in Kirk's world, anyone involved with this movie, that jumps up on your suspect radar?"

"Does this mean you think the killer might be someone trying to frame Kirk?" Ray asked.

"That's a possibility," Tony said. "One that'll have to be considered."

"We asked Kirk about that," I said. "Nicole and I, and Detective Doucet. He said he had no issues with anyone in this crew."

"That was confirmed by Tara and Tegan James," Nicole added. "They probably know Kirk better than anyone and they agreed."

"But he did collect DNA from all the women involved with the film," Tony said.

Yes, Tony's reach was deep.

"Detective Doucet said he wasn't optimistic," I said.

"Really?" Tony asked.

"He watched the women being tested. Said he didn't see anyone with guilty stamped on them."

Tony nodded. "Many of them are actresses, I assume?"

"Besides the twins, maybe a couple," Nicole said. "Most are makeup artists, script girls, and a pair of producer types."

"Regardless, Doucet said we'd have results tomorrow," I said. "Preliminary ones, anyway. Maybe we'll know something then."

"Or not," Ray said. He nodded toward Tony. "Let me ask you this. You knew Kristi. Is there anyone around her that would or could do this?"

Tony sighed. "Believe it or not, I've asked myself that question many times over the past few days. Even though I was, and more or less still am, convinced that Ford is the guilty party here, I had to at least consider other possibilities."

Interesting.

Tony continued. "I came up empty. I mean, Owen would be a consideration, but I don't see him as a viable possibility. He's a good guy. Decent. And he truly loved Kristi. I've sniffed around her friends in college, the folks she worked with over at Café du Monde. No one looked good for it."

"So, where does that leave us?" Nicole asked.

"If the DNA comes up a bust," Ray said, "I think the key will be to uncover who gave Kristi that kicked-up joint." Tony started to say something, but Ray waved him away. "I know. It could have come from Kirk. But, I don't think so."

"What makes you think that?" Tony asked.

"The cops did find several joints. A couple Kirk had, and he said Kristi brought the one they smoked."

"He would, of course, say that," Tony said.

"True," Ray said. "But it's the details that make me believe him. Kirk said he couldn't roll a joint to save his life. Loose was how he put it. Tended to fall apart. The one they did smoke was rolled by someone who knew what they were doing. According to Doucet, that's what it looked like."

Tony's shoulders sagged a little. Not much, but some.

"That leaves us with a problem," Ray said. "And why I wanted to talk with you. Any idea where Kristi would have gotten this?"

"If she did," Tony said.

"If she did," Ray conceded.

"I don't know."

"Look," Ray said. "Let's don't tap-dance here. Okay? We both know little goes on in that world that you don't know. Or couldn't find out." Tony stared at him, face flat, giving away nothing. The consummate poker player. "You know we talked to Ju Ju and Ragman—there's a piece of work. And they both said they knew nothing. My question to you is, are they shooting straight here?"

Tony hesitated then said, "I've had a chat with them, too. They told me the same thing. I'm inclined to believe them."

"Completely?"

Tony smiled. A half smile anyway. "Mostly."

"There you have it," Ray said. "The question is, will you help us find out who the seller was?"

Tony shrugged. "Sure."

"Then what?"

"What do you mean?"

"We know a great deal about you," Ray said. "That you take care of business. To your credit. But here, I don't want to track down someone and then have something happen to them. Outside the courts, that is."

Tony raised an eyebrow. "You mean like floating down the Mississippi?"

"Something like that."

"Life is funny, isn't it? Folks stumble and fall all the time. Nothing is guaranteed. Not even someone's next breath."

"Look," Ray said. "This is your domain. Your world. But it's mine, too. Dark alleys never bothered me."

Now, Tony smiled. "I know about you, too. I'd say we aren't all that different. Aren't strangers to dark passages. To the sordid corners of the human mind. I refer to several things, but mostly that little deal near Kandahar a few years back."

Ray shrugged. "So, we understand each other?"

Tony leaned back in his chair. "We do."

What the hell was that about? I knew Ray had done some tours in the Mideast. Back when he was involved in the spook world. He never talked about it, saying generic things like he was merely a consultant, but I had always had my doubts. I don't know why. Maybe it was the way he avoided that period of his life. Maybe it was because I knew Ray all too well.

CHAPTER FORTY-THREE

"WE SHOULD'VE TALKED about this long ago," Ray said.

We were huddled around a table in the corner of the Carousel Bar. The place was noisy, which made good cover, but required each of us to lean forward to hear Ray.

"Truth is I never wanted to. Wanted to put it all in the archives. Not to mention, much of it I can't talk about anyway." He took a slug of his Knob Creek bourbon, swirled it in his mouth, and swallowed. "None of this leaves this table. Clear?"

I nodded, as did Pancake and Nicole.

"Back then, I was attached to a special operations group with the Pentagon. It will forever remain nameless. From me, anyway. But we carried out black ops. Mostly I was a consultant, just as I've always said. But sometimes, I took on a more operational role. It might be simply dead-of-the-night intel gathering. Or disrupting communication or support centers."

"Like blowing shit up?" Pancake asked.

"Sometimes." Another hit of bourbon.

Our waitress reappeared. Another round was ordered.

"Other times it was more personal," Ray said. He cradled his nearly empty glass in his hands. He glanced around, either checking for curious ears or buying time. I couldn't be sure, but I sensed he wasn't comfortable with any of this. "Maybe a local warlord needed neutral-izing. Maybe an IED team needed to be taken off the board. Maybe a certain so-called mosque needed to evaporate. Our missions took many forms."

"Who is the *our*?" I asked

The waitress returned, placing bourbon before Ray, Pancake, and me and another wine before Nicole. "Anything else?"

"We're good," Pancake said.

"The team varied," Ray said. "Sometimes a Marine platoon or some SEALs or Delta guys. Whatever assets were needed."

Assets. What an innocuous term. Ray an asset. This was all news to me. That Ray had been involved in covert ops at this level. As an operative. It didn't surprise me, yet it did. I was seeing him in an en-tirely new light. Not necessarily a bad one, just different. I had always regarded him as warrior of sorts, but this was different. He was ba-sically saying he had been involved in assassinations. And more. It was weird. I felt a sense of pride to be his son. Not sure why, but the feeling was undeniable.

"So, what was Tony referring to?" I asked. "Kandahar?"

Ray pinched his nose between his eyes, then scanned the area again, before leaning forward. His voice dropped a few decibels. "This ab-solutely goes nowhere else. A Marine sniper, two SEALs, a Delta Force op, and I were flown into a hot zone in the city. Maybe a half mile from where the Marines had wrested control from the bad guys. We came in on one of those super quiet copters. All stealth, all dark. Remember Megan Willis? It was her boat we used to attack Barkov's yacht and pluck you two out of the Gulf."

"We remember," Nicole said.

"She was the pilot on the mission. She dropped us near an aban-doned soccer field in the city and then extracted us from the desert after the mission was completed."

"She flew combat missions?" Nicole asked.

"Many times."

"Wow, that's amazing."

"Megan was all that and more. She could stand her craft on its nose if need be." He took a sip of bourbon. "The mission was to neutralize a mullah and his war dogs. The kind of op no one ever talks about."

"A mullah?" I asked. "You killed a mullah?"

"He was that in name only. He was a bigwig in the Taliban. A commander way up the food chain. And a weapons maker. Mostly IEDs. Big ones. Ones that killed and maimed a lot of Marines over the years. Took a year to locate him. He was hunkered down in a mosque." Another sip. "I use that term loosely. Those guys would name anything a mosque, knowing we considered them off-limits for airstrikes. This was simply a house. With a basement filled with explosives and people working round the clock to churn out IEDs." Again, he scanned the area. "He and eight of his guys were down below. I guess they thought they were safe because they never saw us coming. I remember the thump as one of the SEALs popped the door with a well-placed explosive and then we were through the door." He sighed. "I'll tell you, there is nothing more disconcerting than a bunch of bullets flying around a room filled with explosives. I expected the world to go up in a big fireball at any minute. Our weapons were silenced, of course, each making that soft spitting sound. I was a pretty good shot back then, but these SEALs and the Delta guy were even better. Seemed with every shot a bad guy's head snapped back and he was down. Took about twenty seconds, seemed like an hour, and we were alone. No one else breathing. The silence, the stillness was startling. Like we had suddenly been dropped into a vacuum.

"We set charges and humped it out of there. We were three blocks away, creeping down an alley, when the Fourth of July went off. Shook the ground with explosion after explosion. The sky looked like noon had arrived. Then all hell broke loose. Taliban guys were everywhere. Don't know how many others we took out before we reached the open desert and scrambled down a ravine. Nearly a mile of dead-out running and then Megan swooped in and we were gone. Without a scratch." Ray drained his glass, placed it on the table, and leaned back in his chair. "So, there you have it."

He looked tired, older, even war weary. But I also sensed that a great weight had been lifted from him. As if this was a story he had wanted to tell for years. Needed to tell someone. Even if it meant breaking a handful of federal laws. I felt closer to him than I had since I was suiting up for Little League baseball.

"This is obviously all classified," I said.

"Very."

"How did Tony Guidry know about it?"

Ray smiled. "Not sure he did. Not the details anyway. I suspect he knows someone who knows someone and he discovered I had done a few undercover ops and maybe knew my name was connected to something in Kandahar. My guess is he was fishing. And making a power play. Acting like he knew more than he did. For Tony, the mantle of knowledge and power are necessary illusions in his world."

I considered that for minute and decided that Ray was probably right on in his assessment. "Do you think he'll be of any help here?"

"Not really. Not unless it's in his best interest."

I cupped my glass in my hands, stared down into the amber liquid, running a thumb back and forth along the lip. "Do you think his plan was to kill Kirk if the courts let him off?"

"I do."

"And if we find out it's someone else?" I asked.

Ray stared at me for a beat. "I think Tony hoped the courts would take care of things. Probably didn't want to intervene. I mean, Kirk is an international star. Anything happened to him after he walked would be a media shit storm and the blowback could be huge."

"But he would have anyway?" Nicole asked.

"Probably. For Tony, this is personal. And about power. If someone got off with killing his niece, it might not sit well. Might loosen his grip. Maybe offing Kirk would be the lesser of two evils. For him, anyway."

"And now it looks like someone else is the killer," Pancake said. "How does that change his equation?"

"I think with Kirk off the table, if it turns out it's someone who had it in for Kristi, he'll walk through the fires of hell to take care of business."

"So, he might cooperate with us, and Doucet, until the killer is found?" I said. "Then what?"

"He'll do what he does. Fix it."

CHAPTER FORTY-FOUR

THE NEXT DAY we decided to hook up with Detective Doucet at the Acme Oyster Bar on Iberville, around the corner from the Monteleone. Ray, Pancake, and I, anyway. Nicole had gone out to the shooting site with Ebersole, Kirk, and the twins. Acme was packed, as usual. Also, as usual, a long waiting line extended down the sidewalk. We had just beaten the crowds and were near the front, only two groups of four ahead. Five minutes later, we were escorted to a four-top near the back. As we took our seats, Ray's cell buzzed. Doucet, saying he'd be a few minutes late.

We ordered. Ray and I, gumbo and iced tea; Pancake, an oyster po'boy, fries, and iced tea. And gumbo. And a shrimp cocktail. Our tea arrived before I could unfold a napkin.

"What did Doucet say?" I asked Ray.

"He was at the ME's office. Going over the DNA with the lab guy."

"And?"

"And nothing. Said he'd tell us about it when he got here." He took a gulp of tea. "But he didn't sound overly excited. I'd suspect he came up with nada."

"Not unexpected," Pancake said. "I agree with Doucet. I didn't read any of the women out there as murderers. Or as enemies of Kirk." He played with a pack of sugar, flipping it back and forth across the table with his index fingers. Sort of like sugar hockey. Sort of like a big kid. "In fact, just the opposite. Everyone seems to love the guy."

"Somebody doesn't," Ray said. "Maybe not part of the crew, but somewhere in this city Kirk has a mortal enemy."

"Or Kristi did," I said.

Ray nodded. "Or Kristi."

The food arrived and we dug in. The gumbo was perfect. Thick and the right amount of spice. Pancake added a large dose of Tabasco to his and then it disappeared quickly. He moved to his shrimp cocktail, the po'boy waiting at his left elbow.

Doucet arrived as our waitress was refilling our teas. He ordered gumbo, too.

"What's the story?" Ray asked.

"Dead end. The lab did a great job rushing the DNA for us, but they found squat. The twins of course matched each other, but none of the samples matched what was found beneath Kristi Guidry's fingernails."

"That means we have to look outside the film crew," I said.

Doucet nodded. "Looks that way."

His gumbo arrived. He stirred the rice and the soup together and took a bite. Pancake tore into his po'boy. Literally.

"Any new ideas?" I asked.

Doucet took another spoonful of gumbo, dabbed his mouth with a napkin, and shook his head. "Nothing to shout about. We're still looking into Kristi's life. Friends and really anyone who knew her. So far, no one looks good for this."

Ray pushed his empty bowl away. A busboy immediately snatched it up. Ray then told Doucet about our dinner with Tony last night.

Doucet stared at him. "Tony Guidry and you guys sat down for a friendly dinner?"

"Friendly might be pushing it," Ray said. "But we did have a long chat."

"And?"

"My read is that Tony wanted to know what we knew. Maybe even get in our good graces so we would keep him in the loop in case we turned up anything."

"That would be Tony. He has his eyes and ears everywhere. Knowledge is power." Doucet leaned back in his chair. "The question I have is exactly what Tony will do with that knowledge."

Ray nodded. "That's my take. I think he'll do what he usually does. Get revenge. By whatever means are necessary."

Doucet smiled. "Seems you know Tony well."

"I know his type."

"Where does this leave Kirk?" I asked.

"Doesn't drag him out of the woods, if that's what you're asking," Doucet said. Another bite of gumbo. "Yesterday, after the initial DNA came back, saying it was of female origin, I chatted with Melissa Mooring and asked her the same thing. She said it was bothersome but that she was proceeding toward trial with Kirk Ford as the defendant. Said she had no reason not to do so. That she would argue that the DNA was older and had nothing to do with Kristi Guidry's murder."

"But this is still good for Kirk?" Nicole asked. "Right?"

Doucet shrugged. "Not my call. It all depends on how the jury sees it."

"I called Kornblatt yesterday," Ray said. "Told him about the DNA. He believes that's the end of the case. That he can introduce enough reasonable doubt to gain an acquittal."

Doucet raised an eyebrow. "Maybe. Unless he alienates the jury. Folks down here don't care for outsiders. Particularly some slick Hollywood dude flashing thousand-dollar suits and Rolexes."

"I suspect that's true," I said.

"Take it to the bank."

CHAPTER FORTY-FIVE

AFTER LUNCH, DOUCET headed to his office; Ray, Pancake, and I back to the hotel. Ray and Pancake said they had some work to do on another case. Something down near Orlando. I wasn't involved in that one, but I knew it had something to do with someone embezzling from an insurance firm. Millions had disappeared. Pancake was sorting through all the accounting and computer stuff, Ray looking into the lives of the two guys suspected of doing the deed.

That left me with nothing to do. I called Nicole. She said all was well on the set. The shooting was going smoothly. I lay on the bed and played with my balls. Baseballs. Throwing them up and catching them. I swung my bat a few times, carefully avoiding lamps and chairs. I read another chapter in my self-defense book.

I was restless. Felt I should be doing something.

I walked down to Café du Monde, where I found Gloria. She was due for a break so we walked up the steps to the adjacent Washington Artillery Park. We stood along the black wrought-iron rail, looking over Jackson Square and the three spires of the St. Louis Cathedral. Two tourist couples in a horse-drawn carriage clopped by below. Their wide eyes and enraptured expressions told me it was their first trip to the Big Easy. Not an uncommon reaction. Brochures and Internet pages just don't quite capture the real thing.

"What's up?" Gloria asked.

"This is just between us. For now, anyway. Okay?"

"Sounds very secretive." She smiled.

"Sort of."

"Okay. My lips are sealed." She made zipping movement across her mouth. "Or would you prefer a pinky swear?"

"Just your word will do."

Her smile evaporated. Concern creased her forehead. "What is it?"

"Some new evidence. They found DNA beneath Kristi's fingernails."

Her shoulders sagged slightly. "Let me guess. It's not from Kirk Ford?"

"It's not. In fact, it's from a female."

"What?"

I shrugged.

"What does that mean?"

"Since the ME thinks the DNA was fresh, it could mean someone else was in that room that night. And since Kirk was out of it, he can't tell us who. In fact, he doesn't remember anything."

"This is crazy." She looked down toward the street where a juggler entertained a cluster of tourists, her gaze unfocused. Her grip on the railing whitened her knuckles. She looked back at me. "Why are you telling me this? What do you want?"

"Do you know of anyone—any girl, woman—that might want to harm Kristi?"

"Jesus." She shook her head. "First it's guys. Now it's some chick? What's next? A space alien?"

"I'm as confused as you are about this," I said. "And if it's any comfort, so are the cops." I laid a hand on her shoulder. "But I have to ask. Does anyone's name pop up for you?"

Tears welled in her eyes. She sniffed and wiped the back of her hand across her nose. "No." Now she wiped her eyes with the heels of her hands. "No one here for sure. None of her friends—at least the ones I know—would ever do this." Another sniff. "I guess this means I can expect the cops to come back by to see me?"

"Probably. And don't freak out, but I'm sure they'll want to take a DNA sample."

"I hate needles."

"They don't do it that way. It's simply a swab of the inside of your cheek."

"At least that's some bit of good news."

Gloria returned to work, promising she'd call if she thought of anyone. I humped it across the Quarter to Vaughn Motor Works where I had an almost identical discussion with Owen Vaughn. After his shock at the DNA results, I asked if he knew any women who Kristi had issues with.

"Not that I know," he said. "Kristi didn't have issues with anyone. Male or female." He forked the fingers of both hands through his hair sweeping it back off his forehead. It stood up as if windblown. "Well, there was the one girl."

"Oh?"

"Long time ago. We were sophomores. Sandy London. She somehow got a crush on me. Tried to get me to go out with her. Said some awful stuff about Kristi. It was a big deal for a couple of weeks, but me and Kristi were solid. Sandy and Kristi later made up. Sort of. It was always a sore subject between them though."

"Any idea where she is now?"

"She got pregnant during our senior year. Got married. Moved to Little Rock. I heard she's had another kid since then."

"She been back this way as far as you know?"

He laughed. "If you're thinking Sandy did this, you are barking up the wrong tree."

"Why's that?"

"She's tiny. Five feet and ninety pounds tops. And mousey. No way."

I shrugged. "Still, anything's possible."

"Not Sandy. Trust me on that." He shook a cigarette up from the pack he pulled from his shirt pocket and lit it. "This is crazy, isn't it? I mean, some psycho chick might've killed Kristi? That makes absolutely no sense."

It didn't.

Next stop—the Belly Up. Tony Guidry's bar/restaurant off St. Anne's. I hoped Tony wasn't there, as I wanted to talk with Robert and Kevin. I got lucky and found the brothers at a corner table playing cards. They actually smiled when I walked up. That's the Nicole effect. They obviously felt an affinity for her after the other night and that apparently spilled over to me.

As if to prove the point, Kevin asked, "Where's Nicole?"

"She's out on the movie set."

"Cool," Robert added.

Amazing how their attitudes had changed since our first encounter on the street. Nicole had definitely redirected their testosterone. Away from anger and toward something more lust-driven. Not that that made me happy, but it did make the brothers more manageable.

"Mind if I join you for a sec?" I asked.

"Sure," Kevin said. He pushed back a chair with his foot. "Want a beer or something?"

"Thanks, but I'm good. I just wanted to ask you a couple of questions."

They exchanged a look, then Robert glanced to the bar as if making sure no one was listening. "About what?"

As I did with Gloria, I went through the need for this to remain private, for them only. They nodded and leaned forward creating a conspiratorial cone of silence.

"They found DNA beneath Kristi's nails and it didn't belong to Kirk Ford." Their eyes widened, but neither said anything. "In fact, it's from a female."

"What?" they said almost in unison. Then Kevin said, "How's that possible?"

"Not sure. But it could mean that her killer was a woman and not Kirk."

"Or he had an accomplice," Robert said.

"Or that," I said. "Either is possible. Or maybe this finding means nothing. But the police think it's a game changer." I shrugged. "Truth is, I do, too."

"So what?" Kevin said. "Some random chick broke in and killed Kristi?"

"Not random. This wasn't just someone stumbling in. Remember, someone gave them a loaded joint. Someone wanted them out. That's the someone we need to find."

"We?"

"Sure. I assume you guys want to know the truth. Tony, too."

Another glance toward the bar and Kevin said, "You know this sounds crazy? Right?"

I nodded. "It does. But facts are facts. What I want to know is if you can think of any of Kristi's female friends or coworkers or anyone who could be a viable suspect?"

They looked at each other, neither speaking, faces blank. Finally, Robert shook his head. "No."

"Her best friends are Gloria and Betty," Kevin said. "Gloria, she worked with over at Café du Monde. Betty, she went to school with."

"Betty Smithson left school? Right? Sick mother, something like that?"

"That's right. She ain't been around for a while."

"I've talked to Gloria a few times," I said. "I don't see her as involved."

"No. I don't either," Robert said. "And sitting right here right now I can't think of a single soul, male or female, who would want to hurt Kristi. Except for Kirk Ford."

I nodded. "As I said, he still might be the one. And this could be one of those classic red herrings. But if you would ask around. See if anyone has a name we should look at."

Kevin leaned forward even more. "Tony don't want us doing nothing about this. He made that pretty clear."

Robert nodded his agreement.

"Then don't tell him."

CHAPTER FORTY-SIX

NICOLE RETURNED FROM the set around five. I was lying in bed reading my self-defense book. Now up to Chapter 14. I was learning some seriously aggressive stuff. Ways to break bones and damage internal organs. A long way beyond a simple flick to the eye.

"Are you ever going to finish that thing?" she asked.

"I'm a slow reader."

"No, you're not. I've seen you read."

"That's novels. This is a textbook."

"Textbook? Really?"

"Sure. I'm learning lots of dangerous stuff."

"Don't hurt yourself."

"Funny." I closed the book. "Besides, I've been busy today."

"Doing what? Playing with your bat and balls?"

"That's funny, too." I told her of my visits and how I had gotten Robert and Kevin to scratch around for women in Kristi's life that might have a reason to do her harm.

She sat on the edge of the bed and listened, and then said, "You're becoming a real PI."

Good grief.

Then she had a great idea. "Want to help me shower?"

You bet.

I was slipping on a pair of jeans when Ray called. He said he had a reservation at Mr. B's at seven, adding that Pancake had a date with Sophie. We planned to meet them downstairs in the bar and then walk over.

Dinner was fun, relaxed, and, as expected, outstanding. The wine flowed, the chatter mostly light. Pancake was on a roll, telling stories from our childhood, many embellished, of course, but funny nonetheless. Sophie laughed, red-faced, and seemed to constantly wipe tears from her eyes. She watched Pancake's every move, infatuated with the big guy. And they were more than a little handsy, like a couple of high school kids. I loved seeing Pancake like this. For all the grief I gave him about using my bar as an office and mainly hanging out with the staff and chatting with customers, he actually did work hard. Day and night. And never complained when Ray dumped a bunch of crap on him.

Soon the conversation turned to the Kirk Ford situation. And the DNA results.

"So, the DNA basically came up empty?" Nicole asked.

"No matches, if that's what you're asking. At least not with the materials found under Kristi's nails. The twins of course matched each other, but that's it."

"What does all that mean?" Nicole asked. "If the DNA didn't match Kirk, and in fact came from a female, and it matched none of the women involved with the movie, then where are we?"

"We're swimming upstream," Ray said.

"But Kirk is off the hook? Right?"

"Maybe. The DNA is just one piece of evidence. The DA still has a dead girl in a locked room and a suspect who conveniently remembers nothing."

"Conveniently?" Nicole asked. "He was drugged."

Ray nodded. "And that's good for him. At least it will be in the courtroom. The question is, who drugged them? Who had access to the room? Or at least the skills to get inside."

"The hotel staff?" I asked.

"Nothing there, either, so far. I talked to Doucet just before we came down to the bar. DNA on the staff cleared them all." He rubbed one eye with a knuckle. "And, of course, the room was accessed with Kirk's key. Not one of the staff."

"That leaves us with Kristi's world. Someone out there that wanted to bring some harm her way."

Ray tapped a finger on the table. "The question is who? And why?"

While this conversation bounced around the table, I noticed Sophie pulling back. At first she leaned back slightly in her seat. Head down. Looking at her hands, I sensed she was no longer tracking the conversation. When Pancake threw an arm around her, pulling her toward him, she gave him a kiss on the cheek. But unlike earlier, it was perfunctory. She saw me watching her and quickly looked away, gaze dropping again.

"What is it?" I asked.

She looked up at me again. "What do you mean?"

"Something's bothering you?"

"No. Not really." She looked at Pancake and smiled. Half-hearted. Now he jumped in. "You feeling okay?"

"Just tired." Another half-smile. "Maybe too much wine."

But that wasn't it. I knew there was more.

"Are you sure?" I asked. "I get the sense that something about all this is bothering you."

She looked around the table. All eyes were on her. Maybe I should have kept my mouth shut. Not put a spotlight on her. She looked uncomfortable.

Finally, she sighed. "I don't want to get anyone in trouble."

Ray leaned forward. "What is it?" He waved a hand. "Whatever it is, it won't leave this table."

Tears collected in her eyes. She wiped them away with the back of one hand.

Pancake turned toward her, placing a gentle hand against her cheek. "Whatever it is, it'll be okay. I'm here."

She smiled. At least she tried to. Came off as more of a grimace. She sniffed back tears. "The twins. Tara and Tegan. They aren't identical."

"Sure, they are," Nicole said.

She shook her head. "No, they aren't. They're what's called mirror twins."

"Those are still identical," Pancake said. "Just a special type of identical."

"What do you mean?" Nicole asked.

Pancake explained that with normal identical twins the fertilized egg made its first division and the two resulting cells drifted apart and each went on to develop into a fetus. Same DNA. Identical twins. With mirror twins, this separation occurs later, after a few divisions. Often the two twins will then be mirror images of each other.

"One can be right handed and the other left," Pancake said. "The usual facial asymmetry that we all have is often mirrored in these folks. Say one has a crooked mouth, the other will crook in the opposite direction. That sort of thing."

"Do they have identical DNA?" Nicole asked.

"Mirrors? Yes."

"So that fits the results," I said.

Pancake nodded. "Sure does. Then there are twins that look identical but are really fraternal twins. There, the DNA is different. And to screw things up more, there are semi-identical twins. Here, the egg splits into two before fertilization and each is then fertilized with a different sperm. The resulting twins will have identical DNA from the mother but different DNA from the father. This means that about three-quarters of their DNA will match."

"How do you know all this?" I asked.

He gave me a look like that was a stupid question. Which, since I knew Pancake knew a lot of trivial stuff, it was.

"I'm a curious guy," he said.

I looked at Sophie. "Is that what they are? Maybe semi-identical twins. Did they ever say that?"

"All I know is that they told me they were mirror twins."

"That term is tossed around," Pancake said. "Even when it ain't the case."

"How did you find out they weren't actually identical?" I asked.

"It's their little secret. But one night, I don't know, a few years ago, we were out drinking. Tegan let it slip. I was amazed. They swore me to secrecy."

I looked at Pancake, then Ray. "So, if they are fraternal twins who simply look alike, their DNA shouldn't have matched?"

"Exactly," Pancake said. "Same if they are semi-identical."

"What does all this mean?" Nicole asked.

"Maybe nothing," Pancake said. "If they are really identical or are true mirrors, the DNA results are right on."

"And if not?"

Pancake opened his hands, palms up. "Something's fishy in Denmark."

"You mean like they scammed the DNA test?" Nicole asked. "How? Why?"

"Maybe they have something to hide," I said.

"Whoa," Nicole said. "Are you saying it was the twins that killed Kristi?"

Was that where this was going? The twins? Really? That made no sense. They worshipped Kirk. Didn't they?

"That's a big step," Pancake said. "All this means is they might've tricked the lab guys. And it's not like they don't take pleasure in using their twin status to do just that."

"But the cops?" Nicole asked. "That's a little more than playing tricks on friends and family. It's illegal."

Ray nodded.

I flashed on something. "Remember when they took the samples? Out on the set?"

"Yeah," Nicole said.

"Tegan was in the trailer while Tara was examined?"

"That's right."

"And Tara went to get her?"

"So?"

"What if they swapped shirts and it was actually Tara that was tested twice?"

Nicole shook her head. "You'd make a great screenwriter."

"Thanks. But what if that happened?"

"Sounds far-fetched," Ray said. "But since we are simply treading water on this case anyway, it wouldn't hurt to get their DNA and retest it. Just to be sure what, if anything, we're dealing with here."

"Maybe get Doucet to call them in?" I asked.

Ray shook his head. "I'd rather not spook them. And I suspect Doucet would agree."

"I need to see the photos the police took," Nicole said.

"Why?" Ray asked.

"They took photos and prints as well as DNA of all the women out there. Show me the pictures. If they did pull a switch, I can tell them apart."

"You can?"

"She can," I said. "She won't tell me how, but she can."

"Let's go see the photos, and I'll show you," she said.

CHAPTER FORTY-SEVEN

THE NEXT MORNING, we met Detective Troy Doucet in the parking lot of the NOPD Crime Lab and Evidence Division. It was located along Lakehore Drive in the modern and high-tech Uno Research and Technology Park.

Doucet wasn't happy that Ray wouldn't tell him what this was about over the phone. "This better be good. I got a stacked plate today."

"It is," Ray said and we walked inside.

"Okay, let's have it."

Ray told him what we needed to see. Doucet led us into one of the labs where one of the techs, a young black kid named Alton Mack, sat before a large-screen computer.

"You have the photos from the DNA sampling out at the movie shoot?" Doucet asked.

Mack nodded. "Sure do. Who do you want to see?"

"Tara and Tegan James."

Mack worked the keyboard and a couple of seconds later the twins' images appeared, side by side. Nicole sat down and examined the images.

"Both of these photos are Tara," she said.

"Are you sure?" Doucet asked.

"Absolutely." She turned to Mack. "Can you zoom in on the left eye?"

He did.

"Now the other pic."

He did that, too.

She pointed. "See that brown fleck? About eleven o'clock?"

"Yeah," I said.

"That's Tara. Tegan doesn't have that same spot." She leaned back. "Both of these photos are of Tara."

"That's how you knew?" I asked. "The eye spot?"

She nodded. She pulled her phone from her jeans pocket and scrolled through her photos. "Here's a picture I took of them both in the bar the other night." She looked at Mack. "Can you get these off my phone and on your screen?"

"Sure."

He hooked up her phone and downloaded the picture.

"Now zoom in on each girl's left eye."

He did, first one, and then the other. And there it was. Clear as day. Tara had the fleck, Tegan didn't.

"Well I'll be damned," Doucet said.

"What about the fingerprints?" Pancake said. "Even identical twins have different prints."

Mack worked the keyboard and displayed the twins prints side by side. We all looked at them, no one saying anything for a minute.

"They look the same to me," I said.

"Me, too," Mack said. "But to be sure I'll grab one of our print guys."

He left but returned a minute later with a young woman. Her name tag indicated she was Rebecca Bousset. Took her about a minute to confirm what we already knew. Mack thanked her and she left.

"I take it you guys hadn't looked at the fingerprints before?" Ray asked Doucet.

"No reason to. I mean, we pulled a hundred prints from that room. We've identified where about half of them came from. Mostly staff. Kirk and Kristi, Ebersole, the twins. All had been in and out of that room many times." He shrugged. "And each had innocent reasons to be there." He shook his head. "Until now."

"What's the plan?" Ray asked.

Doucet forked his fingers through his hair. "I guess I could haul them in here and resample them."

"Might be better to do it more quietly," Ray said. "Don't let them know what we have here."

Doucet nodded. "That would be best."

"We can do that," I said, nodding toward Nicole. "We'll meet them in the bar after they get back to the hotel today. Grab the glasses they use."

"That would work," Doucet said. "If you can do it."

"Piece of cake," Nicole said.

"I'll call Sophie," Pancake said. "Tell her we are doing happy hour and get her to invite the twins."

"Who's Sophie?" Doucet asked.

"She's the makeup artist for the shoot," Pancake said. "Been with them since the beginning of the series. She's a close friend of the girls. And she's the one that told us Tara and Tegan were not necessarily identical twins."

"What if she spills the beans?"

Pancake shook his head. "She won't. After we got back to my room last night, I impressed on her the importance of keeping this on the DL. Didn't take much convincing. She doesn't want to be in the spotlight here."

Doucet nodded. "Sounds like a plan."

"Let me ask you guys something," I said. Everyone looked my way. "What if they are identical twins? Or, as Pancake pointed out yesterday, true mirror twins? Wouldn't their DNA be the same?"

Mack nodded. "Yes, they would."

"And if Tara's DNA didn't match, Tegan's wouldn't either. Where would that leave us?"

"Right where we are," Doucet said.

"Are you saying they might have simply been messing with the techs?" Nicole said.

"If so, they've opened a can of worms for themselves. Basically, evidence tampering."

"But if Tegan's is different," I said, "and it matches that found under Kristi's nails, Tegan will have more than a can of worms to deal with."

Doucet rocked on his heels. "That's got to be the understatement of the year."

"I don't get it," Nicole said. "If we're thinking the twins did this, the big elephant in the room is why? What possible motive could they have?"

"Jealousy?" Ray asked. "That's always a good motive."

"Why would they be jealous of Kristi?" Nicole asked. "And why would they do something like that and frame Kirk? They worship him." She looked at me. "That makes no sense."

"Maybe there's something with Kirk we don't know about," I said.

"Like what?"

I shook my head. "That I don't know."

"Regardless of motive, we need to focus on Tara and Tegan," Ray said. "There's something there that we don't yet see."

Then I had a thought. "Remember what Ragman said? About his recent onetime customers?"

"What?" Pancake said.

"He said he sold some ketamine to two young girls. Said they looked like college girls. Pretty."

"Didn't he say they had short dark hair?"

"Unless they were in disguise," I said.

CHAPTER FORTY-EIGHT

AFTER WE RETURNED to the hotel, we walked over to Decatur, looking for Ragman. Three firemen were washing down a firetruck in the station's driveway. A quick check of the adjacent alley failed to uncover one Jimmy "Ragman" Walker.

"You seen Ragman?" I asked one of the firemen.

"He makes himself scarce when we're out here," he said. "Why're you looking for him?"

"Need to ask him a couple of questions."

"Too bad. I was hoping you'd shoot him."

"Oh?"

"We know what he does. Pisses me off he does it right here by the station. Arrogant little prick."

"Why not have him arrested?"

He laughed. "Lord knows we've tried. Problem is he's as slick as goose shit." He wiped his dirty hands with a gray towel. "Always seems to stay a step ahead of the gendarmes." He nodded down the street. "You might check down off Bienville. He sets up down there when we're out here."

And that's where we found him. As we approached, he seemed to exchange something with two guys, who looked our way and scurried up the street. Free enterprise never sleeps.

"What the hell do you mofos want now?" he said. I noticed he maneuvered as far away from Pancake as possible. Without actually running away. I also noticed his gaze traveled over Nicole. Really pissed me off.

"Got a question," I said.

"I ain't got no answers," he said.

Pancake folded his thick arms over his chest. "You want a fucking encore, douchebag?"

Ragman took a couple of steps back.

Pancake continued. "I'd be more than happy to oblige."

"Shit, man. You can't come in here and push me around."

"Actually, Jimmy, we can," Ray said.

I thought using his real name was a nice touch.

Ragman looked over his shoulder. Probably deciding if escape was an option. Instead he said, "What you want?"

"The other day," I said, "you told us about a few of your customers. Not your regulars."

"So?"

"You mentioned two young ladies."

"Yeah?"

Nicole extended her phone toward him. Her picture of the twins on the screen. "Is this them?"

He glanced at the pic. "No. I told you guys they was brunettes. These girls are about as blond as you." He smiled at Nicole.

I wanted to unload a few chapters of my self-defense book on him. Maybe the one on internal organ damage.

"Forget the hair," Nicole said. "Take a close look. Imagine them with short, dark hair."

She handed him her phone.

He studied the photo. Sort of. His gaze kept slipping over to Nicole's chest. Finally, he shrugged. "I guess. Could be. Could not be. They was wearing big old sunglasses." He looked at me. "Told you that."

"Does that mean you can't say one way or the other?" I said.

"Isn't that what I said?"

Yeah, the organ damage chapter. Definitely.

CHAPTER FORTY-NINE

HAPPY HOUR TURNED into a party. Once Ebersole found out we were gathering in the Carousel Bar, he took over. Said the party was on him. Sort of celebration of Kirk Ford's acquittal. I pointed out that Kirk wasn't yet out of the woods, but Ebersole wouldn't be deterred. He was almost giddy—no, hell, he was giddy—and I honestly think his pupils turned into dollar signs. I mean, his meal ticket now wasn't likely to go to jail for life. Would he still be happy if the twins turned out to be involved? Wouldn't that toss a wrench into the money machine?

Also, there was nothing on the shooting schedule for the next day. A day of rest for the cast and crew but maybe not for Ebersole. He said he would sit with the editor and the cinematographer and look through all they had done. See if there were any pickups or reshoots needed before moving forward. Another week of shooting, and their work here would be done. Then back to LA.

Ebersole held court regaling everyone with Hollywood stories. Everyone included Nicole and me, Ray, Pancake, Sophie, Kirk, the twins, and our "fake" friend from Alabama. The "friend" was actually Alton Mack. Doucet had requested—or was it ordered?—that Mack be involved in the collection of Tara's and Tegan's DNA. "To make sure it's done right" was his take. Not to mention protecting the chain of evidence. We introduced Mack as a high school science teacher from Mobile and no one raised an eyebrow. Why would they? He looked like a teacher. And he was smart. And he played the role to perfection. He even had a canvas briefcase, which according to him, held his students' papers. Actually, it held the tools of his trade, including evidence bags.

Sophie was subdued. She did laugh and play around with Pancake, but I could tell her heart wasn't in it. Not that Pancake was the problem, but the situation had tamped down her spirits. She probably still felt like she was betraying friends. Which I guess in a way she was.

The twins were the opposite. Giddy like Ebersole. As if the news about the DNA matching no one on the set, including them, cleared away any lingering black clouds. They jabbered on about, since the next day was a free day, all the shopping they needed to catch up on. To me, they looked like a pair of typical young women. Playful and innocent. Were they?

I had trouble getting my head around the fact that they just might be killers. And if so, sociopathic ones. I mean, this was planned. In great detail. Buying the ketamine, gaining access to Kirk's room, not to mention strangling the life from a truly innocent young lady. Could they do that? Why would they? That was the big question.

Had the green-eyed monster of jealousy raised its head? Did Kristi move into territory claimed by one of the twins? Boy, I surely hadn't detected any evidence of that. Of a relationship between Kirk and one, or both, of the twins. I scrolled through everything any of the three had said, recalling the times they were all in the same room, and I came up empty. Nada. No hint of anything.

I was pulled from these thoughts when Ebersole tapped on his champagne glass with a spoon, raised it, and declared that Kirk had been "completely exonerated." The twins clapped and giggled the loudest. Kirk merely nodded and mouthed a thanks. My impression? He didn't feel as if he had been "completely exonerated." After all, the DA had made no moves to drop the charges or even say a word publicly about the DNA evidence, meaning Kirk was still the guy in her eyes.

The twins took a liking to Mack. They were even flirty, maneuvering him to the sofa between them, asking him questions, touching his arm or leg, laughing at his jokes. Mack seemed to enjoy it. Immensely. I hoped he'd keep his eye on the ball, the reason he was there, and not the twins' low-cut silk blouses. I know I had trouble with that and I was sitting across from them. He did keep his briefcase wedged between his feet.

At least I could tell them apart. With Nicole's help. She pointed out that Tara's blouse was black, Tegan's peach. Good thing because I had them pegged exactly wrong. I knew Nicole's tell, the brown fleck in Tara's eye, but from where I sat, I couldn't see it. Too far away.

I was concerned that the party atmosphere would make grabbing the evidence tricky, or even impossible. Mack looked calm and unconcerned. As if he believed that when the time came to grab the twins' glasses, the chaos might help.

It did.

Tegan stood, drained her champagne glass, and placed it on the table. "I need to visit the little girls' room."

Tara stood, also draining her glass. "I'll go with you." Then she looked at Mack. "I expect those to be refilled with champagne by the time we return." She laughed and they were off.

I could never understand why women couldn't go the restroom alone. Or so it seemed. They went as a pack. I'm sure it was so they could talk about us guys without a filter. Of course, guys are guilty of that, too.

This time it helped.

Mack nodded to me. Ebersole was sitting in a chair at one end of the table. I casually stood and stretched, then maneuvered around the coffee table, positioning myself between him and Mack. I asked him something stupid about how many more days of shooting were scheduled. He told me, in great detail, the scenes they still needed to shoot, but I paid no attention. I hoped he wasn't able to see whatever Mack was doing behind me. Apparently that was the case, as he gave no reaction. When I turned around, Mack sat there like nothing had happened; but the two glasses were gone.

I motioned to the waitress. She came my way. I ordered another bottle of champagne and asked if she could bring everyone fresh glasses. Of course, she could. By the time the twins returned, two filled glasses sat before them.

Tegan lifted hers and titled it toward Mack. "You're the best."

Mack hung around for another twenty minutes before saying he had to go. A dinner engagement. The twins gave him mock pouts, hugged him, and gave cheek kisses before he left.

Mission accomplished.

But there was one more thing I wanted to do.

Soon Kirk headed to the men's room. I waited a couple of minutes and then followed. I loitered in the lobby until he came out and intercepted him before he entered the bar.

"Can I ask you something?" I said.

"Sure."

I glanced around. A few people were looking at us without really looking. I suspected Kirk was used to that because he seemed not to notice.

"Let's step outside."

"Oooh. Sounds mysterious."

We were on the street when I said, "Not really. I just want to know about you and the twins."

Was that a flash of concern that rippled across his face?

"What about us?"

"You've known them a long time."

"Oh, yeah. Since the series started." He smiled. "They were kids then. I think fifteen. Maybe sixteen."

"Do they pull that twin stuff on you, too?"

He laughed. "All the time." He shook his head. "Every time I think I can tell them apart, I'm wrong." Another laugh. "And they use it to mess with me."

"And everyone else, as far as I can tell."

"They do take delight in it."

"Did you and them ever have any problems?"

"Like what?"

"Like anything. Any arguments or something like that over the years?"

"No. Maybe a disagreement on dialogue, or staging, or something like that. Creative differences as they say. But those are always minor and, in the end, not our decision. Ebersole makes all those calls."

I waited until a couple walked by. The woman looking at Kirk, then grasping the man's arm, whispering to him as she gave a quick backward glance. The man kept walking, never looking back, either not interested or possessing the good manners not to gawk.

"Did you ever have a thing with either of them?"

He hesitated. "No." Another hesitation. "Why do you ask?"

I laughed, trying to sound casual. "I mean, we're guys, they're hot, and I know you have a reputation for—what's the word?"

"Being a hound?" He laughed. "I'm afraid that's true. I can't deny it."

"I imagine in your world, that's almost expected."

"Part of the job. You know, being the big movie star. All that crap."

"Does that mean you don't enjoy it?" I ask.

"Are you kidding? I love it. Who wouldn't?"

"But never with Tara or Tegan?"

He frowned slightly. "Where is this coming from? Did someone say something?"

"Not really."

"Not really? What does that mean?"

"No, no one said anything. I just sense they have a big crush on you."

He laughed again. "They do. And I on them. But in an older brother sort of way." He tapped my shoulder with a fist. "Maybe if I'd met them later, and they weren't part of the franchise, then maybe. But I still see them as kids. All fresh-faced and innocent."

Innocent? Were they? Was he?

CHAPTER FIFTY

"WHAT DO YOU mean by hinky?" Tony asked.

He was back at Maison Maralee, Melissa Mooring nestled in the crook of his arm. They were in a postcoital haze when the conversation returned to the case.

"Hinky. Odd or strange."

"I know what hinky means. What I want to know is what it means here. In this context."

"Something with the DNA. The samples taken from those sisters—the twins—Tara and Tegan James—weren't kosher."

"That's it? Not kosher?"

She propped up on one elbow. "You're the one with fingers in the crime lab. Not me."

"You're an Assistant DA. Don't they have to give you that kind of information?"

"News flash. The DA's office isn't always their primary concern. Most things I learn about come from official reports. Or rumor and innuendo. And that can take days, even weeks."

"I know."

"Then why are you busting my balls about this?"

"I'm not. Besides, you don't have balls. I checked."

She laughed, fell back against him, and kissed his cheek. "Are you going to be able to stay tonight, or should I head home?"

"I need to check out a couple of things. But why don't I grab some wine and cheese and come back after that?"

"That works. And bring some of that wonderful capicola salami. I love that."

"Will do."

She stretched and rolled to a sitting position. "I'm going to shower and then do some paperwork until you get back."

Tony called Reuben, dressed, and walked downstairs, climbing into the limo, Reuben driving, Johnny in back with him.

"Where to?" Reuben asked.

"My office."

Ten minutes later they walked into the Belly Up. Robert and Kevin were there, actually working. Well, sitting at the bar anyway.

"What's up?" Kevin asked.

"Nothing." Tony walked by and entered his office. Reuben and Johnny followed.

Tony dialed the crime lab and got his guy on the phone. "What's going on with the DNA?"

"It looks like those two girls—the twin ones—faked their sample. Swapped places or something. At least that's what I hear."

"Why would they do that?"

"Why does anyone tamper with evidence?"

Tony rubbed his eye with a knuckle. "Because they have something to hide."

"Exactly."

"The question is what?"

"I can tell you that Detective Doucet is giving them a hard look."

"Maybe I should, too. Thanks." He hung up. "Okay, I want you guys to shadow the twins. Tara and Tegan James. I want to know where they are at all times."

"Will do," Reuben said.

"And be ready to grab them if I say so."

"You think they're involved in Kristi's murder?"

"The cops seem to."

"Wow," Johnny said. "That changes things. How do you read this?"

"Maybe they were jealous of Kristi. I mean, they had Kirk Ford to themselves until Kristi came along."

"It's not like that dude hasn't done this before. From what we know about him, anyway."

"I get the feeling things between him and Kristi were a little more than his usual dogging around."

Johnny shook his head. "Kristi was special."

"Yes, she was. In many ways." Tony leaned back in his chair and rubbed one temple. "That's why whoever did this won't walk away."

"You thinking you're not going to bet on the police anymore?" Reuben said.

"That's exactly what I'm thinking."

CHAPTER FIFTY-ONE

AFTER THE PARTY broke up, Nicole and I grabbed a table at Criollo, the Monteleone's restaurant. Classy, cool, and quieter than the bar. Pancake and Sophie joined us. Ray begged off, saying he had work to do and would order room service. I think he was tired of watching Pancake act like a lovesick puppy, fawning over Sophie. I could be wrong on that but, trust me on this, Ray lacks the warm and fuzzy gene. The Pancake-Sophie mating dance reminded me of him and Jill Hanks. Back in high school. She the cheerleader, he the star player, their hookup seemed natural, even inevitable. At first, he was lovestruck, like now, as was Jill. But over the year the relationship withered, mutually, and by graduation, each had moved in separate directions.

When our waitress appeared, Sophie selected the Shrimp Bienville; Pancake, the bone-in rib eye. And an appetizer of pork belly with jalapeño cornbread. I chose the grilled pompano; Nicole, the char-grilled oysters, adding that I should order the oysters, too.

"Why?" I asked.

"You might need them. I have big plans for you tonight."

Sophie laughed, and then tossed in that maybe Pancake should consider the same. He did, flagging down our waitress and adding the oysters to his order. I declined, saying I'd be fine.

"Sure of yourself, aren't you?" Nicole said.

"Reasonably."

"Reasonably? That's a ringing endorsement of your prowess."

"Prowess? That's me. Jake the Stud."

"Sure you are." She patted my arm.

"You complaining?" I asked.

"Not in the least." She kissed me on the cheek.

The meal was great, and we continued the champagne train, not wanting to switch alcohol types in the middle of a good buzz. I was never sure that made much difference, but why tempt the fates? Particularly since I had "big plans" to look forward to.

The conversation, which mostly was light and fun, turned toward the day's events. Sophie said she felt guilty about "tattling" on the twins, but I assured her that what she did couldn't be classified as "tattling."

"Seems that way to me," she said.

"Not the same thing," Pancake said. He draped an arm around her shoulders. "You simply offered up evidence."

She gave a half shrug.

He pulled her against him and kissed the top of her head. "You did the right thing. If Tara and Tegan are involved in this, we need to know. And if Kirk is innocent, we need to know that, too."

"I can't even imagine that Tara and Tegan did this," Sophie said. "Doesn't compute."

"All we know is that they fudged the DNA," I said. "Why they did it, I have no idea."

"Maybe they were just goofing around? They do that all the time."

"I'm not sure pulling a stunt like that with the police is a wise choice."

"Probably not," Sophie said.

"Regardless, we should know more tomorrow," I said. "Doucet indicated he'd have the preliminary results by noon."

After we returned to the room, Nicole's "big plans" turned out to be all that and more. She was insane, and acrobatic. I love it when that happens.

* * *

The next morning, I awoke tired and stiff. Not that way. My muscles—back, shoulders, legs—ached, as did my head. The latter from too much alcohol; the former from a whole lot of Nicole.

We skipped breakfast, opting for coffee and a walk along the river. The Tai Chi folks were at it again, as were the tugs that pushed barges here and there on the river. After a shower and clean clothes, we met Ray and Pancake just after one o'clock at Mother's for lunch. Afterwards, as we walked along Tchoupitoulas toward the hotel, Doucet called Ray, asking where we were. Ray told him, and he said he'd meet us at the Monteleone. He was standing in the lobby, talking on his cell, when we arrived. He closed his phone, sliding it into his jacket pocket.

"I take it you have the DNA results," Ray said.

Doucet nodded. He scanned the lobby, then jerked his head toward the front door. "Let's step outside." On the street, he said, "Sophie was right. The James twins' DNA samples don't match each other. But Tegan's matches that taken from Kristi."

Ray whistled.

"She killed Kristi?" Nicole asked. Her eyes were wide.

"Doesn't necessarily mean that," Doucet said. "All it really means is that her DNA was present. Could be an innocent explanation for that."

"Like what?" I asked.

Doucet looked up the street, his gaze unfocused. "Can't really think of one. But maybe they can tell me something I'll believe." He looked back toward us. "Any idea where I might find them?"

"They went shopping," Pancake said. "Sophie went with them."

"What time?"

"Around ten thirty."

"Where?"

"They were on foot," Pancake said. "Headed that way, last I saw." He nodded up Royal Street.

"Shouldn't be too hard to find them," I said.

"I'll get patrol on it," Doucet said. He pulled out his cell.

Thirty minutes later, we had come up empty. That's when Pancake's cell rang. He answered, listened for a minute, and said, "We'll be there in a minute. Don't move." He disconnected the call. "That was Sophie. The twins are gone."

CHAPTER FIFTY-TWO

WE FOUND SOPHIE standing along Royal, right across from Madam Theresa's shop. The front door was closed, so I suspected the good madam had some big-eyed tourist inside, scamming another forty bucks. Still, her words echoed in my head: "But he is not the one. They did it. Not him."

I looked at Nicole. She was obviously thinking the same thing as her gaze angled that way.

"What happened?" Doucet asked.

Sophie was shaken. Her fingers trembled, as did her lower lip. Eyes moist, breathing ramped up. "I was in there." She indicated the antique shop behind her. "They were over there." She pointed across the street. "Through the store window, I saw them being pushed into the back of a black limo."

"Pushed? By whom?" I asked.

"I don't know. Some guy. Tall and mean-looking. I think he had a gun."

Johnny Hebert. One of Tony's goons. No doubt.

She went on. "I couldn't see the driver, but once they were inside they took off. Headed that way." She pointed up Royal. "Turned right and were gone."

"When did this happen?" I asked.

"Just now. Right before I called."

"Fuck," Doucet said. "Has Tony lost his goddamn mind?"

"Looks that way," Ray said. He pulled out his cell, scrolled through his contacts, and pressed a number. He put the phone on speaker so we could hear.

Tony answered after two rings.

"Ray Longly," Ray said.

"Hey, Ray, what's up?" Tony asked. He sounded normal, calm.

"Let them go," Ray said.

"What? Who?"

"You know damn well who."

"I'm afraid I'm at a loss."

"Listen to me, Tony. This is a huge mistake. You have no idea how big."

"And I thought we were friends," Tony said.

"Apparently not. Let's talk."

"I'm busy today. Maybe tomorrow."

"Maybe today. Maybe now."

"Not going to happen."

"Don't make me unleash the dogs of war on your ass," Ray said.

"Tell you what. I don't have a clue what you're jabbering about, but when you want to talk like a couple of adults, give me a call."

The line went dead.

Ray shook his head. "Some people just can't get out of their own way." He looked at Doucet. "Any idea where he might have taken them?"

"Not likely to one of his clubs. That would be too risky."

"Then where?"

Doucet hesitated a beat. "Don't know."

"His grabbing them means he knows about the DNA," Ray said. "No doubt."

"Of course he does," Doucet said. "Probably knew before I did."

"And he isn't going to wait on you guys," I said. "He's going to take care of this his way."

"He usually does."

"We have to find them," Nicole said.

"I've got an idea," I said. I looked at Ray. "Let's start with Ragman."

"Good idea."

I turned to Nicole. "You and Sophie head back to the hotel. Stay there."

Nicole nodded. I was sure she would argue the point, but then again, I guess she saw the danger in all this. She grabbed Sophie's arm, and they headed up the street.

We found Ragman exactly where we thought he'd be. In his alley. Chatting on his phone. His eyes widened as we walked up. Pancake didn't hesitate, but rather charged right at him. Ragman took a step back. Pancake punched him in the chest. The air left Ragman in one sibilant wheeze, and he stumbled. Pancake flattened a palm against Ragman's sternum, pressing him against the concrete wall. With his other hand, he slapped the phone from his hand. It cracked against the pavement.

"Hey, man."

"Hey, nothing," Pancake said. "We have a few questions."

"Fuck you, man."

Bad idea.

Pancake's fist dug into the pit of Ragman's stomach. He collapsed on all fours, gagging. Pancake grabbed the back of his shirt and lifted him. He looked like a marionette without strings, dangling in Pancake's grasp.

"You ready to talk or should I start breaking shit?"

Still gasping for breath, Ragman managed to squeak out, "What you want, man?"

I was impressed that Doucet stood back and let all this go down. Guess he had a low opinion of Ragman. Or maybe a degree of admiration for Pancake's methods. Now he spoke.

"Where's Tony Guidry?"

"How the fuck would I know?"

"Where would he hole up if he wanted to lay low?"

"The Belly Up's all I know."

"Guess again," Ray said.

Pancake slammed a forearm into Ragman's chest, pinning him against the wall once again. "Listen up, you little shit. Start talking or I'll punch your teeth into your lungs. Tony grabbed a couple of folks. Where would he take them?"

Ragman's eyes watered from the impact and again he struggled to breathe. "How the fuck would I know? I don't know nothing about Tony's habits."

He appeared to be telling the truth. Amazing. And after a few more questions it became apparent Ragman couldn't help. Pancake released him, and he staggered again, bending forward at the waist, his breathing ragged. I thought he might fall. Or faint. Or cough up blood. Instead he said, "What about my phone?"

"Send me a bill," Pancake said, and we were gone.

Next stop: Ju Ju's.

Doucet took the lead. Much more polite and controlled. Ju Ju did have his two armed morons with him, after all. Unlike Ragman, Ju Ju wasn't intimidated, or even concerned, and offered nothing, saying he had no idea what we were talking about, that he didn't know where Tony might be, and that even if he did, he wouldn't say. He suggested Doucet get a warrant if he wanted to turn Tony's world upside down.

Next stop: The Belly Up.

No Tony, nor his two guys, but Robert and Kevin were there. They didn't seem happy to see us. In fact, they looked scared.

They knew. No doubt.

"Got a couple of questions for you," Doucet said.

The brothers exchanged a glance, then Robert said, "About what?"

"I suspect you know."

Robert hesitated, glancing at his brother, taking in the room.

I scanned the room. A dozen people in the bar, twice that many at tables in the restaurant area.

"Outside?" I said. "Would that be better?"

Another hesitation, then he nodded.

Outside, in the parking area, we faced off with the brothers. We waited while a pair of young ladies came out, climbed in their car, the driver taking a couple of minutes to check her makeup and hair in the rearview mirror. Seemed to take forever, but finally she cranked the car to life and they pulled away.

"Where's your uncle?" Doucet asked.

Another glance toward his brother. "We don't know."

Pancake moved. Ray stopped him with a hand on his arm.

"Look at me," Ray said. "Tony grabbed the James twins. Right off the street."

Kevin shook his head. "What are you talking about?"

"Tara and Tegan James. He snatched them."

Robert looked confused. "Why would he do that?"

"Because he thinks they were involved in Kristi's murder."

"Were they?" Kevin asked.

"That's not the issue here. Kidnapping is."

"We don't know nothing about it," Robert said.

"But you do know your uncle. My question for you is where would he take them?"

Robert stared at him but said nothing.

Ray stepped into his face. His nose only inches from Kevin's. "You want to be part of this? You want to go down for Tony?"

Robert was now in full panic but said nothing. Like his brain had vapor-locked.

"Tony fucked up," Ray said. "Big-time. And unless you two want to get dragged into the middle of this, I suggest you talk. Now."

Robert took a ragged breath. "We don't know anything."

Ray stepped back, looking at Pancake. "They're all yours."

Pancake smiled, closed on them.

"Wait a minute," Robert said, stepping back, raising his hands in a defensive posture. "Wait just a minute."

"I'm waiting," Ray said.

"He has a house. Up across the Pontchartrain."

"Where?"

"About an hour from here."

"That doesn't help," I said. I pulled out my iPhone and opened the map app. "Show me." I handed the phone to Robert.

Obviously still trying to figure out his options, hoping to find some way to avoid all this, Robert held the phone but didn't look at it.

"Get to it," Pancake said.

Robert worked the screen, moving, expanding, shrinking the map before finally settling on a spot north and west of the city. "There."

"See, that was easy," I said.

I examined the map, Ray looking over my shoulder. It showed a house on the banks of what looked like a narrow finger of swamp water. An access road ran just north of it, the house's drive slanting off and winding through some scrub trees before dumping into what looked like a gravel lot behind the structure. A short dock and small boat house extended into the water. I expanded the view. Nearest other house appeared to be at least a half mile away, farther up the access road. I extended the phone toward Doucet. "You know where this is?"

He took the phone, manipulated the image for a few seconds. "Sure do." His finger traced a snaking river. "This is the Lacombe

Bayou. Just outside Lacombe. North of the Pontchartrain, not far past Slidell."

Doucet now addressed Robert and Kevin. "Here's the deal. Keep your fucking mouths shut. We're going after Tony, but if either of you gives him a heads up, I swear to God you'll never see the light of day again. Am I clear?"

The brothers nodded in unison. Then Robert said, "We ain't part of this. Okay?"

"You better hope not," Doucet said.

* * *

Robert watched as Doucet and his entourage circled the Belly Up and disappeared. "What do you think?" he asked Kevin.

"I don't know what to think." Kevin shook his head. "Maybe he was lying."

"Really? Why? For what purpose?"

"I don't know."

"Tony took them. That I don't doubt," Robert said. He brushed his hair back from his forehead. "The question is why?"

"You know why. He's going to kill them."

"You don't know that."

"If he thinks they did Kristi, he won't even blink."

"Shouldn't we call him?" Robert said. "Let him know the cops are headed his way?"

"What? And let him know we pointed them that way?"

"He'll find out anyway. He always does."

"Shit," Kevin said. "We are so fucked."

"Yes, we are."

"I vote that we do nothing. Say nothing. If later we need to, we can deny everything. Say the cops made it up."

Robert thought about that for a minute. "It's not like we really have a choice."

"Not a good one, anyway." Kevin rapped a knuckle on his brother's arm. "Let's get back to work. Act like nothing's wrong."

CHAPTER FIFTY-THREE

TARA AND TEGAN James were scared. No, they were terrified. It was written all over them. Their tight faces, their wide eyes, their entire body language. Their white-knuckled fingers laced together in one big knot. Their sniffing and grimacing as they fought back tears. Not very successfully.

Tony loved it.

He faced them down the long passenger compartment of the limo. He with his back to the open window that looked toward Reuben, the driver, Johnny to his right, the twins huddled on the rear seat.

He waited, giving them his most malevolent stare. Practiced and perfect. He knew what was coming. Had seen it many times. The questions, the bargaining, the begging. All that sniveling always made the ultimate killing that much easier. He hated whiners.

And then it began: *Where are you taking us? Why are you doing this? Please don't hurt us. We can pay you. We won't say a word. Just let us go and you'll never see us again.*

He wished at least once someone would come with some new tack. But, it was always the same.

Tony, of course, answered none of their questions. He simply stared at them, letting the tension and the fear mount. The gun Johnny held in his lap, its muzzle angled in their direction, though not necessary, added a nice touch. Each twin's gaze had bounced to the weapon more than once.

God, he loved this stuff. The power he could wield over others. Literally life and death. And when the victim knew it, had time to process it, really process it, deep down on a visceral level, that was even better. When death seemed less scary than what might happen before.

That's where these two were. And he knew it. Could feel it as a palpable entity.

It took the better part of an hour to reach his cabin. He always called it a cabin but, in fact, it was a well-appointed, two-story, four-bedroom home. But it was isolated, no nearby neighbors, and it had served its purpose for many years. Not only as getaway from the city, but, like now, as a place where business could be conducted. Business that needed privacy.

He had considered calling in a few of his other guys but rejected that idea. The snatch had been clean. No struggle, no unwanted attention. Reuben had said that anyone who even noticed would only see two girls and a guy climbing into a limo. No big deal. Happened all the time in New Orleans.

And Ray Longly? He was fishing. He didn't really know what had happened. All he could know is that the girls were missing. And he might not even be sure of that. He might call the cops, of course, but so what? They had no way of knowing where Tony was going. The Lacombe house wasn't even in his name. Rather that of a distant cousin. Four states removed. No trail to him.

And if all that were true, no extra muscle would be needed. Besides, the fewer people who witnessed what was coming, the better. He trusted Rueben and Johnny completely. It wasn't like they hadn't done this before. He paid them well, very well, took care of them, and, perhaps most importantly, had enough on each to get them the needle, or at least life without.

Once inside, they settled in the living room, Tony in his large, overstuffed leather chair, facing the twins across a six-foot coffee table. They collapsed on a sofa, fingers still entwined, legs wound into braids. Reuben stood near the window, gazing out toward the bayou, Johnny in the kitchen prepping the demonstration that was to come. A little something to get the girls' attention.

"Tell me," Tony said.

"Tell you what?"

Tony smiled. "Which one are you?" he'd asked the speaker, the twin on the left.

"I'm Tara."

"Good. Now we have the players in this drama sorted out." He tapped a finger on the chair's arm. "Tell me why you killed my niece."

"We didn't," Tara said. She looked at her sister. "We don't know anything about it."

"That's your answer? You know nothing?"

The twins stared at him.

"Then riddle me this—how did Tegan's DNA get beneath Kristi's fingernails?"

Tegan's eyes widened. Tony smiled.

"No way," Tegan said. "The cops must have planted it or something."

"Pray tell, why would they do that?"

No response.

"What they did was smash your little scam. They know you guys aren't identical twins. You just look that way. They know your little switcheroo didn't work."

Tara and Tegan exchanged a glance.

"Yeah, I bet you two have been pulling that shit since birth. Probably worked most of the time. But not now."

The twins seemed to deflate right before his eyes. Time to ramp up the pressure.

Johnny stood leaning against the kitchen doorjamb. Tony nodded.

"Let me show you something," Tony said. He stood and waved a hand toward the rear deck and the dock. "This way."

Reuben pushed the door open and held it while Tony and the girls filed out.

"Look at this," Tony said. "My own little pond, as it were. Sort of hangs there off the Lacombe Bayou." He looked at the girls. "Looks calm and peaceful, doesn't it?"

Tara froze; Tegan nodded.

"But here's the thing about the bayou, about everything in this part of the country—danger always lurks in calm waters." He waved a hand toward the water. "Just when you think all is well, everything changes. Just when you think you've sidestepped the bullet, you discover, too late, that that's not the case."

Johnny came out the door, a deep metal bowl in one hand. Tony gave him a nod. He walked out on the dock and began tossing chicken parts into the water.

Tara and Tegan watched, confusion on their faces. Then Tegan's eyes widened and she pointed.

The first gator slid from beneath an overhanging shrub and glided toward the offerings. No hesitation. His jaws snatched a chicken half and he shook his head. Then another gator appeared, and another, and then there were five of them. Tony ignored them, keeping his attention focused on the twins. Panic didn't quite cover the reaction.

"My little pets," Tony said. "What do you think of them?"

The girls were too terrified to speak. And seemed almost unable to breathe.

"They like my little pond. Hang around here all the time. As you can see, they aren't very cuddly, but they do serve their purpose."

Neither twin could drag her attention away from the alligators, now weaving in circles, looking for more food.

Tony ushered them back inside. They again collapsed on the sofa, sobbing uncontrollably. He sat and waited until they gained some degree of composure. Until they wiped away tears and looked at him. Fear and anticipation all over them.

"Here's what's going to happen," Tony said. "I'm going to feed you to them."

The girls wailed in unison. "No, please, no."

Tony waited, letting it sink in, letting them come down a notch. Then he said, "I'm afraid that's not negotiable. The only question is whether I do it while you're alive, or after my boys put bullets in your head."

"Please," Tegan said. "You don't have to do this."

There it was, more bargaining. "Actually, I do."

"No, let us go. We won't say a word."

So predictable.

Tony leaned forward, elbows on his knees. "Not true. You're going to say a lot. Starting with how and why the fuck you killed Kristi."

"We didn't," Tara said. "I swear. We . . ."

Tony raised a hand, silencing her. He stood and looked at Reuben. "Toss them in the fucking pond."

"No, please," Tara said.

"Then talk."

Tara began to sob, barely able to talk. "Yes, we did it."

Tony stabbed her with his gaze but said nothing.

"We bought some ketamine, soaked a joint with it, and gave it to Kristi. After they were out, we went in and . . ." Her voice trailed off.

"Strangled her?" Tony said. "Strangled the life from my niece?"

The twins sobbed and nodded in unison.

"Where did you get the bump? The ketamine?"

"Some guy."

"What guy?"

"I don't know," Tara said. "Some black kid. Over on Decatur. Near the fire station."

Ragman. Tony would visit him soon. Very soon.

"How did you get in the room?"

"We went to dinner together," Tara said. "Kirk, Kristi, and us. I gave Kristi the joint in the restroom. Told her it was some really good stuff and she and Kirk would like it. After dinner, we went back to Kirk's room for some wine. While there, I snatched the room key. From the top drawer of his dresser."

"How'd you know it was there?"

"It's where he always leaves it. Along with his watch and wallet and things like that."

"So you came back in later and killed Kristi."

Tara nodded.

"It was me," Tegan said. "I did it." She clasped her sister's hand. "Tara didn't have anything to do with it."

"Just fed her drugs and stole the key card that got you in the door? That kind of nothing?"

The twins began to sob again. Softer, resigned.

"Why?" Tony asked. "Why Kristi?"

Tegan swiped the back of one hand across her nose and sniffed. "To get back at Kirk, I guess."

"For what?"

Tegan wiped the back of one hand across her nose, sniffed back tears. "For using me. For dumping me. For breaking my heart. For killing part of my soul."

"What does that even mean?" Tony asked.

"Years ago, right after I turned eighteen, Kirk and I were at a party. One of those Hollywood things. We ended up in an upstairs bedroom. He said he thought he might love me. I believed him. We had sex. That night and many others for the next few weeks. Then he walked away. Said it would never work out between us. He went back to humping the chick of the week as if nothing had ever happened."

"It was awful," Tara said. "Tegan was devastated. I mean, we still had to work with him. Go on location with him. Do all the promo stuff with him. Act like we were still just one big happy family. And watch him with woman after woman while acting like it meant nothing."

"That was hard," Tegan said. "Half the time I wanted to scream and other times I actually considered suicide." She looked at her sister. "I might have done it had it not been for Tara. No way I could leave her."

"Okay," Tony said. "You've lived with this little Hollywood drama for what, four or five years, and now you decide to do something? Why Kristi?"

Tegan expanded her chest with a deep breath and exhaled slowly. "She was different. I think Kirk actually fell for her. She wasn't just another bimbo to him." She squeezed her eyes shut, fighting the tears that cascaded down her cheeks. "With the others, I knew they meant nothing. That sooner or later he would cut them loose, always leaving the hope that he would eventually come back to me." She looked at her sister. "Tara kept telling me to move on, but I couldn't." She let out a ragged breath. "God, I wished I could. I wanted to."

"I'm confused," Tony said. "If you were angry with Kirk, why not kill him?"

Tegan gave him a look that seemed to ask if had been listening to what she had said. "Because I love him. I could never harm him."

"Just frame him for murder? Is that it?"

"He needed to be punished. But I couldn't kill him. Not possible."

CHAPTER FIFTY-FOUR

DETECTIVE TROY DOUCET took charge. No doubt about that. He did so quickly and efficiently and the result was that a whole bunch of stuff happened in a big hurry. We had walked on our rounds to see Ragman, Ju Ju, and Kristi's brothers at the Belly Up, so we had to hustle it back to the Monteleone. On the way, Doucet made a series of calls, barking orders, cutting people off who tried to ask too many questions, and made sure, in no uncertain terms, that what he was saying weren't requests but rather orders. The upshot was that by the time we reached the hotel, he had arranged a helicopter to fly by Tony's place, discreet and distant, of course, a SWAT team to assemble just outside Lacombe, and a hostage negotiator to join the team, because you just never knew how all this would go down.

In the lobby, we ran into Kirk and Ebersole. Kirk said they were waiting on the twins as they had plans to go to a jazz club over on Bourbon. They were late. Ebersole was antsy, which from my view was his usual state. He checked his watch three times in the minute we chatted with them. Nicole ended the discussion by saying they were shopping and probably lost track of time. And that maybe they should go ahead and she would let them know when they showed up.

She was smooth and then some. Said that with a straight face, no hint that she was lying.

We had decided on the walk over that it would be best if Kirk and Ebersole knew nothing about the abduction. Their hysteria would have been another issue to deal with, and right now focus and speed were important. Not to mention that Ebersole liked to jabber, and if the wrong ears locked on, the word might get back to Tony that we knew he had the twins. Surprise would be out the window and that could easily tilt things in the wrong direction. No one wanted a gunfight.

Speaking of which, after they took Nicole's advice and left, Ray and Pancake retrieved weapons from their rooms, a pair of Sig Sauers. I grabbed my baseball bat. Okay, not great in a gun fight, but in close quarters it might be useful. And it was much quieter. If it came to that. Hopefully not.

Then we were off.

I suggested Nicole stay behind, Ray agreed, but she put an end to that line of thinking very quickly.

"Want me to kick your balls up into your throat?"

She has a way with words.

Doucet agreed with her. Said he thought it was a good idea, but I think he was afraid of her, too. Smart man. Then he added that if it became a hostage situation, the negotiator might want to call on her since she knew the girls. Made sense.

We flew across the Pontchartrain on I-59 and then west on 190, which, according to the signs, was the Louisiana Scenic Bayou Byway. This plugged us into the swamp country along the Lacombe Bayou, an anaconda of dark water surrounded by scrub trees and grassy fields. Ray and Doucet rode in Doucet's department-issued sedan; Nicole and me with Pancake. Nicole insisted on shotgun. Rather than being impolite, and of course risk getting kicked in a delicate region, I let her have it. Intelligence is my hallmark.

My cell buzzed three times on the way. Each was Tammy. Each I punched over voice mail. Not that that would change anything. Or deter her from more calls, but right now didn't seem the right time to enter Tammy's world.

Nicole looked back, smiling. "Tammy?"

"Of course."

She and Pancake laughed. I failed to see the humor.

We pulled into a corner service station lot, behind the building, where a military-looking SWAT vehicle sat next to a pair of St. Tammany Parish Sheriff's vehicles. A dozen officers in varied uniforms huddled nearby.

I wondered what jurisdictional hurdles Doucet had to jump through to organize this, but it was quickly apparent that everyone assembled deferred to him. One of the deputies opened a map and spread it across the hood of his cruiser. His name was Paul Harbin and he knew his domain. In addition to the map, he had an iPad with a geographic map of the area displayed.

Buzz. Tammy. Voice mail.

"Here," he said indicating a spot. "This is Guidry's house. About a mile and a half from here. It's snugged up against this little outpouching off the Bayou. Sort of like a big pond. The access road is here, and Tony's drive spurs off here." The map crinkled as he tapped it with his finger. "The access road will put us just north and west of the property. The drive is maybe two hundred feet long." He picked up the iPad. "As you can see on the satellite image, the house is surrounded on three sides by thick scrub brush and trees, so we should have good cover for an approach."

"Good work," Doucet said.

"Got something else that might help," Harbin said. He snapped a finger at one of the deputies who handed him some folded pages. He spread them over the map. "This is the schematic of Tony's house. The first floor is basically one large room. Big picture windows front and back."

"Good," Ray said. "That'll make it hard for them to hide in there."

Harbin nodded. His finger tapped the page. "Here he has a large deck and a short pier that overlooks the pond." He scanned all the eyes that were on him. "As an FYI—rumor has it—Tony feeds the alligators in the area. So they'll hang around."

"Why?" Nicole asked.

Harbin turned toward her. "Body disposal is what we hear."

"He feeds people to the alligators?" I asked.

"That's the rumor. Regardless, I'd suggest staying out of the water."

I nodded. "No problem there."

Harbin looked at Doucet. "Any idea what we're up against?"

"I got a call from the helicopter I sent up. They made a couple of distant passes. Looks like the only vehicle there is Tony's limo."

"He didn't call in reinforcements?"

"I suspect he thinks we have no idea he took the girls. Or that we know where he is." Doucet's face hardened. "And he doesn't want any more witnesses than necessary."

"That means it's probably just Tony and those two clowns he runs with," Harbin said.

"Armed clowns," Ray added.

Buzz. Tammy. Voice mail.

Doucet lifted the iPad and studied the satellite image. "Okay, let's put a couple of your deputies and a couple of the SWAT guys on either side. In the trees. Pancake—you, Jake, and a couple of the SWAT guys take the front. Ray and I and Deputy Harbin will come from here." He pointed to a spot on the iPad screen that would put them near the left rear corner of the house, near the pond, just off the rear deck. "If we can get Tony to come out, maybe we can reason with him."

"You think he'll listen?" I asked.

Doucet scratched an ear. "Normally, I'd say yes. He's not generally stupid. But with this kidnapping, I'm not sure he's of very sound mind right now."

"What if the girls are dead?" I asked.

"Then we have no one to protect," Harbin said. "Sad as that would be, it would make this takedown much easier."

"We have to assume they're okay," Ray said.

"Let's hope," Doucet said. He scanned the group. "Let's roll."

"What about me?" Nicole asked. "Want me to go with Jake and Pancake?"

"No," Ray said. "You stay in the SWAT truck with Billy Jean, our hostage negotiator."

"That would be me." She was short, wiry, dark hair pulled back into a short ponytail. She wasn't uniformed, but rather in jeans and a Sheriff's Department dark-blue tee shirt, a service weapon on her right hip. "I'm Billy Jean Janeway." She and Nicole shook hands.

Everyone climbed in vehicles, doors slammed, and we were off. My cell buzzed. Tammy, of course. I answered. Might as well get this over with.

"Jake, are you avoiding me?"

"I learned long ago that's not possible."

"Where are you?"

"In a swamp."

"What?"

"I'm a bit busy right now."

"Doing what?" Tammy asked.

"Something important."

"What could be more important than my happiness?"

"Just about everything."

"Don't be an ass."

"Look, I've got to go. But I'll call you back. I promise."

"We know about how good your promises are."

"I'll call you."

"When?"

"Soon." I disconnected the call.

CHAPTER FIFTY-FIVE

TWENTY MINUTES LATER everyone was deployed and ready. Pancake and I squatted among the trees, maybe a hundred feet from the front door but well hidden by drooping branches. Two SWAT guys, armed with assault rifles, flanked us but I could no longer see them through the thick brush and trees. Everything suddenly seemed eerily quiet. No breeze to rustle the trees, no birds, nothing. Just the dank odor of the swamp water. It was as if all the local fauna knew something was coming.

The floor plan Harbin had showed us was right on. The large front and rear picture windows allowed a clear view of the interior as well as letting plenty of light inside. We could even see through to the rear. I saw no one inside and no movement. Had they gone somewhere else? Tony's limo was still in the drive, only a few steps from where I squatted. Had they left in another vehicle? If so, where? Were the twins already alligator food?

To my right, I saw Ray, Doucet, and Harbin creep toward the house, each with a weapon in hand. At about twenty feet from the deck, they spread out and knelt, weapons leveled before them.

My heart raced. I could feel my pulse in my neck, even in my eyeballs. I gripped the bat, my palms leaking sweat.

Pancake shifted his weight from one heel to the other, holding his Sig loosely in his hand. "Showtime."

Harbin kicked off the proceedings, one hand cupped near his mouth. "This is Deputy Paul Harbin. Saint Tammany's Sheriff's Department. Come out right now."

I saw movement inside. Tony had been sitting. Not visible from where we were. Now he stood and scurried toward a window that faced toward Harbin. He peeled back the curtain and peered out. He then turned, looking back into the room. Now I saw Johnny and Reuben stand, each pulling one of the twins upright. They herded the girls toward the back door.

"Let's go," I said.

Pancake didn't hesitate. He lurched forward. I followed. One of the SWAT guys said something, but I couldn't hear him well enough to know what. Probably something like, "What the hell are you doing?" We pressed on, staying low, running toward the front door. Tony and his two goons, each dragging one of the twins by the arm, stepped through the back door and onto the deck.

Through the open window to our right we heard Harbin shout, "Don't move!" and Tony reply, "Or what?"

Pancake and I crouched near the window, peering through the screen, trying to take a read on the situation.

"Mr. Guidry, don't do anything stupid here," Harbin said. "There's no need for this."

"The hell there isn't."

"Take a breath," Ray said. "Think for a minute."

"They killed my Kristi!" Tony screamed, his voice cracking. He seemed borderline unhinged. Maybe not borderline.

The front door looked solid, oak most likely, with an intricate stained-glass inset. I tried the knob. Locked.

"They aren't going to get away with it," Tony said.

"If they did do it," Harbin said, "they'll pay for it. But not like this."

Right," Tony said. "I'm sure a couple of attractive rich bitches will have to pay for their sins."

"They will, Tony," Doucet said. "You know me. Know I'll take care of business."

"And you know me. One step and I'll kill them both."

Reuben stood to Tony's left, his gun pressed against one twin's head. Tony held the other, his gun near her shoulder, pointed upward. Johnny stood behind Tony. Relaxed, gun to his side.

"Tony, you can't win this." It was Ray. "You can only make things worse."

"Things can't be worse," Tony said. "And if you think I won't die right here, right now correcting this wrong, then you don't know me."

"Listen to me, Tony," Doucet said. "There's a half dozen SWAT guys with a bead on you and your guys. They have orders to take you down if you so much as flinch."

"A flinch is all I need," Tony said. "This one," he said. "Tegan." He tapped the barrel of his weapon against her temple. Tegan flinched. "She's the one that killed Kristi. If I go down, so does she."

There was brief silence. Brief. Then things happened quickly.

A pair of rifle cracks. Almost as one. Reuben's head jerked sideways and he went down. Tara fell with him. Was she hit? Two more pops. Tony stiffened.

Then, Pancake went into full Pancake mode. His shoulder shattered the doorjamb. The door literally flew off its hinges, clattering across the floor, wood splintering, glass shattering. We raced inside.

Tony's head swiveled our way, shock on his face. Johnny spun through the door, gun raised in our direction. He snapped off a round, and I literally felt the bullet zip past my head. Pancake didn't flinch, but rather steadied himself and put three hollow-points in Johnny's chest. Pop-pop-pop. Just like that.

Through the window, I saw Tony stagger to his left. He clutched Tegan by the arm and spun her from the deck. Tegan screamed, arms flapping, airborne until she struck the water. Hard. Two more shots. Tony grabbed his chest and spiraled to the deck. Pancake and I raced through the rear door.

Tegan flailed in the water. Gasping, coughing, trying to clear her lungs. She had obviously inhaled a healthy dose of swamp water. Then she managed to gain her footing, and steadied herself. The water was maybe five feet deep, up to her chin.

Then the game changed. From beneath the overhanging brush along one side of the pond, a flotilla of alligators appeared. Seven or eight at least. They immediately locked on Tegan and with sharp tail kicks torpedoed her way.

Then all hell broke loose.

Gunshots came from every direction. Peppering the water, slamming into the gators, killing most, damaging others. The injured ones began to roll and thrash, churning the water. Tegan froze, as if unable to move. The shooting suddenly stopped, the following silence a vacuum. As if all the air had been sucked away.

Reuben lay to my left, Tony to the right, both very dead. Tara struggled to her feet, unharmed but shaken. It was over.

Or so I thought.

Another gator appeared. From beneath the pier. It motored toward Tegan. She seemed to sense it and turned. Her scream pierced the air. I saw a couple of the SWAT guys scurry around the edge of the pond, weapons raised, looking for a clear shot. They had none. The gator closed fast.

I had no idea what I was thinking but likely I wasn't. The idea that this could go very badly jumped in my head but only after I was airborne.

It seemed to take forever to reach the water. As if some undetectable breeze lifted me and held me suspended. I flashed on the jump from the back of Victor Borkov's yacht. There the drop had been three stories, the water dark, cold, and chopped by a storm—and deep. Very deep. Here the water was shallow, brackish, and warm. A much easier jump. But here, a ten-foot gator waited.

What the hell was I doing?

I hit the water feetfirst, driving straight to the bottom. Nearly lost my balance in the slimy silt.

"Jake!" I heard Ray yell.

The gator looked bigger now. And committed. It never lost focus on Tegan. I waded into its path. It veered toward me. Uh-oh. Brown water waked over its snout, its eyes large, round, with prehistoric slits for pupils. It didn't blink. Or waver from its mission.

I raised the bat and slammed it into its head. Hard. A sharp thwack. The gator shuddered, jerked its head to one side. I struck it again, and again. Confused, or more likely stunned, it turned away, its tail rippling the water. To my left I saw one of the SWAT guys had gained the deck. He raised his rifle. Pop, pop. The gator's head jerked. It shuddered briefly and then sank.

I stood there, swirls of alligator blood around my chest. I scanned for any of its buddies, bat raised, but the only two gators I saw were dead. The others had obviously sunk from sight. Or were they triangulating me? I turned to Tegan. She stood stone still, her face pale, and then she collapsed. I caught her, wrapping one arm across her chest. I shuffled toward the pier, lifted her up on the boards. I scrambled up beside her.

My heart felt like it might explode. I suddenly felt cold. So much so that I was shivering.

Nicole ran across the deck and down the dock, dropping to her knees, hugging me.

"Jake, you're an idiot."

"Hard to argue with that."

"And I love you."

The day just got better.

CHAPTER FIFTY-SIX

WHILE HARBIN'S GUYS secured the scene, and the SWAT crew packed up, Tegan jumped in one shower, me another. Fully clothed. The warm water leached most of the swamp debris away. I stripped off my clothes, wringing them as best I could. I dried off and then wrapped a towel around my waist. Tegan had done the same, her towel like a dress. We waited while Nicole tossed our clothes into the drier for a few minutes. Not long enough to dry them completely but enough so that we could wear them back across the Pontchartrain.

I checked my phone. Dead. Swamp water and cell phones didn't mix.

"You trashed that thing," Nicole said.

"At least Tammy can't call."

She laughed. "There are silver linings everywhere."

More deputies and the crime scene techs showed up as we were leaving.

Nicole grabbed shotgun again. I didn't argue. She twisted in the seat to face me.

"That was brave," she said.

"Stupid's what it was," Pancake added.

"Seemed like a good idea until I hit the water," I said.

"You saved Tegan," Nicole said.

I nodded. "So she can spend the rest of her life in jail. Maybe on death row."

There it was. Tegan's future. Tara's, too, most likely. We rode in silence, the only sounds the hum of the tires and the hiss of the wind outside the windows. The lake was flat, gray, like a massive metal disk.

*   *   *

Back at the NOPD, while Tara and Tegan were booked, we each gave a statement, telling them everything we knew. Nicole called her uncle, waking him up, it being early in Paris, bringing him up to date. To say he was shocked didn't quite cover it. Ray and Pancake headed back to the Monteleone while Nicole and I hung around. Doucet had arranged for us to talk with the twins once their processing was complete.

It was after eight when we were directed into an interrogation room. Tara and Tegan sat at a table, now dressed in jail garb. At least they weren't cuffed or shackled. They looked pale and worn, resigned. Still beautiful, yet each seemed lifeless as if the magnitude of their situation had now come into focus.

We sat across from them, Doucet leaning against the wall. They had already told their story to Doucet, and according to him, had been very straightforward and honest, as best he could tell. They had declined to have an attorney present. I was sure Kornblatt would be thrilled at that.

Now they related their tale to us. It wasn't easy, and came in fits and spurts. They held hands, continually looked at each other, and more than once sniffed and wiped away tears. They told of Tegan's affair with Kirk Ford. How it had started at a party one night. At some producer's home in Holmby Hills, near the Playboy Mansion. Both had been drinking. They had explored the house and had somehow ended up in an upstairs bedroom. Party going on downstairs. It was like a dream, as Tegan related it.

They continued the affair for a few weeks, but that's it. Kirk said it would never work and moved on to a new adventure. This one an eighteen-year-old brunette who was starstruck and then some. Kirk's favorite type. Tegan told of her pain and humiliation. Of her smoldering anger that she couldn't shake. Couldn't rationalize away. Regardless of how hard she tried to tamp it down, it visited her day and night, when she least expected it. Maybe on the set, doing a scene with Kirk. Maybe in the middle of the night, jerking her awake. It seemed relentless. And she seemed powerless to make it go away.

But the truly cruel part? Her pain and anger were laced with hope. Hope that Kirk would one day return to her. That all his roaming would end when he realized she was best for him.

That was before the appearance of Kristi. Tegan quickly realized that she wasn't just another one of Kirk's dalliances. That she was special and that Kirk was falling for her. Really falling.

Tegan then told of how she had hatched the plan, of convincing Tara to go along, of getting the drugs from "some dude," who by her description was obviously Ragman. Of how they gave Kristi the loaded joint, clipped Kirk's key card from his dresser drawer, and then the long wait. An hour, two. Seemed like forever. They then returned, after Kirk and Kristi were out.

Tara told us of Tegan's second thoughts, and that they had even discussed killing Kirk and not Kristi, as they stood beside the bed and stared down at their drugged forms. But in the end, Tegan loved Kirk and couldn't follow that path. They talked of how they almost decided to walk away and of how Tegan ultimately swept those doubts away and strangled Kristi. Of the fear and regret that had gripped them since that moment. Of how they managed to use "all their acting skills" to appear as if they supported Kirk, while hoping he would pay for his abuse of Tegan. Even as she loved him.

They cried, Nicole hugged them and cried, I cried. Even Doucet's eyes glassed with moisture.

* * *

Doucet drove us back to the hotel. We met with Kirk in his suite. Ebersole was there. I let Nicole take this one. She wanted to, and she really was the one who should tell Kirk about all the dirty laundry he had dropped in his wake.

It was a gut-wrenching half hour. Filled with moans, and tears, even from Ebersole—maybe it was seeing his franchise go up in smoke— but I thought he looked truly hurt.

"I can't believe this," Kirk said. "I never suspected."

"Tegan is an actress," Nicole said.

Kirk nodded. "But this? I always thought of our fling as just that. I thought she did, too. I thought she realized, like I did, that it would never work. That it wasn't good for either of us."

Nicole laid a hand on his shoulder. "She fell hard. Very hard."

"I never knew." He looked at Nicole. "I should have. How could I have missed seeing it?"

"Guys are pretty good at missing clues," Nicole said. "Particularly when the new shiny thing comes along."

He looked up at her, eyes now welling with tears. "And that's me, isn't it? Always looking for that next thrill?"

Nicole shrugged. "Kirk, you're not alone in that pursuit." She glanced at me. "I think it's a guy thing."

Me? How did I get into the conversation?

Kirk sighed. "But this? How could it ever go this far?"

"It's an old story," she said. "Happens all the time. Unrequited love and all that."

Kirk broke down, buried his face in his hands.

We left him curled in a ball on his bed, sobbing.

The life of an A-List actor.